TALES OF THE
HEXAGONVERSE
2, FAMILY BUSINESS

TALES OF THE HEXAGONVERSE

2. FAMILY BUSINESS

Stories by
**Nelly Chadour, Anthony Combrexelle,
Robert Darvel, Willy Favre, Amaury
Fourtet, Raphael Lafarge, Jean-Marc &
Randy Lofficier, Ghislain Morel, Blanche
Saint-Roch, Artikel Unbekannt**
and **Patrice Verry**

Edited by
**Romain d'Huissier
& Jean-Marc Lofficier**

Translated by
Michael Shreve

BLACK COAT PRESS

Visit our website at www.blackcoatpress.com
and
www.hexagoncomics.com

TABLE OF CONTENTS

Black Lys by Juan Roncagliolo Berger

Introduction

For the uninitiated, this is a collection of short stories featuring characters from the Hexagon Comics universe.

All stories are pretty much self-contained, and you do not need to have read any of the comics to enjoy them— although, of course, you might experience more fun if you are already familiar with the characters.

A short introduction before each story provides all the basic information about who the characters are, and what their powers are. We have also included pin-ups from the comics to help the reader visualize what they look like if you have not encountered them before.

These stories do not violate the established continuity of the comics. They fit within the "empty spaces" existing before, between, and after the comic book stories.

A short biography of each writer is provided at the end of this book; the great majority of them are distinguished French science fiction or fantasy writers who have had many other works published. I do not like the term "fan fiction," and this anthology, just like *Tales of the Shadowmen*, relies on established talent.

Romain d'Huissier, who edits the original French series (published under the name "*Dimension Super-Héros*"), is himself not only a popular and prolific author, but a major creator of role-playing games—including one devoted to the Hexagon Comics universe. Romain has also penned two novels featuring the Hexagon Group of heroes, *Dark Matter*, already available, and *War of the Immortals*, which will be available later this year.

Michael Shreve is one of Black Coat Press' most distinguished translators. If you like pulp heroes, we strongly recommend his translations of Leon Sazie's classic, *Zigomar*, or of André Caroff's *Madame Atomos* series.

Finally, readers interested in delving into the history of Hexagon Comics, France's oldest shared comics universe, are encouraged to buy a copy of our illustrated book, *Hexagon Comics: The First 70 Years*, available from our catalog.

Hexagon began in 1950 as Editions Lug, and published a great number of digest-sized comic magazines until 2003. During its first four decades, it published many original stories, as well as translations of popular Italian and Marvel series—they were, in fact, the very first publisher to translate Marvel Comics for the French market.

The company was relaunched in 2010 under the brand new name "Hexagon Comics" by the undersigned, with a line of reprints of the classic stories, as well as the launching of new series such as *Strangers* and *Guardian of the Republic*.

Now, read on...

Jean-Marc Lofficier

A founding member of the Hexagon Group, the Black Lys, a.k.a. Cendrine de Merignan, is a magnificent swordswoman with the power of materializing energy blades from her hands. She is descended from Lucas de Merignan, the original Black Lys, who had many adventures as a privateer at the end of the 17th century. The following story takes place shortly after the events of the novel Hexagon: Dark Matter.

Amaury Fourtet: *Family Business*

Outside, the sound of seagulls mingled with that of the colony. In the master bedroom of the Governor's mansion, the curtains fluttered in the warm breeze. Lucas de Merignan gazed at the man bathed in sweat. Tranchelard, his old brother-in-arms, to whom he had loaned his bed, looked pale and weak. The privateer looked on with compassion and sorrow at the bandage around the stub of his companion's arm, which had been amputated at the elbow. The doctor had managed to save Tranchelard's life, but his sailing days were over.

"I'll fight with my teeth if I have to!" his friend had growled in a lucid moment before the fever had struck him away again.

But Lucas knew that losing his arm meant retirement for Tranchelard. He, too, had retired after killing his father's murderer and taking over as Governor of Saint-Pierre… and finally marrying the lovely Louiselle.

So many years at sea had given him memories to last a lifetime, but it had also given him a thirst for adventure that had been hard to quench. That was why, even though Lucas had finally settled on land, Tranchelard had not.

But now, Lucas would not let him go back to sea. When he had found out about his friend's injury, he had set up a healthy pension for him, but would that be enough for a man who, all things considered, had been his only family during their pirate days? Consequently, he had made another decision. It was a fair one, and after a few days of opposing it, Tranchelard had finally come to see its merits.

For the moment, Lucas de Merignan could only watch over his friend while waiting to be called back back to France. Sitting in an armchair next to the bed, he gazed at the tired old face and patted his wife's hand which rested on his shoulder when she stood behind him. She had been told of her husband's latest decision and had accepted his choice—in the name of their family.

I

Cendrine de Merignan planted her fork delicately into the bit of pork chop she had cut and brought the meat up to her mouth. It was delicious, as were the hash browns. Eating a simple meal in an ordinary place like this would have been unthinkable in Bordeaux or Paris, two cities where she knew lots of people.

You can't belong to the jet set and still eat pork chops at Eugène's—that would be indecent.

But here in Lyon, she was just another face. Across from her, half-hidden by a pile of empty mussels, Beatrice looked just as pleased with her meal. Her cousin smiled at her and took another sip of wine.

"It's funny, I was expecting to drink one of your bottles," she tapped on the label.

Cendrine shrugged. "I never order my own wine. Besides, it might give away my other identity." She winked. "And there would be no thrill of discovery, no new exotic pleasure."

Her cousin nodded and went back to work on the marinated mussels.

"How is it going with the police?" Cendrine inquired after another mouthful of potatoes.

"Oh, not much going on. We did have a missing child, but the kid was found hiding in his grandfather's old cabin."

"Safe and sound?"

"Yes. Who knows why he was hiding there, but he didn't want to come out. You remember when we used to do the same thing?"

"Oh, sure, when we were kids. The servants looked for us everywhere and during that whole time…"

"…We were in the moldy old wardrobe in the attic!" Beatrice finished with a grand, theatrical gesture. "I can't remember what we did in there, but what a laugh we had!"

Beatrice came from a more modest background than Cendrine, a commoner branch of the family. They had been close as children, playing together during family gatherings, but had lost touch with each other as they'd gotten older. Beatrice had joined the French police, and become caught up in the real world, while Cendrine moved in the elite circles of European high society, something which she had gotten used to at a very young age.

"You must have gotten rid of that wardrobe since, right?" Beatrice wondered.

"Actually, no. I haven't thrown anything out since I inherited the estate. They keep telling me to find a good husband who will take care of things for me." Cendrine rubbed her cheek. "And what about you? Still a confirmed bachelorette?"

"You should talk," Beatrice giggled, slapping her with her napkin.

The brasserie was rather quiet. The quality of the cooking hid their conversation from the other patrons who were busy enjoying their own meals. Cendrine was really happy to spend this day out with her cousin.

Since the destruction of Ghool, the last Fomore, who almost destroyed the Hexagon Group and the human race,[1] Cendrine had decided to take little breaks once in a while. Nobody blamed her. She had been so devoted to her work as a super-hero that she sometimes forgot about simply being Cendrine de Merignan and having a life beyond cybervillains,

---

[1] See *Hexagon: Dark Matter*.

mutant sharks and other threats to humanity. Moreover, after all their ordeals, the other crime-fighters had encouraged her to do this, swearing that they could get along without her for a few weeks.

No costumes, no lasers, no Hexagoneers expecting me to make the right decision in a critical situation.

As the last heir in the Merignan line, Cendrine had adopted, out of necessity, her fellow Hexagoneers as her family. Therefore, taking time to visit her cousin, was a way for her to reconnect with her real family without involving her super-powered comrades.

It was during a period of mild depression, a year or two ago, that she had decided to get back in touch with Beatrice, an anchor of normality in a universe normally inhabited by super-villains and space stations. Since then, she had seen the police officer regularly, when her missions or obligations as a socialite allowed it. Her cousin knew about her double life, but very rarely asked her about it, only when something seemed to be bothering her. Cendrine appreciated this, and had frequently offered to introduce Beatrice into the circles of high society, but the policewoman had always refused with the excuse that her life was just fine as it was. At most she sometimes, but rarely, accepted to go to a gallery opening or some other cultural event usually reserved for the elite.

Completely absorbed in her conversation, Cendrine did not notice the man who had entered discreetly soon after her, ordered the fish, and was now following them out the door. He got into an inconspicuous car and remained on their tail. The scheme, which had been carefully planned in order to not attract Cendrine suspicions, was apparently working.

All afternoon, the two cousins were followed by either a man or a woman, but they showed no sign of realizing it.

Beatrice was now dragging Cendrine into a small gift shop, filled with cheap, replica swords and cat figurines made in China. Cendrine sat on a little stool watching her cousin looking through the knick-knacks.

"What are you looking for?" she finally asked.

Beatrice glanced at her thoughtfully.

"A present," she replied.

"For whom?"

"A birthday. What do you think of this?"

She showed Cendrine a copy of an Egyptian canopic jar. The monkey head had a lopsided, twisted grin because of the cheap reproduction.

They didn't even try to get close, Cendrine thought since she had had a real vase like this among her precious possessions.

"No," she said, "Don't waste your money. Maybe get something simpler, but with some personality. Who is it for?"

"For someone who forgot their own birthday."

"Seriously? What kind of person does that?"

"The very busy kind, I guess."

Beatrice kept looking over the shelves. She finally decided on a pretty, shiny, bronze clock, which Cendrine approved of—it was in good taste.

As they left, Cendrine smiled at Beatrice,

"And now what do you say about a movie? We'll go and grab a bite somewhere afterward."

Before her cousin could answer, a man bumped into Cendrine just as she was stepping onto the sidewalk. He was a handsome young man with blue eyes and dark hair, but his ready smile looked forced. The crime-fighter's quick mind identified him right away, because she recalled having seen him already several times, but without paying him much attention. He had been following them for a while. His fumbled excuses for bumping into her could not hide the cold flame in his eyes and her senses went on high alert.

She stepped in front of Beatrice to shield her. Cendrine de Merignan had spent a pleasant day in carefree activities with her cousin, but this was Black Lys facing the intruder. Beatrice, being a police lieutenant, could feel that something was wrong, and she took a self-defense stance.

The evening is starting off great, she thought.

When the stranger stepped to the side, Lys tensed up, ready to take him down, but instead, he just bowed eagerly.

"I know you! You're the famous Cendrine de Merignan! You're a long way from your wonderful vineyards, Fraülein."

His German accent sounded real and his manners were courteous. Cendrine did not let her guard off, but she held out her hand.

"Pleased to meet you, monsieur...?"

Briefly taken aback by the rather unfeminine gesture, the man shook her hand.

"Dieter Bauchwunde. Delighted and surprised to meet you so unexpectedly."

"I can imagine."

He had a curious name that did not sound natural. *Belly wound*, Lys translated to herself. She preferred not to jeopardize her cousin by introducing her and she was not exactly jumping into the conversation. The man could be an agent of any evil organization that had fought Hexagon before.

I've seen his face before even today, I'm sure of it. Maybe in the mosaic of faces on the computer at HQ...

The crime-fighter only listened with half an ear to the German's slick chatter, answering him automatically. She chose to stay on guard, watching for an imminent attack that could come from any direction. But strangely, nothing happened.

She caught a woman spying on them, hidden behind a notice board, but she just noted it without trying anything. She wondered if her career as a superhero had not made her overly suspicious. Maybe this really was just a coincidence. Maybe that woman watching them was Dieter's shy friend, or even a *paparazzi*.

And maybe I believe in Santa Claus.

"I'm sorry, but I have to be going now," she heard the man say.

She snapped back to reality, trying vaguely to remember if he had said anything that demanded an answer, but she couldn't, so she just nodded and smiled.

"It was nice to meet you, *Herr* Bauchwunde. Maybe we'll see each other again in Paris, or even in Bordeaux sometime."

"*Ja*, very likely. As I said, we're planning to expand our operations in France. *Auf Wiedersehen* and watch yourself!"

A minute later, he had turned the corner, accompanied by the other woman who had been watching them. Cendrine went into action and rifled around in her purse.

"What do you think that was all about?" Beatrice asked.

Cendrine pulled out her cell phone. On the screen there was a dot moving.

"Seriously? Is that what I think it is?" said Beatrice.

"Tracker on his sleeve when I shook his hand. I never leave home without one," Cendrine joked. "Anyway, I am sorry, darling, but this means that we're going to have to cancel our plans for the evening."

"Do you think he was really suspicious?"

"I'm a hero, we can feel these kinds of things. As a cop you should know that."

"Yes, of course, clear as day," Beatrice laughed. "Go on then, follow him, I understand. I know what it's like never leaving your work behind." Beatrice hugged her. "And by the way, happy birthday!"

There was moment of silence before Cendrine understood and then, in the blink of an eye, she graciously accepted the gift her cousin was holding out.

"It's true! How did you know that I forget my birthday!"

Beatrice kissed her on the cheek and smiled.

"Because it happens to busy people. That's what family's for."

II

Cendrine rushed back to her hotel. She put away Beatrice's gift and jumped into her uniform, all the while keeping an eye on the screen.

The tracker was still for the moment and a quick internet search gave her the address as that of a small garage downtown.

After slipping out of the window, she stood on the roof. The long flaps of her costume fluttered in the evening air and her face was hardened with determination. Black Lys was on the hunt.

She jumped from roof to roof in the direction of the signal, appreciating the constant training that the members of Hexagon did to stay in top physical condition. Down in the streets below, people were waiting for late friends in restaurants or hurrying back to their homes.

Black Lys had a rendezvous with a stranger who had dared to approach her in broad daylight to taunt her. His cold eyes, which had drilled into her during their encounter, left no doubt about it.

I'd bet anything he's not just an ordinary businessman.

Their meeting had been no accident. It was a clear attempt at intimidation: *we know who you are and we can get to you whenever we want.* She hated threats, even veiled ones.

When she got to the roof of the garage, she looked through a dirty skylight just in time to see Dieter crush out a cigarette while the woman he was with hung up the phone.

Now that she had a little time to observe them, it was obvious that they were brother and sister. She resisted the urge to confront them as they put on their coats. Making sure that the tracker was still working, she let them drive out of the garage and cruise away without noticing her presence. Then another car stopped in front of the building as she was climbing off the roof. The Bauchwunde sedan was already out of sight.

"Shall I drop you somewhere, Mademoiselle?" Beatrice said as she opened the door.

"Bea? How did you know?" Lys jumped into the car.

"I thought you might need a hand so I went by your hotel," she said as the car took off. "You left your computer on and I checked your search history, which gave me this address."

Lys nodded, "Thanks. I always feel a little bad when I have to borrow a car off the street, so you've saved me the trouble."

"'Borrow,' ha! Some day vigilantes like you who make their own laws are going to have serious problems," she laughed. "And now what do we do?"

"Cabbie, follow that car!"

Beatrice slipped expertly through the traffic. In no time at all, she had caught up with the Bauchwunde and followed them a few cars back. This was not the first time the police officer had tailed someone. On the other hand, she had never had to deal with two black vans barreling out of an alley to chase her. In a symphony of honking horns, the vans boxed in the unmarked police car. With one van behind her to cut off any escape and the other on her left, she was caught.

Lys clenched her jaw and unfastened her seatbelt.

"I'll take care of this. Keep going and try not to swerve too much."

"Huh? What are you doing?"

The crime-fighter looked at her. Above her right eye appeared a black *fleur-de-lys*, the sign that she had "activated" her powers. A second later, Lys had swiftly slid onto the roof.

The van in the rear revved its engine and hit the car's rear bumper. Lys used the shock to jump onto it. Energy blades sprang out of her fists and she dove through the enemy's windshield. The glass exploded on contact and the driver yelped comically. Lys thought that he looked like the typical thug, with a rough, hardened face like a cheap copy of Lino Ventura. She glided straight into the backseat where she knocked out the other goons who were struggling to pull out their guns.

One final kick laid out her last foe. She jumped into the seat next to the driver, who did not look so fearless now, and one good punch in the nose took care of him. A second later, she was on the hood and leaped onto the back of the other van just as the first crashed into a dumpster.

She used an energy blade to stab through the flimsy metal to announce her arrival, but the rear door flew open. Hanging on with two hands, her boots scraped the pavement every time the van hit a bump. The man standing in the back pointed a submachine gun at her and smiled. But his smirk turned into a sickly grin when Lys swung her two feet up and knocked away his weapon. The gun went bouncing down the street and fired off a few random shots before vanishing from sight.

The thug had no time to be surprised because Lys was still moving, swinging her legs up to hang onto the door, upside down. In the same movement, she grabbed the guy's collar with her free hands and threw him into the traffic, which was becoming increasingly chaotic behind them. She did not forget to snatch up the gun he had tucked into his belt, which she used to shoot out the two rear tires.

The van swerved off to the right as the driver tried to keep control, but Lys was already back on Beatrice's car, which had been able to get into position after the van behind it had crashed.

"I really think that Teutonic Don Juan wanted to hurt us," Beatrice shouted out the window to her cousin who was hanging onto to the side of the car.

It was this very moment that Lys' communicator buzzed in her ear and the honeyed voice of Hexagon's computer wiz came through.

"Hey, Lys, they're starting to talk about your little street show on the social networks. Having fun?"

"Sweet! You couldn't have called at a better time. I'm going to need your help."

Beatrice took her eyes off the road to shoot a questioning glance at Lys who pointed to her ear.

"Find me everything you can about a certain Dieter Bauchwunde and his sister. I don't know if that's his real name, but the jerk could very well have given it anyway."

"Nothing more specific?" Sweet asked sarcastically.

Lys could already hear her expert fingers tapping away on the keyboard.

"Search among the known and suspected members of CRIMEN, The Hundred, maybe Phantom... Something like that..."

"OK, and by the way..."

"Hold on, Sweet, the party's not yet over. I'll call you back."

Lys broke off abruptly. She had just seen a third van pulling up to them and she took a deep breath when the side door slid open to reveal a bunch of goons armed with assault rifles. Time stopped for a moment.

As if on cue, everything went back to normal in an instant. The guns sprayed the car. Beatrice ducked to avoid getting hit by the bullets or the shattered glass. Lys was not exposed because her cousin had moved the car so that the van was on the opposite side of the superhero. Lys opened the rear door and crawled into the back.

"Bea, you're still with us?" she asked

"My poor car..."

"OK! When I tell you, swerve into them and stay right next to them as long as you can."

"Why?"

"Until you see me cracking some heads."

Beatrice jerked the steering wheel and the car scraped against the van.

"I said on my signal!" Lys complained. "Ah, the hell with it!"

She cleared out what remained of the window and dove through it to land in the middle of the assault team. Her energy blades went straight through the barrels of half the guns before they could turn on her. A hard kick in the guts of one of the three men still armed sent him flying into the other two, who fell down like dominoes. All three of them fell out of the van.

With her leg still extended, Lys pivoted theatrically on one foot to face four other goons who were now holding useless guns. They dropped them to pull out combat knives. The superhero smiled. *How cute!* She thought.

She brought her foot down to the floor, raised the other at the same time and made a smooth, swinging kick at the closest two. Their hands went flying to their throats as she stood straight in front of them—they dropped to their knees, choking. Meanwhile, one of the other two slashed her arm. Lys moved into a fencing stance and used her two energy swords to attack. One strike disarmed one of her opponents, and the other stabbed the man next to him, forcing him to back off.

Another thug saw his chance, but Lys easily blocked his knife, grabbed him by the collar and head-butted him in the face. He staggered back and tripped over his comrade on the floor. A swift kick in the jaw put him out for the count. The last man standing came at her, yelling. She stepped out of his way, grabbed his hair and smashed his face into her knee. He collapsed in a heap of broken cartilage. After that, the driver was easy to convince to pull the van over. Police had it surrounded in no time.

All the bystanders were kept at a distance, while Beatrice explained what had happened to her colleagues. Meanwhile, Lys got back in touch with Sweet.

"So, did you find anything?" she asked.

"Dieter Bauchwunde, alias Raymond Tranche, alias John Cutter," the young woman informed her. "You were right. Despite all his pseudonyms, he gave you his real name. He must like you."

"Or he's taunting me."

"Possibly. Anyway, he and his sister, Astrid, used to be agents of S.P.I.D.E.R. We'd lost track of them. Until today, that is."

Lys bit her thumbnail and thought. Why would two former members of an international terrorist organization decide to attack her? And so brazenly, with vans full of armed men in the middle of Lyon? Why? Maybe it was just their style? Super villains had an annoying tendency to develop a "style." But that didn't explain their motive...

And those vans... Did it mean that they knew I was following them? Or was it standard precautions?

She could not back down now. According to the tracker, the Bauchwunde were heading straight for the airport. It was still possible to get there in time and Beatrice could set up a police roadblock. The vans were a perfect excuse and it would even make the two criminals think that, if they got through, no one knew they were the ones behind it all.

"Sweet, who can I count on if there's trouble?"

There was a frustrated click of the tongue.

"That's what I wanted to tell you before. The whole team is busy right now. Something to do with Hyperbrain trying to hijack a nuclear submarine."

"Great, just my luck. OK, I'll keep you up-to-date anyway. If things get really bad, I'll pull out."

"You really think I'll believe that?"

Lys could not help smiling. Sweet was clever, insolent, and very perceptive.

"No, not really, I guess. Later, Sweet."

"Be careful, Cendrine."

The superhero went to join Beatrice. She made a quick statement and told them about her idea for the roadblocks.

III

The tracker had led her to the section of the airport reserved for private planes. Lys could see the brother and sister climb out of the car and talk for a minute before getting into an ultramodern jet with vertical takeoff capabilities. They seemed to be alone; they were probably the kind of people who preferred to fly their own toys, just like their car.

She covered the distance from the plane by slipping through the shadows, unseen by the patrols she had spotted while on lookout. Except for two guards who had broken their routine, probably to have a quick smoke—she came up right behind them. One of them turned around, a young woman with her hair pulled back wearing a paramilitary cap and tactical sunglasses. Lys hit her hard, then kicked her back against a crate. In a graceful movement, the crime-fighter ducked under the second guard's gun swinging at her. She leaped forward, head first, into the man's gut and he fell to the ground. She did not want to attract attention by bringing out her energy blades so she simply knocked them out and threw a tarp over their bodies.

She was at the plane in no time. As she was inspecting it, she heard a patrol making its round so she quit dawdling and snuck inside. Before she had taken three steps, the door slid shut behind her and the hum of the engines suddenly filled the space.

Oh, come on!

The door in front of her was closed. She tried to force it open but the acceleration threw her against the wall. They were in the air and climbing fast if she could believe her stomach. She finally got the better of the door and found herself in an empty cockpit. The lights from the city sparkled through the window, so close and yet so far. The smooth voice of Dieter Bauchwunde came through the speakers.

"As you can see, my dear Cendrine, we had to leave the party when you got here, but please, make yourself at home. You're the guest of honor."

They must have left during the brief time she was not watching the plane—her fight with the two guards. The whole thing had been staged.

"Quit playing around, Bauchwunde, and get to the point," she hissed, angry with herself. "What do you want from me?"

Astrid's voice took over, harder and colder than her brother's.

"Your death, Cendrine de Merignan. Nothing else. Is that clear enough for you?"

"I already figured that, sweet Fraulein. I just wonder why. I'm sure I never saw you with the other flunkies of S.P.I.D.E.R. when I kicked their ass."

There was a pause before Dieter broke in.

"So, you know who we are, and you still fell in our trap. I don't know if we should consider you brave or just plain stupid."

Cendrine rolled her eyes.

"Is your plan to kill me as corny as your dialogue? A heads up would be appreciated."

Dieter did not react,

"I consider our plan elegant in its simplicity. The plane is already high enough to prevent any means of escape. It's going to get higher, up to its usual cruising altitude, before having a terrible accident that will take the life of the famous Cendrine de Merignan. That's what happens when you fly alone in an untested prototype."

Cendrine looked through the window. Even cutting through the hull would do no good now.

"Yes, you've thought of everything, Bauchwunde," she tried to buy some time. "But why do you want to kill me so badly? You didn't answer."

"We have our reasons," Astrid growled.

"It's an ancient oath," Dieter explained. "Your ancestor Lucas de Merignan ruined the life of our ancestor, and the hand of destiny must eventually wield the hammer of retribution."

The speakers went silent. Cendrine looked into the sky. An ancestor from the time of Lucas de Merignan... Perhaps the descendants of one of the many pirates he had defeated were coming back to kill her? Families had different impacts on different people. For some, just spending a day off with a cousin was fine. For others, plotting to avenge an ancestor who had died a long time ago was an obsession. She decided not to linger over the cause of her predicament.

That's the way the ball bounces.

The most pressing matter now was to search the plane. Indeed, five minutes later, she was standing in front of a big bomb with a blinking light.

An accident, eh? We'll see who's smarter.

She pressed her earpiece. "Sweet?"

"Online, boss."

"I'm going to describe a bomb and you're going to tell me how to disarm it."

"I appreciate the boundless confidence you have in my unlimited knowledge, but I never got my bomb disposal degree."

"No, but you have access to anti-terrorist databases and a whole bunch of ways to get that kind of information," she replied, "Unless you can't pull off something that complicated, in which case I'd understand."

Silence.

"OK, I'm listening," said Sweet. "Start by describing the casing and we'll figure out how to open it."

Once the insides were exposed, the bomb was easy to identify. It was a recognizable model that had been used by S.P.I.D.E.R. in the past, and was not difficult to disarm with Sweet guiding Lys all the way through. After ten minutes, the bomb was as dangerous as an anvil.

Although this was a step in the right direction, Lys still had the problem of being trapped in a plane remote-controlled by two lunatics who sought to kill her for really stupid reasons. Nevertheless, she allowed herself a smile of satisfaction.

Back in the cockpit, Lys began planning her rescue with the help of Sweet. The GPS showed her plane to be somewhere over Bavaria, but the craft remained undetectable to radar. Hexagon was still busy with Hyperbrain so Sweet was now trying to contact C.L.A.S.H. to arrange an interception.

"We've reached our destination," Astrid's voice hissed, out of the speakers. "Farewell, Black Lys."

"Not so fast," Lys said, a little disappointed with the sister's curt manners. Dieter was much more theatrical and certainly more pleasant to thwart. "I'm afraid your bomb is out of commission. It was a nice plan, simple and direct like most good plans, but come on, a big bomb in the middle of the plane? Maybe a little too simple."

"I agree." Dieter was back at the mic. "That's why the bomb was only a decoy to keep you busy, Cendrine."

Lys' smile vanished. It had all been too simple from the start. The meeting, the chase, the airport, and now the bomb.

"I'd love to tell you that you were just about to escape, that your failure was due only to a bit of bad luck, but that would be false. You alone are responsible."

What are you planning? What did I miss?

"By working alongside your team of do-gooders and relying on them, you forgot how to work alone. Be wary. Vigilant."

"Let's get this over with, Dieter." Astrid was in the background and then at the mic. "If you believe in God, now's the time to curse Him for abandoning you, de Merignan."

Everything suddenly shut off. All the instruments died, then the engines, which whirred more and more slowly, then fell silent. The only sound was the wind lashing against the hull of a plane that had turned into a flying brick.

Electromagnetic pulse. They burned everything with an EMP. I'm dead.

The first thing Lys did was to inform Sweet. Their communicator—a product of NeroTek—was immune to EMPs.

"Put me in touch with Dominik," she ordered as she paced the length of the plane like a caged tiger. "I don't care if he's in the middle of a battle. We're superheroes. We can talk while we're fighting. And instead of laughing at his foes, he's going to tell me how to get out of here."

Dominik Nero—the Dark Flyer—was a genius engineer who had designed his own armor. If anyone could guide her blind to fix the plane's electrical system, it was him.

"Cendrine," Dominik's voice came through the earpiece. "Sweet explained everything. We're going to get you out of there."

"Forget it, Dom. By the time you find me, I'll be a pretty red blot over the Black Forest. I've got a better idea. Remember all the boring tech talks you had with me when you thought I was listening?"

"Er, thanks?"

"I remember hearing you say that a plane hit by an EMP could be fixed."

"Sure, but it depends. You need equipment. It's also possible that some components are protected from the pulse, but you'd have to be able to restart the system after."

"OK, one thing at a time." Lys could feel the engineering fever rise up in her partner.

"Right, right, let's start with fixing the less important parts of the system and see if we can get a basic nav system going."

"Should I go into the hold?"

"Are you joking? Stay in the cockpit. If you can't find what you need there, you won't find it anywhere else because you don't have time to take the plane apart. You either make do with the instrument panel, or you're done with."

"This is getting better and better. OK, I'm listening."

For the second time that day, Lys was guided by a disembodied voice through the various steps of a delicate operation. She worked quickly, wiping away the sweat that dribbled into her eyes. Her anxiety, which she tried to control as best she could, made her rush. That madman Bauchwunde was not completely wrong: she was too used to working with a team. Alone in a flying coffin drifting towards certain death—it was a miracle that it had not yet dropped into a vertical nosedive— she felt pretty helpless.

You're not alone, however. Your team is here. Listen to Dominik, He knows what to do.

Easy to say. When she asked for the time, she had spent only three minutes inspecting and replacing the vital components. But time was of the essence. Sweet cut in to tell her that she had just reappeared on the German radar. But no plane was around to come to her aid, and the crash would happen in twelve minutes. She tried to swallow, but her mouth was dry; for how long she did not know, but her throat felt like sandpaper—every breath was painful.

"That's it!" the Dark Flyer's voice finally said. "From what you tell me, we can get back control of part of the rudders and engines. Now you have to restart it."

"Right," she panted. "I'm going to find the power source."

The superhero found it right away and cursed out loud. The EMP had obviously come from there. The heart of the plane, a big, rounded box stuck in the compartment, was blackened and smelled like burnt rubber.

Dominik welcomed the news with a mixture of encouragement and distress.

"It's not possible. There's got to be another solution. Let me think... I can't believe that..."

"It's all right," Lys broke in. Her voice was calm, almost loving. In the ears of Sweet and the Dark Flyer, it was the voice of a person finally accepting her death sentence.

"Lys... Cendrine?"

She tossed away her earpiece and walked slowly toward the cockpit. She noticed that the floor was sloping—and becoming steeper and steeper at every step. The lucky streak that had kept the plane horizontal was over.

Standing in front of the windshield, Lys watched the clouds swirling outside. She put her hand on the Plexiglas. It was cold. She pulled it back and looked at it. She turned it over and stared at her palm, spreading her fingers, and watched the eddying clouds through them.

In the windshield, she saw the image of the Black Lys reflected over her eye like an ink flower on a blotting paper.

"An accident," she said in a calm voice to her imaginary companion. "You've trapped me. Bravo! You've carried me into the skies and turn off the power. Less messy than a bomb. More like a technical problem. And me, thinking that I was invulnerable—but I can't even fly.!

The angle of the fall became sharper.

"I don't breathe fire, I can't read minds..."

She now had her right hand raised as the left gripped the pilot's seat in order to keep herself from falling.

"I'm just a fighter..."

Her face was bathed in an unreal light.

"...A swordswoman who creates her own blades..."

Immaterial and luminous, the swords of Black Lys sprang out of her hands, silhouetted against the gray skies.

"...Blades made of pure energy."

She slammed a fist into the instrument panel. Then the other. And she let her bioelectric energy pour into the dead circuits of the airplane.

The engines coughed and started up. All around her in the cockpit, the lights started blinking, the screens lit up, digital numbers appeared and the needles suddenly went crazy.

It took incredible willpower for her to stay conscious. But then everything stabilized. Half of the plane did not work—the half she had cannibalized following the Dark Flyer's instructions. But when she pushed the control stick with all her strength, the plane responded sluggishly. Partial control was better than none at all. It was the difference between life and death.

She still did not know, and maybe would not know for a long time, the name of her ancestor's enemy for whom the Bauchwundes had almost killed her. And even if she found it, she did not have the energy to care.

She collapsed into the pilot's seat and saw her earpiece rolling nearby. Without thinking, she snatched it up and began to slowly guide the plane back toward the land of the living.

Epilogue

Three months earlier...

...and experts have confirmed the authenticity of the document. It's a legally binding under certain conditions, or at least all the lawyers I've talked to say so... Extended family is not an issue. It concerns Cendrine de Merignan herself. If she dies, her lineage becomes extinct and this clause comes into effect... Even if others decide to fight it, we've got better

and less scrupulous lawyers than them. I've already hired a genealogist to trace the Bauchwunde family tree all the way back to their French ancestor, a man named Tranchelard.

Dieter, believe me, when S.P.I.D.E.R. no longer needs us, this inheritance will be a windfall. This piece of paper hidden behind that hideous painting is the key to our future. I know that you think we have enough money with our family business and all that S.P.I.D.E.R. paid us, but get your head out of the clouds. There's never "enough money."

If Governor Lucas de Merignan (because he was a Governor, apparently! Nice ending for a pirate) wanted our family to inherit his fortune because of the stupid matter of an amputated arm, who are we to deny his last will?

I'll be in Hanover soon. If you manage to get away at the same time, we can talk face-to-face. So, listen to your sister. When Black Lys is out of the picture, it'll be smooth sailing. We just have to figure out how to get rid of her without her damned team coming to her rescue.

But we're a family too, and with two of us working in concert, nothing is impossible.

Astrid

The Time Brigade by Edmond Ripoll

The Time Brigade, *based in the 41ˢᵗ century, is responsible for the protection of Earth's various timelines, up to about 1 million A.D. It is composed of teams of four agents dubbed "Hands" and managed by a giant A.I. known as the Thumb. Hand 28 is made up of Khanor Rhi (coordinator, former chronoprogrammer, 40ᵗʰ century), Varna Zelton (time sensitive, a former student of Khanor), Jason Spell (archeologist, 20ᵗʰ century) and Minus-3 (an augmented ape).*

Anthony Combrexelle: *Boundless is Space*

"Ohhh!" Jason moaned.

The time agent got up rubbing his temples. His chin hurt and his knees ached. Around him Khanor, Varna and Minus-3 were doing the same thing. All of them were wincing from an intense migraine.

The agents of the Hand 28 were disoriented. None of them could remember how they got here. They looked around, trying to get a handle on the situation. The four of them were in a huge, underground cave with dark tunnels winding down through the rock.

Khanor rubbed his sore neck while making sure that the rest of his team was all right, uninjured, and that no immediate threat was lurking in the shadows, waiting to pounce on them. Their Temposcaph, the bubble-shaped Chronosphere that was their means of transport through space and time, was a few yards away, hidden in the gloom of the mysterious grotto.

"I'm not tipping anyone's hand when I say, uh... *What the hell is this?*" Jason asked.

"I wouldn't put it in such primitive terms," the augmented ape replied, "but that is the general idea."

"I have a splitting headache," Varna said, "and the strange feeling that something is terribly wrong."

"Does anyone remember what we're doing here and why we all obviously passed out?" Khanor questioned.

When he realized that no one was going to answer, the coordinator and operations chief went to the Chronosphere.

"We're not gonna hang around, right, boss?" Jason grumbled as he walked around the grotto. "I'm starving and I don't wanna start snacking on dirt and rocks. Let's go back to HQ quick and have us a little feast."

Khanor did not answer. Once he was through the wall of the Temposcaph, he activated the vocal command to contact the Thumb. In a fraction of a second the AI popped up in front of him. The former chronoprogrammer had learned not to jump when the Noh mask plugged into dozens of cables came out of the wall so abruptly. He only had to ask where they were in the Continuum, and the artificial intelligence answered immediately.

"Agent Rhi?" the computer-generated voice asked.

"Thumb, can you tell me what happened here?"

"Khanor, your sense of humor is starting to get a little repetitive," the white porcelain face grumbled. "If I were not programmed to help you under any condition, I would simply stop answering."

"I don't understand. What's got into you?"

The cables behind the metal mask shook and it came close enough to touch the human's graying temples. The cold face seemed to want to verify that the man was not mocking him, checking to see if it could see any sign of a tired, old joke. To no avail.

"Well then, I will repeat for the 17th time: we spotted an anomaly in the space-time continuum. Ships have been disappearing for decades in the part of the Rhamno Sector where you are, and had been for decades. The epicenter of the disorder is the planetoid that you are currently occupying. The asteroid measures four miles in diameter, and from its core produces an electromagnetic field that prevents us from monitoring both it and space-time from a chronosphere. Furthermore, we have not yet been able to identify its exact composition, nor the reason for the disappearances. The Hand 28, therefore, was sent on a fact-finding mission."

"I guess that when you say the 17th time it's not just a figure of speech."

"You guess correctly, Agent Rhi."

"How long have we been here?"

"You left 36 hours ago. The analysis of the air by the nanosensors of the Temposcaph reports a sleeping gas being intermittently vented through certain cracks in the surrounding rocks."

Khanor pressed a button hidden in the collar of his orange jacket.

"Did you hear that?" he asked the other members of his team.

"Loud and clear," Varna replied, following Jason to the entrance to the network of tunnels. "That explains the cause of all us passing out together."

"36 hours? Does that mean we haven't eaten for that long? I didn't sign up for a mission of fasting! No wonder my stomach's growling," Jason said. "And what does the AI say about this weird loss of time?"

"I say that you did not sign up for anything at all and I say that I am not just a simple AI. I am a powerful calculator, a computer for whom the Copenhagen School is nothing but a building in Denmark. A little respect please, Agent Spell. Remember that a hand without a thumb is nothing. And I say that the more we talk, the more this weird loss of time really becomes one."

"I didn't know machines were so touchy," Jason joked, stepping into the depths of the asteroid.

He had been recruited in the 20th century while digging around in Mesopotamia and looking at the rocky landscape here reminded him of his archeological days. Intrigued by the unknown nature of the rocks around him, he started exploring.

"I much appreciate these communicators the Thumb put in the collars of our uniforms," the super-ape raved. "Pleasantly functional and discreet."

Minus-3 examined the ground around the Temposcaph. He had noted some rock material to take samples of but also a bunch of strange, laminated objects. Intrigued, he picked up one of them, which looked as much like an organic gas mask as a rubbery manta ray. At his feet and scattered around at random were a dozen other similar objects.

Observing the oddity from all angles the augmented ape found a kind of sense to it and put the creature up to his face. As he suspected, it stuck to his breathing device, wrapped its wings gently around his neck and covered his nostrils. He breathed in and out slowly to test the appendage, and it seemed that, despite the strange smell and ugly appearance, the cartilage mask filtered the air. His breathing was clearly improved and his headache slowly faded.

Nearby, Agent Zelton started showing signs of weakness. She had barely taken a few steps when she got dizzy. Her vision blurred as she tried to lean against a wall, to hang on to something so as not to fall. At the last minute she was held up by the ape.

"Varna!" he shook her a little. "Here, use this!"

Minus-3 laid her on the ground and gave her one of the strange accessories he had just discovered.

"What's this?" she sputtered. "What are you wearing?"

"These creatures filter the sleeping gas coming out of the rocks," he explained. "If you put one over your nose and mouth you'll breath more easily."

A little reluctantly, the former student of Khanor Rhi put the mask on her face. Once the creature was comfortably in place, she relaxed.

"In fact, I... am starting to feel the difference."

Minus-3 pressed his communicator to talk to the two other agents.

"The creatures you see on the ground are..."

"Air filters, I know," Jason broke in, already having stuck one on his face. "Meanwhile, instead of twiddling your thumbs, you should come see this. There's a huge network of tunnels over here. The rock is shiny in some spots and it lights up of the underground."

"Khanor, Jason's right," Varna said as she stood up. "The masks seem to protect us from the gas. I still feel kind of weird, but my headache is going away."

"Let's get moving," Minus-3 told the young woman. "If we don't keep a close eye on him I'm afraid Agent Spell will get lost by himself," the ape added sarcastically.

At the same time, the conversation in the Chronosphere between Khanor and the Thumb was coming to an end.

"Agent Rhi, do you need the help of another Hand?"

"No, Thumb. That won't be necessary. The situation doesn't call for it yet. I'll get back in touch with you when we know more. Thanks."

In Jason's famished mind the rock he was examining had turned into a giant hunk of Swiss cheese with its multitude of winding passageways and interconnected tunnels. The rocky walls had a strange texture, almost organic, and the feeling was strengthened by abnormally loose soil. Several times he saw jets of gas spewing from the rocks but fortunately his mask kept him from being affected.

After choosing one tunnel over another, the most impulsive of the agents of Hand 28 had gone just a few yards before he was facing another crossroad. The planetoid had a whole maze of underground passages. Stopping at the junction, he was surprised to find that, besides the hooked stalagmites, looking like mammoth tusks, there were piles of bones. Where they came from was a mystery and trying to identify them only made it more puzzling.

Standing up, he noticed that some animals—a kind of giant wasp—had been crushed against the sharp walls. The remains were of all sizes, some measuring no more than a few inches while others were over a foot long. Before he had a chance to press his communicator to give his location, he heard them coming. The advancing buzz was obviously hostile. He looked for a place to hide, but there was nothing around. Before he could turn back, they were there, huge, ugly, flying creatures with sharp stingers.

"Sorry, I didn't mean to disturb you. I…"

Jason did not have time to finish his sentence because the quartet of flying parasites—very similar to the proto-wasps smashed on the wall—attacked, stingers out front.

Jason dropped to the ground, dodging the first onslaught of the hysterical creatures. He rolled away and grunted when his back hit a pile of bones, but as he got back on his feet, he grabbed a long thighbone that must have belonged to some tall alien. The extraterrestrial bone was like a spear in his hand.

"OK, you want to play it like this then?" he smiled savagely.

The agent never felt more alive than when he was facing an enemy. He loved feeling the adrenaline in his blood and the challenge represented by the violent creatures facing him.

The bellies of the pseudo-wasps were huge and bumpy, the carriers of the venom that he figured was very fast-acting if it had killed all the creatures whose bones he was stumbling through. Fast maybe, but not as fast as him. Jason made his first strike at the leader of the buzzing, venomous squadron.

"If you wanted to be squashed like your old buddies there, you just had to ask!" he sneered as he picked off one of the parasites in mid-air.

The puffy wasps smashed against the sharp rocks while Jason ducked under the repeated attacks of its flying comrades. When he stood up, he spun the extraterrestrial leg in the air to fend off his enemies.

"Mom was right—the cheerleading practice wasn't completely useless."

When the fighting hornets bumped into the spinning shield, they got the message: they were outmatched. After a few vain attempts to get through, the creatures beat a hasty retreat and disappeared down a dark tunnel.

"Varna, Minus-3, you got to come see this. Two or three good swings and the evil bees buzzed off in a jiffy."

The two agents did not respond. Not even one of those smartass comebacks the augmented ape always had ready. Jason called again but received only silence in return. His communicator seemed to have stopped working for no apparent reason.

"Hey, is anyone there? My friends?"

At a bend in one of the tunnels Jason had disappeared. The number of passages was no help as the echo of their footsteps bounced eerily off the stone walls. Once he was lost from view, it was impossible for Varna and Minus-3 to follow Jason in the maze.

"Jason? Where are you? We've lost sight of you and..."

Varna was cut off by a sign from Minus-3. The sound of footsteps was coming closer through the darkness.

"Jason?" the ape asked into the dark.

He was quickly answered by the appearance of a bizarre creature walking straight towards them. Well over six feet tall, the frog-faced humanoid was wearing a kind of spacesuit riddled with tubes full of liquid and vapor and on the back a bunch of valves and hydraulic pumps.

"You-just-sleep," the frog astronaut said.

"We are friends," Minus-3 replied.

"You-just-sleep," it repeated.

Varna and Minus-3 looked at each other, wondering how to interpret these words.

"Do you think it's trying to tell us we were just unconscious or...?"

The creature rushed at Varna in order to restrain her. The young woman jumped back and ducked to her left to evade, for the most part, the attack.

"Let her go, you filthy frog!" Minus-3 shouted as he grabbed the spacesuit.

The creature struggled and tried to wave to the ape to let go. Minus-3 bared his teeth and held fast. Varna rained blows onto the metallic arm of her attacker but to no avail: the creature seemed unaffected.

37

"You-just-sleep!" the toad repeated and it tore off the young woman's breathing mask.

"You're the one who's going to sleep!" the angry ape yelled out.

The creature threw itself against the wall and stunned the augmented ape.

"Minus-3!" the young woman screamed.

When she tried to do something to help her partner, she got dizzy. The gas in the air hit her hard and before she could cry out for help she passed out.

When the ape stood up, his body hurt and all he could do was assess the situation: Varna Zelton had disappeared and the creature with her.

"Varna? Minus? Jason? Will somebody answer me?"

Khanor was sure that something was wrong. He did not yet understand exactly what or how, but he felt it. They should have been together, not separated. Together, they could face things. Separated, they were at the mercy of whatever was living here. On Minus-3's orders he, too, had put on the animal-mask and had noticed how the air, despite its peculiar smell, was easier to breath.

The Temposcaph was not able to scan the inside of the asteroid. On the other hand, the Thumb could still provide Khanor with some satellite images of its exterior appearance. They had located the openings most likely for the vanished spaceships to enter and had landed here, alone. Now, the communicators were no longer working. And he cursed the fact that Jason was always off on his own and never listening to anyone. He was the leader and since that troublemaker had joined them, his authority was deteriorating.

After a long, forced march into the tunnels only lit by the natural radiance of the rocks, guided by his unerring sense of direction, the chief of the Hand 28 came into a huge room with a high ceiling, which must have served as some kind of loading dock or space dump as well as a cemetery for ships. As far as the eye could see, there were all kinds of flying vessels: alien aircraft and various UFOs lying all around.

Khanor was on alert, looking around for inhabitants, scrutinizing the nooks and crannies in search of some trace of a passage, but he saw nothing and heard nothing. Never too careful, he unbuttoned his holster to free his laser gun and… realized that it was empty. He did not have his weapon, which was a big surprise. Had he lost it? Had someone taken it from him while he was passed out? Something was terribly wrong and now he felt like he was being watched. Even more vigilant, he marched slowly through the maze of scrap. A vast quantity of ships was piled up, of every age and size. But there was no sign of any alien crew who apparently just vanished into thin air.

While he was kicking through some bent sheets of metal on a pile of junk, looking for an explanation for the absence of life around the ships, he was caught off guard by an earthquake. At first, he barely felt it, but the shaking got stronger. Before Khanor could scramble down the mountain of metal, the cause was made clear in the form of a creature that looked like a giant, biomechanical worm. A good fifty feet-long and a foot-wide, the worm-like thing was feeding on metal and machinery. Khanor had disrupted its meal.

"Don't worry, unidentified life form, I don't want to hurt you. I was just leaving," he tried to reassure the worm.

Khanor slowly backed away, but kept facing the creature. He accidentally stepped into a puddle of foul liquid. Glancing down at the smelly sludge, he saw his laser gun. What was it doing here? He had no idea. He swept it up and automatically went into a fighting pose. He wanted to shout 'Hands up!' at the creature, but it had no hands and it was already coming at him before he could give it any warning.

Khanor dove out of the giant earthworm's line of attack and almost got away… Almost—because the worm had closed its mouth around his hand, the one holding the weapon.

"You're going to force me to shoot, you know that?"

As if the creature understood what he was saying, it bobbed its head and turned around, spewing out gastric fluid along with Khanor's hand as it went. When he cleared his mind and went looking for his gun, he realized what had happened: the creature had swallowed it! Worse, when the leader of the Hand 28 was about to do something about the theft, the worm turned back on the metal mountain and made it shake enough that he could not run after it on the unstable heap.

Feeling a little angry and very alone with no way to contact his team, Agent Rhi looked around and saw a kind of path winding across the top of the piles of junk. If it was a passage—taken by the giant worm or the vanished survivors—it might be the best way to find out what happened here.

"Finally!" the ape grunted. "Jason, what were you doing?"

He was jogging toward him.

"I was trying to get some rock samples, OK?" the young man grinned.

"Why didn't you answer my calls?"

"Maybe I was busy fighting monsters."

"Monsters?"

"Let's say, giant wasps."

"You were too busy fighting giant wasps to answer?" Minus-3 was getting upset.

"Giant alien wasps! But that's not the problem. I didn't hear you. In case you haven't noticed, our communicators are on the fritz. I heard the Thumb and Khanor loud and clear from the Temposcaph, but here, away from it, between you and me, nothing."

To prove what he said Jason pressed the button. "Minus-3? Minus-3? Little Minus-3?" he spoke into the collar of his uniform.

Nothing. No sound came out of the ape's communicator except fuzzy interference.

"See? Weren't you the one who said they worked nicely?" Jason jeered.

"I also said they were discreet. Follow me. Varna's just been kidnapped. We have to find her."

After of few minutes of climbing down through the junk, Khanor reached the end of the path. He entered a big room with a vaulted ceiling but no other exit. The ground he had clambered over to get here was rough and chaotic, but in this round room, it was even worse. Cut through with cracks and crevasses, with walls studded with strange cavities, like ulcers dug into the rock. Khanor smiled at the thought of Jason (if he'd been here) comparing the bulges in the ceiling to goose bumps. When he'd taken the winding path, the leader of the Hand 28 was hoping to find out why the ships had ended up in the belly of the asteroid, but this place looked as deserted as the tunnels.

He moved around in the room scrutinizing every detail in the rock, everything worth noticing in order to maybe understand the specifics about the planetoid. He could not see the gas emitted intermittently from the cracks in the ground and walls, but his mask kept him from falling asleep. The more he thought about it, the more surprised he was not to see any denizens of the place. The giant worm he had pathetically confronted was probably just a survivor from one of the spaceships and its need to eat metal kept it in the junkyard. The asteroid apparently hypnotized the ships that approached it and he had to remember that they themselves had passed out and completely forgotten what they had done during the previous 36 hours.

He was about to return to his ship when one of the big dents in the ceiling opened up. When Khanor saw outer space through the weird opening, he understood, almost immediately, where he had gone wrong.

"But that would mean…"

"And after you laughed at me because of my giant wasps, you're going to tell me about a seven foot-tall toad man in a diving suit? Now, we've really seen it all."

"When you say it like that, it does sound ridiculous, but believe me, there was nothing very funny about it at the time," Minus-3 sounded upset.

"You've got a laser gun—why didn't you use it on the thing? You could've fried it in a split second."

"Is that how they did things in the 20th century? Deal with every conflict with weapons?"

The two agents were exploring the tunnels through the giant rock without any clue to tell them which way to go. There was no sign of the creature, nor any trace of Varna. So, they wandered aimlessly for a long time until they ended up on a walkway over a stone alcove that looked out on a huge room.

"Look at that!" Jason was amazed.

"No, I can't," Minus-3 whined.

"What do you mean you can't? Just open your eyes!"

"I can't… I get dizzy."

They were standing over an immensely long room full of cocoons as far as the eye could see. The place was some kind of hatchery or incubator, and when they went down into it, they were astonished at the size of some of the containers. All the species of the universe seemed to be archived here. Most of the cocoons were paired with another, side by side, and lined up to form interminable rows.

"Are you thinking what I'm thinking?" the former archeologist asked.

"A kind of Noah's Ark in space?" Minus-3 responded. "Looks like it."

"Where we're going to find Varna, banana?"

The ape glared at him. "Did you just call me banana because I'm a form of an ancient primate?"

Jason avoided the question. "Do you have any idea how we're supposed to find Agent Zelton among all these cocoons? I doubt there's a sign-in list by the front door."

"Scent."

"Scent? You mean…"

"We all have a personal body odor. Even with the masks, my sense of smell is highly developed. Walking down the aisles of this zoological museum, I should be able to smell her without too much difficulty…"

"OK, let's get going!" Jason was laughing now.

"For your information, you smell like hamburger and fries."

"Note that I didn't ask anything."

"Hush!"

"Hush yourself. You're the one who…"

Minus-3 put his hand on Jason's mouth and pushed him behind a cocoon. He froze for a few seconds, then relaxed his hold.

"I know I'm irresistible, Minus-3, but still…"

"Jason, be quiet! That's not it."

He peeked around the cocoon they were hiding behind trying to see through the shadows and mist from the geysers.

"What is it then?"

"I saw it… the frog-man… but I can't see it now."

Jason turned serious again and pulled out his gun.

"Varna must be close. Breathe, Minus-3. Breathe in deep and smell if she's around here. I'll watch your back."

"I don't know if I should feel better, but I'll take it. Let's go."

They advanced slowly, passing by the coupled cocoons, watching, searching, Jason covering the blind spots with his gun while Minus-3 sniffed the air through his mask.

"Do you smell anything?"

"Hold on, I've got her… left nostril…"

The augmented ape followed his nose and finally stopped in front of a cocoon the size of a human. He turned to Jason and pointed to the container.

"This is it, I'm sure!"

The two agents started opening the cocoon. The sepulcher felt rough, organic and bumpy like the surrounding rock. The sleeping gas being spit into the room clouded their view more than six feet around them. They pushed and pulled at the opening with all their strength, but nothing happened. It would not budge.

"Jason, you don't like me because basically you know I'm more intelligent and more clever than you," Minus-3 suddenly spoke out.

"Oh, augmented bonobo," the archeologist grumbled as he struggled with the opening, "you who are so wise, do you know what the word *minus* means?"

The two agents gritted their teeth. The veins on their foreheads and necks were popping out.

"Why does everything that comes out of your mouth sound insulting?" the ape punched the cocoon. "Besides, I've already told you many times that I prefer Encultured and Augmented Pan Paniscus Bonobo to Minus. And to address your question more precisely, do you know that, in our training center in Borneo, when we want to insult someone, we call them a 20th century man? It's like you calling someone a Cro-Magnon, I believe. Does that answer your question?"

"Did you take classes in sensitivity with the Thumb? You're upset with me because you know that, despite you being an ape, I'm a lot stronger and more agile than you!" Jason grunted as his muscles flexed.

"Cro-Magnon!"

And with this last surge of pride, Jason tore open the cocoon.

"You are very sensitive and particularly easy to manipulate," the ape was glad to see his ploy had worked.

Inside the cocoon, just as Minus-3 had said, was Varna, but the beauty kept sleeping. The super-ape looked around for something that ended up being only a few feet away. He picked up the mask and saw that there were hundreds of the creatures strewn over the ground. He went back and put the thing on Varna's face. She woke up abruptly and opened her eyes.

"What happened?" she asked worriedly.

"The mechanical toad kidnapped you," the ape sounded guilty.

"We were afraid he took you for a bath with him and that you'd be lolling around while we went searching for the cause of this mess. But luckily I was there and I saved you from the cocoon where you'd have stayed for an eternity."

"Jason, you're impossible…"

"Impossibly mighty? I know. Stop fighting it. That's why you let yourself get kidnapped, right? Just so that the valiant knight would rescue you? Mighty and chivalrous?"

"Don't overdo it. How'd you find me?"

Varna looked at the augmented ape and raised an eyebrow. Did she fully understand what Jason had just said? She was getting a bad migraine again.

"Agent Zelton, how do you feel?" Minus-3 asked.

"Still got this killer headache…"

"You were without your mask for a long time," Jason observed, "so you breathed in a lot of sleeping gas."

"It's not the gas. It's the… the sense of time in this vacuum of an asteroid. Space-Time is out of whack here. I feel it."

Jason did not understand what she meant and he looked at the ape to clear it up a little.

"Varna was exposed to the Continuum from a very early age," Minus-3 explained. "She's very sensitive and can feel when a temporal imbalance is at work… and surely the reason for the ships disappearing."

"OK," the young man replied without fully understanding everything. "Tell me, your mechanical toad, did it look like a spacesuit full of tubes with a frog's head?"

"Exactly," she was waking up now. "Why?"

"Because he's right behind you."

Varna and Minus-3 swung around in a flash, sparked by surprise and fear. Varna was still a little groggy and Jason did not like this kind of surprise. Minus-3 was determined not to get beaten this time.

Steam was spitting out by the pumps and tubes of the creature's suit. It was impossible to decipher the expression on the frog face that stood before them, but all three of them were ready to fight.

"You-stay," the creature said.

"We leave," Minus-3 snapped back.

"What did you do to me?" Varna sounded a little scared.

"Sorry, but I just invited my friends to fast food. I'd like my primate friend here to taste a real good 20th century burger. I'm a man of my word so don't make me break my promise. And I do believe I can smell the grill."

The humanoid amphibian stepped forward.

"Watch out, my friend has a bad history with toads. It's better not to get him riled up, if you please, Mr. Astronaut."

"Like he says," the angry ape agreed.

"Explain yourself, please," Varna pleaded. "Why? I don't understand. What's happening here?"

While the two others faced off against the creature, Jason went around the cocoon and grabbed the creature from behind. The amphibian struggled fiercely.

"You-stay-for-your-good!" it moaned.

"For your good too!" Jason said.

Agent Spell bent his back and, as the creature tried to shake free, he threw it down. The creature fell hard under the weight of its spacesuit. Some tubes broke off, shooting oxygen into the air. The toad struggled more, frightened now.

"No! Put-back-tubes!"

"Put back nothing at all," Jason snarled as he kept the creature pinned to the ground.

Minus-3 came over with Varna right behind him.

"Who are you and what do you want with us?" the ape asked.

"Help-human-female."

"How?"

"Breathe-air-good-in-cocoon."

The three agents looked at one another, not sure they really understood what the creature was trying to say.

"You want to help Varna breathe better?" Minus-3 asked. "You kidnapped her to help her?"

"Yes."

"Oh."

While he was putting the tubes back in place, making sure the outside gas could not get into the suit, Jason saw that the creature had passed out. He scratched his head, feeling even more bumbling, and sat the frog-man up to wait for him to come around.

"Sorry," he whispered to the sleeping creature.

"I'm a man of my word, don't make me break my promise?" Minus-3 repeated with a laugh.

"I was trying to scare him," Jason barked.

"Only someone who knows you could be scared by such an assertion."

"You're probably right," he nodded to the simian agent. "It even sends shivers down my spine!"

"Varna? Minus-3? Jason? Do you read me?" a worried voice came over the communicators.

"Khanor? Loud and clear," Varna answered still feeling nauseous.

"Why'd you call me last?" Jason grumbled.

"Because you're always the last to listen. I'm back at the Temposcaph. Get back here immediately, it's urgent!"

"Are you all right, Khanor?" Varna ran up to him.

The mission leader was taking samples of the weird rock in the grotto where the Temposcaph was parked.

"Yes, yes, and you? No injuries?"

"Jason accidentally knocked out an amphibian in a spacesuit."

"It's the ape's fault. I thought he'd kidnapped Varna when he was really just trying to save her from the noxious air."

"What exactly is happening?" Agent Rhi stood up and turned a gloomy face to them. "I should have understood immediately! I don't know why I didn't make the connection sooner..."

"Just because we're time traveling doesn't mean you're getting any younger, Khanor."

"And your recklessness is going to get you killed, Jason."

"What can I say, I'm ahead of my time!"

"You're just twenty centuries too late," Minus snubbed.

"Excuse me, children, could we get back to our problem," Varna complained. "Khanor, what's going on?"

"You're right about the distortion of Space-Time. The asteroid... it's the host! We're inside a huge alien head! Each of the tunnels is one of its arteries. The junkyard I saw must be its mouth and stomach and I stumbled into the place where its eyes are..."

"And we found the pantry!"

"The cerebral activity is causing the electromagnetic disturbances and the Space-Time anomaly. The gas circulating through its body is putting to sleep all the crew that fly within range."

"And I suppose we'd be considered a virus wandering through its veins?" Varna wondered.

"Pretty much, but it's not up to us to decide what to do with this form of extraterrestrial life."

"Are you saying we're done and we can go eat?" Jason asked.

"Right, let's make our report to the Thumb and get out of here."

"I am getting hungry, too, I have to admit," Minus-3 agreed.

Jason was the first to take off his mask, but when he struggled with it, the others came to help him.

"What the...?!"

Each of them tried to remove the ray-shaped creature that was clinging to their necks.

"*No!*" a voice screamed into all heads at the same time.

"What the hell is that?" Jason asked.

"Who are you?" Khanor demanded telepathically.

"*We are the Hive. We are plugged into your synapses. We filter your air and, in return, we feed on your memories—*

your short-term memory. We can't live without you. Please stay."

"Stay? Like the others? The ones you stored up down there?" Jason shouted.

"Yes. Like them. We breathe together. We share our memories. We live together and forever."

"You let out the gas so that we need to have an air filter, right?" Khanor asked. "These things, these masks, these creatures are your antibodies, your agents that lure your victims, isn't that so?"

The Hive did not reply. The leader of the Hand 28 tore off his mask by pulling hard on the tail of the alien ray and the organic device slipped off. When Minus-3 saw this, he did the same, imitated right away by Varna and Jason. They threw the masks on the ground and Khanor picked up the samples he had taken before heading back to the Temposcaph. Unfortunately, the last of them had just removed the mask when Khanor fell to the ground, unconscious. When Minus-3 tried to help him, he, too, succumbed to the sleeping gas that had spread quickly. By the time Varna and Jason realized what was happening, it was too late. They both dropped to the floor.

"Ohhh!" Jason moaned.

The agent got up rubbing his temples. His chin hurt and his knees ached. Around him Khanor, Varna and Minus-3 were doing the same thing. All of them were wincing from an intense migraine.

The agents of the Hand 28 were disoriented. None of them could remember how they got here. They looked around, trying to get a handle on the situation. The four of them were in a huge, underground cave with dark tunnels winding down through the rock.

Khanor rubbed his sore neck while making sure that the rest of his team was all right, uninjured and that no immediate threat was lurking in the shadows, waiting to pounce on them. The Temposcaph, the bubble-shaped Chronosphere that was their means of transport through space and time, was a few yards away, hidden in the gloom of the mysterious grotto.

"I'm not tipping anyone's hand when I say, uh... *What the hell is this?"* Jason asked.

"I wouldn't put it in such primitive terms," the augmented ape replied, "but that is the general idea."

"I have a splitting headache," Varna said, "and the strange feeling that something is terribly wrong."

"Does anyone remember what we're doing here and why we all obviously passed out?" Khanor questioned.

Excerpt of official report from the Thumb, dated CTA 4004
To: Admiral Rom Hagan, Commanding Officer of the Time Brigade and Secretary-General of Earth.
cc: Kobul Shan, Head of the Time Brigade.

(...)

The agents of the Hand 28 got out of their predicament 48 hours after the start of their mission, after Agent Jason Spell, on the verge of starvation, decided to go against the orders of Coordinator Rhi and return to the base on his own initiative. His impulsive behavior and disrespect of orders allowed them, to the great surprise of all, to disengage from the time loop.

The zone near the living planetoid called the Hive is now under surveillance so that no other vessel can approach it. The geological singularity is being studied by the agents of Hand 27 led by Coordinator Jeremiah Watson and this in order to determine the degree of danger and any possible solutions the Time Brigade might be able to provide if need be.
(...)

The Sea King is the nom-de-hero *of Daniel Cluny, whose uncle performed an operation that gave him incredible underwater breathing powers that made him amphibious.*

Robert Darvel: *11,000 Underwater Gorges*

For Juliette's father, Joko Smartcucumber

A mysterious shipwreck

It all started with the wreck of a ship off the coast of Brittany, a few miles from the Glénan Islands.

The news made headlines in the French papers. The photo accompanying the article, taken from a rescue helicopter, showed the site of the tragedy, an empty sea covered with debris. The article did not mention the exact circumstances of the drama and for good reason—there were no survivors to talk about it.

That morning, Scilla Cadot had moored her boat not far from Loctudy. She was supposed to pick up her father, the famous industrialist Michel Cadot, coming back from a meeting at the Industrial Center and take him to Pine Island (*l'île des Pins*), where they had their family home. Behind the wheel of the car she had borrowed from a friend, she waved to her father at the bus station. But while Michel thought they would head out right away, his daughter had decided to enjoy the drive and took the road to Quimper.

"But, good heavens, why such a detour?"

"I have a few things to buy."

Michel tried to make the best of a bad situation. While his daughter was doing her shopping, he stayed in the car to read the paper he had bought. When Scilla got back, she found him preoccupied and pensive.

"Bad news?" she looked at the newspaper but said nothing more on the way back to the port.

The Sea King & Scilla by Mario Cubbino

Heading for Black Island

As soon as he was aboard the yacht, Michel Cadot told his daughter to head for Black Island, which belonged to Emile Cluny, a respected scientist in the field of oceanography and ichthyology.

"Does this have anything to do with that horrible news?" Scilla asked.

"Yes. I've heard Daniel talk about the ship that sank, the *Sitnalta*. He might just know some of the people that were on board when the tragedy... I need to be sure and be there for him if that is the case."

Scilla was happy to visit Daniel Cluny, so there was no need to protest. She headed for the last island of the Glénan archipelago, Black Island, where he lived. As soon as the yacht docked, Daniel, fair-haired with a black streak, a manly face with honest eyes, was there to greet them. He kissed Scilla warmly on the cheek and said hello to Michel Cadot.

A little later, when they were in the laboratory, Daniel told them the truth about the ship.

"I know that behind its new name, *Sitnalta*, the ship really belonged to the French Navy. That shipwreck bodes nothing good because I'm afraid it might be connected in some way to a secret project of theirs. Early tomorrow morning, I'm going to the site of the wreck..."

The next day, Daniel Cluny was at the helm of his boat. Scilla insisted on going with him and was at the railing examining the waves. Soon, she cried out:

"Look, here's Pegasus! Hey, Pegasus!"

Pegasus was a tamed dolphin that Daniel had saved after he had gotten caught in a fishing net.

"He really is as loyal as a dog."

"Especially since my uncle..."

But Daniel did not finish his sentence, leaving Scilla puzzled. What did he mean? Could Professor Cluny, who had operated on his nephew to give him extraordinary underwater breathing powers and abilities, have used his science on Pegasus the dolphin?

Scilla had to stop wondering because they had reached the site of the tragedy. The sea was calm, as if nothing had happened. Daniel got ready to dive. Scilla insisted again on accompanying him. She slipped into her wetsuit and buckled on her oxygen tanks.

Two minutes later, they were swimming in the deep, accompanied by the faithful Pegasus who darted around them making lots of sounds as if he was trying to talk to them.

A creature of the laboratory

They found the *Sitnalta* lying thirty meters down—one hundred feet underwater. Daniel gestured to Scilla to wait outside because there were serious risks in exploring a shipwreck. She agreed.

He swam through a crack in the hull and found himself in a familiar environment. During his career in the French Navy, he had been on ships like this one. With a wary but seasoned eye, he looked through the various rooms, including the laboratory with all its electronic and surgical equipment. As he was about to leave, he noticed a dark bundle lying under the remains of some kind of aquarium...

Scilla Cadot saw him suddenly shoot out of the wreck with a bundle in his arms. He waved at her to go back up.

Soon, they were heading back to Black Island. Scilla could not get Daniel to tell her what was in that package.

Later, when she was in the kitchen preparing their meal with the new utensils she'd bought in Pont Croix, Daniel put his bundle on the steel table in his lab.

"What's weird," he told his uncle, "is that I didn't see any corpses, except for this one stuck under some pipework. I'm forced to conclude that all the drowned sailors were eaten by predators."

"In such a short time? I know predators like giant moray eels can swallow entire bodies , but they're rare in these waters—too close to the coast."

While talking, Daniel opened the wet tarp and Professor Cluny was speechless upon seeing the torso of a man stuck in the body of what looked like a huge sea cucumber.

"It sure looks weird, uncle, but it's just as I thought: a herd of sea cucumbers were attracted by the corpses and devoured them all."

The scientist leaned over the jumble of flesh.

"Daniel, I think you're mistaken. You think you see a man being eaten by a predator that died in the process…"

"You don't agree?"

"No, I don't. What we're looking at is a *laboratory creature*. Someone tried to graft these two bodies together. It's the *human* part that couldn't handle the benthic surgery and it killed the holothurian."

"A half-man, half-holothurian! This would be proof of secret bio-engineering experiments conducted by the Navy!"

Daniel paced around the room, deep in thought. Emile Cluny added:

"The reason why you found no drowned corpses is because they came and took them away."

"Why would they do that?" Daniel was skeptical.

"Because it's in the interest of the Navy to keep such experiments secret—*especially if they're still going on!*"

Daniel looked at him without saying a word.

Project Second Atlantis

Later, Daniel Cluny started his investigation. He got in touch with some old acquaintances. One evening on the terrace, a week after the tragedy, he told his uncle and Scilla what he had learned.

"I got definite confirmation on the existence of a secret project being conducted by a shadow department inside the Navy and called Project Second Atlantis."

"Ah, yes!" Scilla said. "Their ship was called *Sitnalta*. That's *Atlantis* spelled backwards."

"The project aims at getting personnel capable of living and working in the depths of the ocean in order to exploit its riches," Daniel continued. "It is headed by Professor Georges Pichard. My contact at Department X, Joel Laubau, whispered to me that they call him *The Merman*. Unfortunately, Pichard was one of the men who vanished in the wreck of the *Sitnalta*. Project Second Atlantis has now been completely crippled."

"This project raises serious ethical questions. Why was it authorized?"

"What are you thinking, uncle?"

"Faced with poor results, possible failure even, one could easily imagine the Navy wanted to wipe out all traces of their, er, questionable work."

"Isn't that being a little too hard on them?" Scilla asked. "You have a very negative image of the Government if you think they wouldn't hesitate to sacrifice their own people."

The professor smiled at her. "I hope you're right. Perhaps I'm judging them far too harshly. Still, keep in mind, young lady, that the goal of exploiting the ocean's natural resources, which could be an honorable pursuit for the well-being of a nation, can also be the cause of bitter conflicts."

"Yes. We might be looking at a case of sabotage by a another country defending its interests," Daniel interpreted.

"It's just a hypothesis," his uncle reminded them.

Daniel Cluny decided to expand his investigation. That evening, he scheduled a meeting with Joel Laubau in Douarnenez. As he got there, he saw a crowd gathered in front of their meeting place—a local café. He rushed over, a growing anguish gnawing away at him, and elbowed his way through the crowd.

"A guy jumped off the bridge into the Pouldavid River," a police officer explained.

After a short conversation, using his title of Navy Captain, Daniel got the name of the victim: it was indeed Joel Laubau!

The giant sea cucumber

From that moment on, Daniel Cluny was determined to solve the case. He spent whole days exploring the shipwreck of the *Sitnalta*. However, he didn't make any significant discovery except finding that the ship had been torpedoed or harpooned almost vertically from under the waterline, which disproved the idea of it being sunk by a submarine.

One astonishing fact was that the edges of the breach were covered with some kind of thick mucus that, according to Emile Cluny who studied its toxins, belonged to a holothurian.

"A giant sea cucumber then!" Daniel exclaimed. "A sea creature able to split a steel ship in two!"

He searched harder, dove again and again, explored the area around the wreck looking for evidence. He had found nothing of interest until, one day, when he was floating through some huge rocks covered with algae, he suddenly found himself being enveloped by a huge shadow. Pegasus had already swum off, troubled by some unexplainable anxiety. Fearing it was a prowling predator, Daniel hid in the algae and looked up.

Above him, a monstrous sea cucumber was passing by, identifiable by its tube feet, its soft tissue, and especially its mouth surrounded by tentacles. The specimen measured over fifteen feet long and a good seven feet wide. It was the most massive and magnificent sea cucumber he had ever seen! A real sea monster! Bigger than any echinoderm ever discovered!

But that was not the most extraordinary thing. As the side of the creature brushed against the rock where he was concealed, Daniel saw a sharp, steel spur sticking out in such a way that it looked like a big swordfish. And a transparent membrane hidden by a row of filaments, round, the size of a bull's eye. Behind it was *a human figure*! The giant sea cucumber was, in fact, a kind of living bathyscaph piloted by a man!

This, obviously, was what had speared the *Sitnalta*!

Daniel could not miss his chance. Without a moment's hesitation, he grabbed the back end of the animal and hid among the filaments, not worrying about the toxins because he had his wetsuit on. Then he hung on for the ride.

While the sea cucumber was swimming away, Daniel saw Pegasus a good distance away, looking suspicious and distrustful. He waved to him to come closer. The dolphin obeyed and he used sign language to tell him to go back and warn Scilla who was aboard their boat. He pointed in the direction that he thought the sea monster was taking, and where he hoped the dolphin would lead her.

Armed with all this information, Pegasus—thanks to its augmented brain improved by Emile Cluny—darted up to the surface.

Into the Deep

The holothurian dove deep into the sea. Daniel Cluny silently thanked his uncle for giving him his extraordinary underwater powers. But there was a limit to his powers. If the sea cucumber dragged him too far, too deep and too long, he might have to give up and return to the surface.

The voyage continued. Darkness slowly took over the light. The perpetual underwater twilight settled in and blotted out the amazing seascapes. Soon, it was pitch back, pierced only by phosphorescent lights, some of them moving—the deep-water organisms or mineral formations covered with luminous algae.

A beam of light shot out of the sea cucumber's mouth and lit up the space in front of it. Sticking his head out of the filaments Daniel Cluny was surprised to see a kind of pale circle in the distance—impossible to tell how far. Was it another creature from the depths? The sea cucumber seemed to be swimming toward the glowing phenomenon. It dove down and headed straight toward it.

Daniel was suddenly struck by an astonishing revelation: what he had first thought was another kind of jellyfish was in fact a shining underwater dome, around ten yards in diameter, an artificial structure with glass walls being lit from the inside!

The holothurian approached a shaft abutting the dome—an airlock. It moved its tentacles over a round mechanism, the airlock opened and it went in.

Daniel had no choice but to go along. Whether he liked it or not, he entered the fabulous structure, even if he knew he would eventually be discovered by whoever lived in that base. He stayed lying against the sea cucumber while the airlock closed behind them. The water level went down. Soon, a pool was revealed with a crescent-shaped deck that allowed the sea cucumber to remain in the water but its pilot to step onto the dry quay.

Daniel witnessed how the creature released its pilot. A shiver ran down the entire holothurian body and white filaments popped out of its anal orifice. Then it pushed out a kind of pod that looked like a cocoon, out of which emerged a man dressed in a yellow, black and spinach green wetsuit. He brushed off the filaments and stood on the landing. When he took off his helmet, Daniel grunted in surprise. He recognized the man. It was Georges Pichard!

What to do now? How should he proceed? This was the critical moment. Luckily, Pichard had not seen him. The scientist left through a thick door in the back that he opened by turning a wheel next to it. Daniel was left alone. The sea cucumber was flopping around in the water. The Sea King knew that it was regenerating after having released the internal organs that had held its passenger. He noticed several round openings under the surface of the water, all closed. When one of them finally opened, the holothurian slipped through and the panel shut behind it.

Meanwhile, on the surface, Scilla saw Pegasus returning alone. What had happened to Daniel? She watched the dolphin's dance, jumping and rolling around in the waves very urgently. After a moment of bewilderment, she understood: Pegasus was showing her where she had to go. Yes, Daniel had given him a set of directions for her to follow. He had surely found something important about the shipwreck.

Scilla lifted anchor, turned on the engine, and headed south-south-west.

In the secret base

Daniel Cluny went to the door through which Georges Pichard had disappeared. He did not hesitate for a second; his decision was made; he took hold of the wheel and turned. When the wheel stopped moving, he pushed the door open slowly. Then he entered a room that looked like the airlock control room. It had screens, levers and pipes, and a communication system. A man was sitting at the console. When Daniel stepped into the room, the man swung around and pointed a gun at him. The screens had showed him that an intruder was present.

"Don't move!" the man ordered. "I don't know how you managed to get down here, but now, you're a prisoner. If you move, you're dead!"

While he was talking, his free hand pressed a red button and an alarm went off. Daniel had nothing to lose, so counting on the element of surprise, he jumped and before the guard could fire, he hit him as hard as he could and knocked him out.

Daniel was surprised that the man's body seemed so soft, but was even more surprised when he fell out of his chair to discover that only the upper part of his body was human. From his pelvis down, instead of legs, there was just a long mass of soft flesh! He truly was a merman!

Without lingering on this astounding sight, Daniel looked around the room. He saw two steel doors. This secret base had obviously been well designed and solidly built. Was it the secret goal of Project Second Atlantis that Georges Pichard had masterminded? Was the sinking of the *Sitnalta* a mere accident rather than a cover-up as Professor Cluny had suggested? If that were the case, Daniel had just punched a Navy officer! Half-man, half-fish, yes, but still a former colleague. He was lost in speculation. The best way to solve the mystery was to go forward. What door should he choose?

60

Trusting his instincts, he went for the left. It opened onto a corridor that, judging from its slight slope, went down into the bowels of the base. Counting his steps, Daniel figured that he had passed the area under the dome, which must have been only the visible part of a much bigger complex. Could the French Navy have built such a huge underwater structure without anyone knowing it?

With his head full of questions, Daniel kept moving. He was calm enough to have taken the merman's weapon and he was ready to shoot as he descended into the secret base.

Who is Georges Pichard?

He reached a room that he thought was huge because his footsteps echoed in it like in a church. Before he had a chance to get a good look, a spotlight suddenly blinded him and a voice rang out:

"Drop your weapon!"

Daniel obeyed and laid the gun on the floor. Even when he shielded his eyes, the light was still too bright for him to see anything. Not knowing whether he was dealing with villains or the Navy, he declared:

"My name is Daniel Cluny and I'm an officer in the French Navy! I mean you no harm!"

"We know who you are, Daniel Cluny—the so-called Sea King! In fact, we knew you'd be coming sooner or later."

The voice sounded familiar. It was Georges Pichard talking. Daniel had met him two years before on a mission. He decided to take a shot.

"You can spare me the spotlight because I, too, know who you are, Professor Pichard!"

A burst of laughter broke out. "Is that right? So, tell me, Cluny, *do you know who Professor Pichard really is?*"

The light switched off. Daniel blinked. He was in a vast room whose floor was bare and decorated only with a mosaic representing hideous creatures. Six feet up on the wall, a line of lights proved that the room was indeed circular. Cluny saw two figures dressed in green, yellow and black suits on either side of a man standing on his own two legs. Daniel blinked and saw his face clearly: it was indeed Georges Pichard.

The man raised his hand under his chin, spread his fingers and lifted what turned out to be a mask, revealing the face of a stranger.

"My real name is Isambard," the man said. "I used Pichard's identity to sabotage Project Second Atlantis."

Sabotage? So, now Daniel knew now that all this—the base and the shipwreck—was not the result of some secret Navy project. More likely, it was the warped plan of evil organization...

"Do you want to know why, Daniel Cluny? Well, I can tell you everything. It makes no difference if you know the truth, because either you will join us, or you will die! Ha ha!"

And Isambard let out a shriek of laughter that split the eardrums...

Daniel Cluny had been dragged behind Isambard by his escort. The Sea King was in for more surprises. The men he thought were dressed in wetsuits were really hybrids with green sides, yellow bellies and skin that made a hideous transformation into thick, black dorsal scales. Their faces were still human, which made them look like something out a nightmare. Faint but visible lines at the base of their neck were the only sign that they had gills and were thus real amphibians.

The Mermen

They finally arrived at Isambard's private rooms and his henchmen stopped—they were not authorized to enter. Daniel walked into the room. Isambard closed the door and was alone with the Sea King, but he only needed to make a simple signal and the guards would come rushing in.

"Do you know what that secret department of the French Navy was trying to achieve with Project Second Atlantis?"

"It had to do with the colonization and exploitation of the deep sea, right?"

"Exactly. The natural resources on land are diminishing as the needs of the population increase exponentially. Inevitably, the riches of the sea will be exploited. And that means two things: one, more competition between nations, and two, better technology to meet the challenge. But Project Second Atlantis came too late. The deep sea has already been colonized... *by me*! I've worked on this for a long time, not waiting for the lack of food and coal and gas and cereal for my breakfast to make me panic like those shortsighted brass hats. I've been down here for years now. I staked my claim before all of them, and what could their stupid little project, doomed to failure, might discover? My secret base, of course! Those idiots were trying to take over my territory. I couldn't let them do it, so... Sabotage! Annihilation! Using the Pichard identity, I got myself recruited, which was easy with my knowledge. I even gave them some key information regarding the mutation of deep-sea workers. Then, with a snap of my fingers—I can gloat about it now—I destroyed all their work. Ha, ha, ha!"

"Why was no body found in the shipwreck?"

"You really didn't find anyone?" Isambard asked. "Not even the holothurian man?"

"Just him, yes."

"He was left on purpose to convince people how absurd the project was in case they went looking for new funding after their fiasco. Myself, I am far beyond their stupid experiments. The guards you've seen are half-men, half-pelagic fish with modified metabolisms and can survive at great depths. My Mermen have both lungs and gills like certain amphibians like axolotls. You can consider them your relatives, Cluny."

"But if I understand you correctly, if your own achievements are so much greater than what the Navy could accomplish, why attack them? Couldn't you just get them to accept your control over the underwater resources?"

"To become *King of the World* for ten minutes, like James Cameron, then get taken over by Big Money? No, thank you!"

Isambard stepped close to Daniel Cluny, who could see how sick and twisted the man looked.

"My goal is exactly the opposite of the Navy's. It is not to save the world, but to drown it once and for all! It is not their *Second Atlantis* but my *New Atlantis*!"

New Atlantis

Isambard jumped out of his seat and approached the giant control screen. He pushed three cursors and the black turned gray.

"Look!"

Daniel Cluny raised his head and looked at the image appearing on the video circuit. At first, he saw a slow tracking shot over the seabed. Frightened sea creatures were darting off to the right and left, proof that the scene was being filmed by a mobile camera. Then, it crossed a flat space lacking all signs of life.

"We owe these images to the sacrifice of one of my Mermen with an underwater camera," Isambard announced without the slightest trace of emotion.

Daniel gripped the arms of his chair. What did Isambard mean? What hideous sight was he going to subject him to?

All of a sudden, the edge of a precipice came in view. With a low-angle shot, the camera revealed a crater of enormous size, hundreds of yards across, at least. Like a crater on the moon, a *living mouth* that opened onto a blood-red abyss out of which shot beams of light...

"An underwater volcano! Lava!" he raised his voice.

"Not at all," Isambard corrected him. "Mucus! It's a mouth opening onto a gorge. A voracious gorge. Look!"

The Merman cameraman was filming the edges of the crater that were quivering under some weird, telluric wave, a force moving in opposite directions. The gorge was literally *devouring* the rock, chewing it, swallowing it until it disappeared.

Abruptly the image started shaking. Then the camera floated and filmed its own fall into the gorge. As it spun around, it caught a glimpse of the Merman who was sucked down and vanished... diving into red, crimson, purple... then black.

"It's..."

"Spectacular?" Isambard proposed. "Prodigious?"

"Terrifying!"

"The fate of that Merman will be that of the rest of the world," Isambard said. "My Mermen were created to sow their pelagic seeds. See, the bottom of the ocean is a base formed by the mixture of antediluvian minerals and cells from long-vanished pelagic organisms that just need a little push to come back to life. Then the ocean floors will become living, breathing, eating creatures that will literally devour the dry lands. You just saw one gorge, only one... there will soon be eleven thousand underwater gorges!"

"But why?" Daniel Cluny asked.

"To follow the path that Atlantis carved before it was destroyed by the madness of men. Men were always wrong about Atlantis. They didn't disappear in some kind of cataclysmic extinction, they showed us the path! Yes, Earth will become a vast ocean that no one can spoil and defile!"

Daniel didn't want to tell the madman that it wasn't at all what had happened to Atlantis, and that the real Atlantis, which he had visited several times with his friend Marino, was still alive and well. Instead, he asked:

"And you? Are you going to sacrifice your own existence for this plan?"

"Me? Dear boy, I've thought of everything. You saw how I developed a symbiotic relationship with the holothurian that I use as a bathyscaph. Well, I'm on the verge of connecting with the underwater heart of the Earth, the heart coming to life, with its neural pathways, synapses, a whole network of nerves... I shall become the consciousness of the Earth! I will

be the Earth, pure consciousness, stripped of material tempta-
tion, pure mind forever submerged in an amniotic bath! Ha ha
ha!

My God, Daniel thought, *he is completely mad.*

The Sea King's last chance

Counting on the element of surprise, the Sea King
jumped on Isambard. He wrapped around him like algae and
then, once on his back, he grabbed his throat to keep him from
calling his henchmen.

"Yell and I'll snap your neck," Daniel said, determined
to treat his host like a fisherman treats a minnow.

"You'll never get out of here alive," Isambard coughed
out.

"We'll see about that, you damn lunatic!"

He dragged his prisoner to the door and opened it. The
henchmen, three of them, were still on duty.

"Stay back and don't try anything, or I'll kill him!" Daniel warned. "Now get inside!"

The thugs obeyed. None of them wanted to take the risk
of sounding the alarm, which they would have done if
Isambard had shouted out. Daniel relieved them of their
weapons, still keeping a firm grip on Isambard's throat. Then
he closed the door and jammed one of the weapons to block
the handle. He pointed another gun at Isambard.

"Try to run and I'll shoot. All that will change is how
you'll die."

"You won't get thirty feet before they stop you."

"Just show me the way to the airlock."

With the spear gun stabbing his back Isambard did as he
was told. The two of them went back down the corridor to the
room where the blinding light had flashed before. The six
mermen inside turned around when they entered. The Sea
King had no choice. He did not like gratuitous violence, but an
example was needed to show the superior number of Mermen
that attacking him would be foolish. He pointed his second

66

gun at one of them and pulled the trigger. The harpoon flew into the merman's chest and he dropped to the floor, mortally wounded.

"Stay calm and drop your weapons. Now back up or I'll skewer you like the fish you are."

They did not think twice. Staring at their dead comrade, they laid down their spear guns and cleared the way. Daniel Cluny and his prisoner went through the door and into the long, sloping corridor that led to the control room. After locking the door, they marched forward.

In the control room, Daniel saw that they had taken away the body of the guard but not replaced him. Keeping Isambard in his sights, he glanced over the room until he found what he was looking for: a group of screens showing submerged cells where sea cucumbers were floating. He pointed at what looked like the biggest.

"We're going there," he ordered.

"What do you think you're doing?" Isambard sputtered.

"Bringing you back to the surface to be judged for your crimes. Unless you want me to lay a waterlogged corpse at the feet of French justice?"

Isambard shrugged. He obviously figured he would find a way to escape the Sea King sooner or later. It was a long way back to the surface and besides, how did Cluny expect to get the holothurian to obey him?

A sea cucumber for two

Being watched more carefully than ever, Isambard pulled the lever for the cell containing the chosen sea cucumber. The water drained out of it. Then he pressed a button and the air-lock opened.

"After you," Daniel said.

The two of them went through the second door that led them to a row of airlocks. They entered the opened one. Isambard pointed to a kind of strap full of sockets hooked up to cables.

"That's the harness needed to bend the animal to your will," Isambard said.

"So, gear up and get in."

Isambard broke out laughing.

"I don't see how you're going to make me follow you through the sea once I'm at the commands."

"That's why I chose the biggest of your protégés here—there's room for two. Now, get inside!"

With the spear gun still threatening him, Isambard slipped the strap around his neck and bent down to step into the sea cucumber. The Sea King was right behind him, poking his ribs with the harpoon the whole time.

The sea cucumber had plenty of room for the two men to lie down side by side. Thanks to the windows letting in light from the airlock, Daniel could see that the inside of the animal was a soft, silky white, like an intestine.

He let Isambard connect the cables to the electrical extensions surgically implanted in the brain tissue of their strange host.

Soon, the sea cucumber, piloted by the scientist, left its cell, which automatically closed behind it. Isambard pressed a button on a box attached to the strap so that all the necessary procedures were carried out: the room filled with water, the exterior door opened and the sea cucumber began its voyage in the depths of the sea. The scientist had not neglected to equip it with a headlight so they could see the ocean floor, gray and furry looking, as they moved forward.

"Go around the base," the Sea king ordered his prisoner.

They made a tour of the dome whose exterior airlock was still open.

"Give me that box!"

Lying too close to him like in a sleeping bag, Isambard could not disobey. Daniel grabbed the box and pressed a button like he had seen Isambard do earlier.

He had opened the interior airlock!

Water flooded into the base.

"You're going to drown everything!" the scientist shouted.

"Exactly!"

"My machines! My neural center! My Mermen!"

"Who I'm sure can escape and survive."

"They'll be eaten by predator fish!"

"Would you rather they take part in the upcoming trial?
Now, enough of this, Isambard! Head for the surface!"

"Never!" he screamed. "I'd rather die!"

And shaking his head violently, he thrust the holothurian
forward and it shot off into the depths of the ocean!

Into the gorge!

Daniel Cluny could do nothing. Isambard kept pushing
the sea cucumber. They raced deeper into the sea for a quart of
an hour, farther and farther, faster and faster. The Sea King
knew that he could swim back to the surface safely thanks to
his extraordinary powers, but he refused to abandon the man
responsible for the sinking of the *Sitnalta*.

"You can't escape the justice of men."

"Nor you that of my New Atlantis!" Isambard yelled.
"Look! Over there!"

Through the porthole, Daniel saw their dreadful destination and the ghastly end toward which the mad scientist was
driving them: a mouth, like the one on the screen, just a few
miles off the coast of Brittany!

It was a stunning sight. It looked like a living crater, a
hungry crater, ringed with two rows of jaws or rather a double
band of fibers bristling with teeth, gnawing away with a weird,
revolting movement and crushing all the rocks and fish in its
reach. Was this hellish mouth getting bigger the more it ate?
Daniel was not sure. It was hard to see through all the sedi-
ment being kicked up.

"Ha ha!" Isambard bellowed. "I'm taking you down with
me! We will be forever united in the heart of my New Atlantis
while Earth is being devoured!"

"I don't think so," the Sea King said calmly as he ripped the strap off Isambard's neck.

He obviously thought of wearing the harness himself and using his own will to control the sea cucumber, but Isambard would not give it up. He got a grip on the metal jacks and plunged his fingers into the bloody tissue. Maybe he was trying to pilot the animal directly from its nerve center...

It was an utterly desperate move and the sea cucumber bucked, throwing the two men against each other and the spear gun went off, the harpoon shot out... and Isambard screamed. The harpoon had gone through his ribs and nailed him to the flesh of the sea cucumber.

Looking through the window again, Daniel saw that they were heading straight into the greedy gorge! It was a foregone conclusion, tragic but inevitable...

Daniel had to get out of the sea cucumber. He had to give up the idea of delivering Isambard to French justice. He could not carry him away since he was nailed to the holothurian and dying. Besides, even with his gills, the scientist could never survive the ascent.

Quickly, the Sea King swung around, shot out his arms, crawled and slithered until he finally slid out of the animal. When he was free, he had to swim hard to get away from the grinding gorge. He called on all his strength, reaching deep down in his body hardened by so many adventures...

He finally saw light breaking on the surface. Figuring that he was now far enough away and out of danger, he turned around—just in time to see the sea cucumber vanish into the ravenous gorge.

Epilogue

Later, a powerful, underwater explosive charge would be set y the Navy, following the Sea King's directions. The gorge would disappear after swallowing its creator. Over the next few months, the fishermen would drag up the remains of the mermen, which added another mystery to the countless legends of the sea.

Did Isambard have time to open up gorges elsewhere? Nobody knew, but for the moment Daniel was not thinking about it. He was in a restaurant with Scilla Cadot, a restaurant that did not specialize in seafood, unlike most of them in coastal Brittany. He was at *Gargantua's* in Audierne, sitting in front of a huge rib roast cooked in the brick oven.

"You see, Scilla," he said, "seafood is wonderful but sometimes *you have to know when enough is enough!*"

Kidz by Alfredo Macall

Kidz *are a team of teenage superheroes brought together by the eccentric British scientist* **Archie Bolt**. *It is comprised of* **Motoman** *(Tommy Spencer), an ace biker riding a souped up motorcycle;* **Qube** *(Tom Tanner), able to materialize any energy construct he can visualize thanks to an alien medallion;* **Marino**, *an amphibian;* **Fl@mbo** *(Gaelle de Neuchatel), a wheelchair-bound girl with the ability to patrol cyberspace;* **Superbill** *(Bill Thomas), a computer prodigy; and* **Ivan Wolinsky**, *a teenage psychic.*

Willy Favre: *Our Common Enemy*

> *"If I had the power to forget, I would forget.*
> *All human memory is laden with sorrow and trouble."*
> Charles Dickens

The ceiling in his room was gray and grimy, spotted with damp stains. Lying on his bed, his arms crossed and his mouth dry and cottony, Motoman took a few long minutes to get his eyes used to the daylight.

A thin ray of light snuck through the thick curtains that were torn in parts. The room was an unbelievable mess, a chaos of dirty laundry, lone socks and odd clothes that had never seen the inside of a washing machine. Tommy Spencer's fingers still tingled, his leg hurt and his head was screaming in pain. He could not remember what he had drunk last night, but it must have been strong enough and plenty enough to knock him out like a brick wall without even a single nightmare. His first night of rest. The only one in maybe thirty years. Just the sort of calm and serenity he needed before starting out on his last day of existence on Earth.

"Shit, it's already one o'clock."

So, his last half-day of life on Earth.

Ticked off by his lateness, he tried to jump out of bed. His broken kneecap, which had put an end to his career, once again complicated his life. Motoman felt a painful shock when he put his foot on the floor between two pairs of underpants and some thick leather pants. Sitting on the edge of the mattress, hunched over, Tommy rubbed his salt and pepper beard twice before heaving his carcass out of bed. It was like pulling up an old tree stump, stiff and heavy.

Sweat was running down his back by the time he finally limped into the bathroom. The tile was dirty, cracked in spots, the grouting blackened with microscopic mushrooms. And Motoman's was not much better. A shaggy head stared back from the mirror, looking haggard. It was an angular face, scarred, with dark circles under the eyes.

After a quick wash, the former member of Kidz sat on the toilet seat and put his leg into a jointed brace. He tightened the leather straps, turned the screw three times, then stood up, creaking. And he got dizzy again.

While he was making himself an espresso, Motoman put on his old red and white suit. A little squeaking in the joints reminded him that he was no longer a teenager. But his diet was composed of almost nothing but cheap whiskey and cigarettes, which kept his body from getting too fat. Sucking in his breath Tommy managed to get the zipper over his belly and pull it up to his neck. Then it was time for the steel-toed boots, the chrome elbow and knee pads and finally the autogyro belt that gave him control over his bikes. A few drops of scotch in the little black coffee, a final glance at the cat huddled in the armchair (Mrs. Martelli would take care of it after he was gone), the first cigarette of the day lit up, and Motoman headed for the garage.

Like a calm sentinel, the superhero's helmet was still guarding the entrance of the lair. Sitting on its shabby pedestal, the high-tech helmet was the only thing in the house that was not covered in dust or mold. An antique that Tommy took great care of, cleaned and polished as regularly as a metronome. Especially when dark thoughts crossed his mind. Lately, slumped on a chair in the kitchen, this brain lost in an alcoholic fog, Motoman watched his old alter ego sitting on the edge of the table. Silent and sparkling clean he brought back to Tommy Spencer forgotten memories, traces of a former life. The one where he saved innocent people with the other members of Kidz: Marino, the merboy; Qube, he of the alien constructs; Superbill, the young genius; Ivan, the psychic; and Fl@mbo, queen of cyberspace...

Until that terrible day when they had all entered the Octagon.

Stop dwelling on the past! The others are waiting for you! There's no time to lose! an electronic voice brayed in his head.

"OK, OK, don't get your panties in a bundle," Tommy snapped back.

Standing in front of the garage door, he took a deep breath. He grabbed his shiny helmet and his holster, then punched in the code to open the airlock. The heavy door, like a bank vault, slowly swung open. Without the fortune left by Archie Bolt, their old mentor, it would have been impossible to finance this fortressed lab. And even harder to keep his uncle's house, hiding in the middle of a residential area in Brooklyn.

Although Archie had disappeared in an attack on London in 2033, the founder of Kidz had made sure that his old protégés would never be destitute. Even after the terrible ordeal of the Octagon, which had put an abrupt end to their team, the billionaire scientist had never really abandoned them. He was a good man, a true gentleman. And Tommy missed him a lot, too.

"Lights!"

With this order, the pale neon lights lit up the room. It looked like an old museum full of statues under dusty sheets. One whole wall was taken up by a modern workbench cluttered with electronic parts, tools, dismantled handlebars and old carburetors. Chains hanging from the ceiling suspended the hero's first motorcycle like a trophy for all to see. It was a *full power* machine, more than 800ccs with a lightweight, armored wind fairing. At the time, he had a hell of a time painting the yellow lightning bolts on the metallic red background. The same for designing the protective shield with jagged edges (strong enough for a tank) welded in front. The missiles built into it worked two out of three times at best and there was too much recoil, but following his uncle's recommendations, Tommy had adjusted to these parameters.

Above all, this first prototype had given birth to a dozen more, faster, stronger, able to reach unbelievable speeds and crash through any obstacle. But for thirty years Motoman had lost his taste for thrills, just like for tinkering. His fingers would not stop trembling. They kept him from working on the electronics. Worse, Tommy Spencer stopped coming up with new inventions. After the death of his uncle Shane, "Motorboy," his genius for engines had melted like snow in the sun, consumed by bitterness and gloom. Moreover, he was bored.

The road veteran limped up to the motorcycle he was going to take on his last ride. It was an armored Chopper, a three-wheeled, crimson monster. With a flick of his hand Motoman tossed aside the white sheet covering the bike before straddling the seat. A cloud of dust float off to land somewhere else.

Out of the corner of his eye Tommy saw the only wheeled box in the garage. It was the one "car" parked there in a dark corner of the lab: a kind of military Hummer, open like a Jeep, with crazy, Monster Truck tires. It was the all-terrain "Crazy Bang" that had belonged to his uncle, who had bequeathed to his nephew his love of engines and gadgets.

"Farewell, old wreck," he nodded to Crazy Bang as he rolled the heavy Chopper onto the exit platform.

There was no door in the garage wide enough to get outside. Motoman pressed the starter. The bike's control panel lit up like a cockpit. For an instant, Tommy wondered what all the buttons were for. There were so many of them. His willpower ended up getting the better of his indecision. He turned the grip to rev the engine and then pressed the red button. The cement platform screeched loudly before swiveling slowly and sinking into the floor like a giant screw.

While he disappeared into the depths Motoman put on his helmet whose tinted visor was immediately covered with a bunch of data: speed, temperature, satellite location, scopes… All these parameters superimposed on his view like a fighter pilot. He was ready.

"We're late, baby. Better choose the right door," Tommy thought.

"Take Exit 3," a voice responded.

"Linden Hill cemetery?"

"It's the shortest route to Roosevelt Island. You've wasted enough time already."

"Sorry, dear," Motoman said, "I usually take public transportation. Exit 3 it is!"

The rotating platform froze in front of a huge, dark tunnel that reeked of sewage. The number 3 was painted in white on the walls every ten yards. Tommy spun the grip and sped off. He shot down the exit with a will to put an end to it, once and for all, like a wild "run" that he had to come out the winner. The needles maxed out. He whizzed around the corners of track 3 until he saw the exit. The Chopper's headlights were like the eyes of a raging monster charging out of its lair after a long sleep to obliterate the town with its fiery breath.

The daylight greeted Tommy in an abandoned flood drain in Linden Hills where the secret exit came out. It was a concrete channel that crossed Linden all the way to Maspeth Creek. It was rainy with a light wind. After smashing a grill locked with a chain Motoman slipped into the traffic on Metropolitan Avenue, but it was a matter of seconds before he shot past the New York cars like a red meteor and reached the gray water of the East River.

It had been a long time since he had felt the thrill of speed. In his wake, two old bikers waved to him. Motoman was just a distant memory now. The vanished icon rekindled some forgotten feeling in the riders who had the fleeting impression of seeing a legend for the last time. Just before the purring, whirring machine did one final stunt for them. Tommy went full throttle, smoked a sports car and disappeared doing an amazing wheelie. One rear wheel was spitting flames of Hell.

Roosevelt Island was cloaked in a thin layer of fog. Two figures had been waiting for fifteen minutes on the sidewalk by the Octagon work site. The two men gazed silently at the Manhattan skyscrapers on the banks of the East River. The peace and quiet was broken only by the lapping water and honking horns from cars taking the Queensboro Bridge. It was Sunday. All the workers were gone from the new residences being built.

The first guy was big. Long hair, as black as a crow, fell over his square shoulders and a thick beard covered his craggy face. He wore a brown raincoat over a kind of black wetsuit. He was barefoot but he had bracelets, charms and various silver trinkets. Marino's skin was bruised in several spots. Bites and scars from the suckers and corrosive acids of the underwater fauna had turned his skin into a roadmap of the depths. Water was still dripping from his earlobes, the tip of his nose, his moustache and from between his spread fingers. Fifteen minutes was not enough time for him to dry off.

The second figure was much smaller, fidgety and tense. Dressed in a magnificent gold business suit. Qube always had an eye on his smartphone. Market data about his company came to him in real time on his touch screen. The chain with Urnus' medallion was barely visible under his Dolce & Gabbana shirt. On the other hand, his elegant, saffron-hued Borsalino could not hide the spreading baldness.

"It wouldn't surprise me if he stood us up," he sneered.

"He'll come. Be patient," Marino answered in his French accent.

"It's easy for you to be patient, Captain Nemo, you don't have a multinational corporation to run!"

"To each his bone, Little Cube."

"Don't call me that!"

"I'll call you what I want, Tom Tanner," Marino threatened while staring the man in the golden suit straight in the eyes.

"Don't push me, fishface, or you'll end up fried in a roach-infested dive in Chinatown," Qube shot back.

"Dare you."

"You're on."

Qube's amulet had just enough time to light up before Marino threw a killer uppercut. The body of the little genius went flying fifteen feet into a tree that smashed to pieces. Leaves and branches were scattered over the dock.

The years had weakened the merman and he could not dive as deep anymore but he was still the strongest of the team.

"Asshole!"

A different form crawled out of the debris. Raging mad the CEO of Qube Corp tore the branches holding him down. He split the biggest one in two with his fist and tossed it aside. His gold suit had turned into heavy armor of the same color. His forearms were covered with lethal weapons that were just waiting for orders to deploy. The mark of Marino's punch was visible in the middle of his chest, dented like a car bumper.

"You could've killed me!" Qube yelled through his golden helmet.

"I just wanted to see if your magic talisman still worked," Marino grinned.

"My inventions don't last as long as before but my imagination still has no limits! Tell me what kind of pain you prefer, old tuna, and it will be my pleasure to create it for you."

Qube was finally free of his vegetal chains. Now he was walking slowly toward Marino like a lone cowboy ready for a showdown in the sun. The smile was wiped off the aquatic man's face—he was all business now. He awaited the second round with balled fists.

"For an amphibian like you, I think a flamethrower would be a good idea," Qube sounded sadistic.

The Urnus talisman started glowing. Right away, the right forearm of the armor changed into a long, brass cannon fitted with weird tubes. Tom Tanner had the power to create anything he could imagine. Weapons, armor, vehicles, suits, nothing could elude his mind. He just had to visualize an object for the pendant to spawn it in a few seconds. The key to Urnus' power could assemble and disassemble the atoms via unknown nano-organisms in order to generate an insane arsenal or change his suit as he pleased.

Like his old teammates, age had put a dent in Qube's power. His creations did not last as long even though their power was still optimal. Above all, however, this inventive capacity had allowed Qube to patent a few things and become a leader in weaponry and new technology. The former runt, bundled up in his golden suit, was now worth billions of dollars.

Fire spit out of his weapon at Marino. The flames shot just over the Atlantean's head as he dove to the side. As quick and agile as an eel, Marino jumped over to the gate. He took hold of an iron post and yanked it out of the ground. The fence collapsed as he did so and Qube lined up his second shot. Marino stood facing him with the post in his hand, the base of it still stuck in a heap of cement.

Motoman's headlights cut into their joust before either could react. The machine spluttered out of the fog, flying over the water. The wheels of the Chopper had pivoted and transformed the bike into a hovercraft. It had drifted silently over the East River before reaching the dock and rising up like a Harrier fighter jet to land between the two combatants. The Chopper's three wheels were now back in position and alighted gently on the asphalt. The engine cut. And all was silent, almost.

Tommy laughed, "You could've waited for me to celebrate the reunion."

"Shut up, Tommy!"

"Shut up, Tommy!"

Motoman struggled off his bike. His leg was stiff but he could not help smiling.

"It took us less than half an hour to come to blows, Tommy, so don't count on me to stick around here," Marino said as he dropped his improvised weapon.

"This damned sushi tried to kill me, Tommy! He started it! Do you even know who I am, Flipper? Don't you realize I've got better things to do than commemorate the disappearance of Fl@mbo?" Qube complained.

"We know, Little Cube, you've got a super important meeting about a new brand of Tupperware," Motoman joked.

"Don't call me that!" With an evil grin on his face, Qube aimed his cannon at the biker.

"Nice gadget. Fl@mbo was right, there were never enough girls in Kidz."

Motoman's reaction threw the golden veteran for a loop. He lowered his arm. All of a sudden Qube felt pathetic. He realized that he was threatening his old friends with a flame-thrower like some petty criminal. It was so childish.

"Listen, Tommy, Kidz have been dead for a long time. Whatever it is you want to tell us, say it quick, please."

Marino had turned pale. His fingers were tapping nervously on an invisible piano. It was land-sickness. The aquatic warrior could not stand being out of the ocean for long, walking around on dry land. He felt the call of the sea and had to bite his lip to stay focused on Motoman's words.

The biker was standing between his two old partners. He had taken off his helmet, hung it on the handlebars, and was breathing in the salt air. He took a deep breath, then explained to his former partners the purpose of the rendezvous.

"OK, I won't waste any more of your time. I didn't bring you to this island just to see you again. It's been thirty years to the day since our last battle in one of these buildings. And since we left behind the body of Fl@mbo. We failed, we split up and we each went our separate ways. We're not going to go over it all again, there's no use. No, I contacted you because I have something important to show you."

Qube and Marino listened avidly to Motoman. With their brows furrowed, it looked like they were trying to read his mind. And while the one had used his talisman to make his weapon vanish, the other was still sweating and nauseous.

Tommy went on, "In truth, Fl@mbo never left me. She's still here in a corner." He tapped his head. "Sometimes she talks to me. She says things aren't what they seem. She bitches when I drink too much whiskey or when I take a taxi home 'cause I'm afraid of wiping out on my bike. She thinks it's really uncool. For a long time, I thought it was me going nuts, that the battle of the Octagon had broken more than just a kneecap. I really thought I was losing it. And then I understood…"

The two others with him on Roosevelt Island stood there speechless. Motoman had hit a nerve. Tommy spoke again in a softer voice and with tears in his eyes.

"I understood what you saw too, for a long time, but that you had repressed. You thought you were going crazy so you did everything possible to put blinders on. It must have been hard for you to shut out her comments, her advice. But it worked, didn't it? She disappeared from your heads. She told me. Me too, I tried. And I never dared to say anything about it or see anyone about it. But I didn't have your willpower. There was only me for her to talk to. And to listen to her. To believe her."

Marino was disturbed. He tried to speak up, "I… I don't see where you're going with all this, Tommy."

Motoman smiled. He looked relieved. His eyes sparkled in the heat of the moment. He was winding it up and feeling the weight lifted from his shoulders.

"What I want to say… is that it's time to go home, my friends."

Neither of the two old superheroes had time to react before Tommy pulled his automatic pistol. Who would have expected this? Motoman, who had never used conventional weapons before, had managed to captivate them, to hypnotize them, to confuse and stun them. The biker in red was not just a simple mechanical genius doubling as a daredevil. He was as quick as Marino was strong and as accurate as Qube was clever... as agile as Fl@mbo was intuitive.

His leg posed no problem when his hands were still working.

The first bullet hit Marino right between the eyes. The big carcass of the merman fell backward. His long, dark hair seemed to swing like the tentacles of a sea anemone before the body hit the pavement with a plop. His glaring eyes were drained of life. Marino's last vision was of the pale, stormy sky.

Qube was hit with the second bullet before his reflex could light up his extraterrestrial medallion. The lead lodged in his neck, severed his carotid artery, the only spot not protected by armor. The impact pushed the billionaire to the edge of the dock where he hit a mooring post and dropped to the ground. Lying on his side Qube took one last, painful breath before giving up the ghost and turning back into a regular human, dressed in regular clothes.

Motoman was satisfied as he put away his pistol. Calmly he dragged his bum leg to the sidewalk that ran in front of the Octagon. The building—obviously in an octagonal shape— was almost rebuilt and would soon be welcoming new, wealthy clients from Manhattan. The only witnesses to this double murder were three big, yellow cranes left swaying in the wind.

Tommy leaned against the railing and pulled a cigarette out of his suit. His lighter had been a gift from Archie Bolt. It was an old, silver Zippo engraved with the symbol of the Kidz. With his second puff he let his mind wander back to the day of Fl@mbo's death.

Her beautiful death.

July 5, 2011.

Motoman's memories were so cloudy about the end of that infamous day and yet so clear about the way it began. His memory was like a yellowed photograph damaged by bleach drizzled all over it. The more he concentrated on the details, the less lucid he saw. The old hero felt like he was staring into a bottomless pit, a rift that opened up into the heart of a void, into the emptiness of his own existence.

However, Tommy still remembered Terry's hair and Mirna's t-shirt, which was too tight. The two famous cheerleaders from the football team that he led as their popular quarterback. The mint-colored lycra top that Mirna wore matched her eyes perfectly.

He remembered how hot it was in the classroom that morning thirty years ago. The rambling lecture by Beckett that had turned the classroom into nap room. You could not even hear a fly buzzing. The old man with his receding hairline and his pasty yellow suit was babbling about the Big Bang Theory. Motoman had stopped taking notes long before and was doodling some bike ideas in the margin. Maybe a new prototype to develop, who knows?

Terry ogling him while nibbling on her yellow pencil while Mirna pretended to ignore him. As for James, his faithful friend, he had decided to go back to sleep with his head buried in his crossed arms. A thin line of drool was dripping onto the graph paper with only the date and subject noted down: Physics. His glasses were crooked because of his uncomfortable position which made him look like a drunk sprawled on a bar.

At this time, Tommy Spencer had already become Motoman and a member of the famous Kidz. But nobody knew his secret identity, except for the other superheroes of course. Qube was in the same school, but not in the same class. He had already been labeled a brainiac, a nerd, which did not make it easy for him with the girls and the jocks. But he liked to study, which was not the case with Tommy who would rather have left school altogether to dedicate himself to a life of crime fighting. Unfortunately Archie did not see things his way and had even managed to get Marino and Fl@mbo enrolled in senior year. They all had to ignore each other or at least try not to break their cover, which made for some weird scenes when vital information was texted in the toilet or the cafeteria or by secret hand signals in the yard.

Of course, being an anonymous superhero in a New Jersey school also had some perks. Marino kept breaking his own record in the 100-meter butterfly. Qube had started a robotics club, Fl@mbo tutored the computer teachers in their own subject and Tommy had designed a real chick-magnet. It was a pretty standard motorcycle but just cool enough and wild enough to attract a few dizzy girls.

So, July 5, 2011, the teacher droned on interminably in a voice as gloomy and dull as a mortician. At least until he got off the beaten path of lecturing to illustrate the theory with something more personal. His voice trembled in this throat when he started, which stopped Terry abruptly from drawing pretty circles over all her "i"s. The blonde popped her bubble gum before looking up at the Physics teacher.

"The Big Bang is scientific proof that an explosion can give life. With the energy released, the particles fused together and gave birth to the Universe. It doesn't matter what name people give to this ancient explosion, it was this chain of events that created human beings. But what about the other explosions? The ones around us? Can you imagine that breaking the sound barrier with a supersonic plane or the atomic bomb tests in the middle of the desert might have repercussions on matter? On the unseen? On the atom? Who knows if slamming a door might not have a direct effect on a part of molecules—or of reality—that we can't perceive? Could the concentrated energy of the Big Bang break down over the millennia and crack open from these tiny but innumerable explosions? Could it be that..."

The teacher's enthusiasm, as well as his minute and a half of glory—which had managed to pull the students out of the doldrums—was cut off by the sound of *Coco the Worm*. It was the stupid ringtone of James' cell phone with *Coco the famous maggot* complaining about the size of his bean.

The whole room started laughing as Jason was startled awake and grabbed his backpack. The poor kid rifled it in a panic to turn off the screeching song before he had time to read the guilty SMS.

The teacher looked very upset by the interruption. "James Duncan. It is strictly forbidden to leave your phone on inside the building. You know the school rules I suppose? See me after class. Together we will figure out the most appropriate punishment but an hour of detention is the minimum, I think, to refresh your memory."

The kid was beet red. A tomato proudly wore this color but was never so ashamed. While Terry giggled on and Tommy struggled to hold back his laughter, Mr. Beckett resumed his monologue.

"Let's continue, shall we? As I just explained, the Big Bang is the original explosion but nothing proves that it was the only one. If we believe the recent research of Lord Sullivan Paddington, the resonance…"

All the cell phones started ringing at the same time. All of them, except for Motoman's. The seasoned teacher lost his Olympian calm, which had been worthy of the captain of the Titanic, and exploded in total fury. The old man babbled incomprehensible orders, pointing at every student, barking names and hours of detention. In the middle of his torrent of words and gestures, the students scrambled to turn off their phones, making the cacophony that much noisier. Most of them finally managed without even looking at the message, but others, like Mirna, could not resist her curiosity. Such a phenomenon was too weird.

The text was the same everywhere. It repeated the same message on all the phones turned on in the room.

"It says you should turn on your phone, Tommy," Mirna blurted out. "And it's signed 'Fl@mbo'," she added with a pouty face.

All eyes turned on him as he took his smart phone out of his jeans. No battery. Bad luck.

Mr. Beckett's wrath was cut short by the bell. Fate seemed to be set on interrupting him every time he put a little spirit into his speech. Still, he promised fire and brimstone in their next class. Which did not sound so bad if it could at least keep them from falling asleep.

Tommy saw Qube in the hallway. He was wearing a ratty sweater knit by his mother.

"Did you get Fl@mbo's message?"

"Is this like candid camera or something?"

"No, I don't think so," Qube still sounded skeptical. "They need us on Roosevelt Island. Marino and Fl@mbo are already there, apparently. Archie detected a bloop and wants our help."

"A what?"

"A bloop. An unexplained, underwater sound. Apparently pretty loud, like an explosion. But even weirder when you look at the spectrogram. Did you hear about the one in 1997?"

"No, but did you know Harley Davidson came out with its custom Bad Boy that year?"

Qube did not blink. "OK, it's a draw. I've already printed notes for our absence. All we have to do is give them to the office. We good to go?"

"I'm right behind you, Little Cube."

"Stop calling me that!"

After handing in their pass saying someone was sick, the two heroes rushed outside. Glancing around they found a quiet spot way from prying eyes. A small courtyard off the street was isolated enough for them to get ready. Motoman fired up his autogyro belt, camouflaged by holding up his regular pants, before putting on his lightweight suit that had been folded up under his street clothes. Qube focused his mind. He was already imagining what he wanted to wear to get to Roosevelt Island. Young Tom Tanner never liked to show up in the same outfit more than once. It was the "showman" in him.

"How long until your chauffeur gets here?" Qube asked.

"Ten minutes tops. I improved the autopilot so it'll take the quickest route."

"Good. What model did you call?"

"The Flying Red Devil. For this trip I figured it'd be the fastest."

"Great. We'll go together."

"Why? You like riding on the back?"

"Are you kidding? I just want you to eat my dust, lousy Metal Thunder."

Nine minutes later a magnificent riderless bike pulled up near the courtyard. It was lightweight, constructed of an aluminum frame and a slim, red body. Four mini-turbines were fitted to the engine.

Motoman ran to his bike, got the helmet from under the seat and hopped on. When he revved the engine the Urnus talisman covered Qube's body with a golden diving suit that looked like a rocket. He shot up into the air without forgetting to give Tommy the finger.

"Watch and learn, pokey."

Motoman pressed one of the buttons on the control panel and retractable wings fanned out. The jets fired up and then after a quick burst of speed it soared up over the buildings.

The flying biker could not remember who was the winner that day. Except that he could never really accept Qube's victory. But one thing that was sure was that Fl@mbo and Marino were waiting for them at the exact place where his teammates would one day be lying. The buildings on Roosevelt Island gleamed in the sun; the lanes were primly lined with trees; and the East River was the color of jade. Everything was still intact. And she was there.

"So, Spencer, we're not turning on our phone?" the pretty brunette said as he landed on the tarmac. Fl@mbo always knew how to greet Tommy with such tender words.

Marino, dressed in his suit of scales, stood there silent and stone-faced.

"You're afraid of Fl@mb'. Is it a fad now with the French to make this kind of stupid joke? How am I going to explain this to my friends?"

The teenager was small in stature but big in charisma. She was around 17 years-old, which made her the oldest of the group next to Marino. The only girl in the Kidz wore a tight-fitting black suit with electric blue symbols that looked like patterns of a computer chip. She had long, jet-black hair that cascaded down her back and she wore platform shoes worthy of an emo girl and a perfect smile. But what fascinated the other Kidz, besides her power to transform into an electronic entity, was the mystery surrounding her. Because no one knew where her powers came from.

"Just say there was a bug. Or that it was Qube who was supposed to meet you. Everyone hates him already so it can't get any worse."

"What?" Qube only heard the end of their exchange.

Motoman lowered his voice and put his arm around Fl@mbo's shoulder to turn them away from the others. He whispered, "And you know that you don't need stuff like that to make Mirna jealous. I'm with you now. I don't care about anyone else."

"We're not here to talk about this, Motoman," she said coldly. "We have a mission to accomplish or did you forget?"

"No, of course not. Sorry."

"Guys?" Marino pointed up like a teacher in class. "Sorry to interrupt but there's smoke coming from that building." He was pointing directly at the Octagon now.

It was without a doubt the most beautiful apartment building on Roosevelt Island. An old building completely re-stored that blended the style of a Victorian dome with more modern lines. Build on the waterfront the Octagon had an incredible panoramic view of Manhattan.

A long, gray plume of smoke was rising out of the main entrance. People were starting to evacuate in a panic. Then the ground shook violently under the Kidz.

"What the fuck?" Qube swore. "Fl@mbo, can you give us a quick rundown?"

"OK, let's go. I'll explain on the way."

The four teenagers in their colored suits hurried to the octagonal building, which was shaking spasmodically. Motoman's bike followed the Kidz like an obedient dog behind its master.

"Here's what I know," Fl@mbo began while Marino helped an old man shuffle down the front steps. "About an hour ago, Archie's private satellite spotted a bloop, a strange wave."

"Oh yeah, a bloop. Like in '97, right?" Motoman blurted out proudly.

"Exactly," she looked suspiciously at him. "After a thorough analysis, Archie confirmed that it was some kind of electromagnetic explosion. A kind never seen before, physically impossible."

"Extraterrestrial?" Qube asked.

"That's all I know. But you know the best thing about it?" Fl@mbo sounded enigmatic as they entered the Octagon's lobby.

The Flying Red Devil had stopped on the porch, unable to go any farther. The acrid smoke had spread throughout the building and was starting to choke the Kidz. A muffled noise was echoing down through the floors. It was the very fabric of the building that was convulsing. The French girl had to yell to be heard. It was like being on a construction site.

"This... this island was called Minnahanock by the Indians. It was turned into a place for asylums and prisons. On this very spot once stood the Insane Asylum of New York. It closed down in 1894. Today there's almost nothing left of it except the dome and the foundations."

"It's an old loony bin?"

"Yes. Horrible things happened here. All the patients were abused and neglected. They lived in filth. Charles Dickens talked about it back in 1800."

"Charles who?" Tommy sneered.

"Forget it."

The young superheroes made sure that no one was in the apartments before starting their investigation. They went through the five floors with a fine-toothed comb, meaning more than 500 doors, shouting for the residents to get out. The building was not going to last long. The support columns were bending like rubber, the walls cracking, all the metal parts were breaking off.

It was Qube who first noticed the magnetic attraction when he could not climb the stairs. He was being pulled to the basement. When the Kidz got back to the ground floor, they saw that all metal objects, computers, security cameras, plumbing, cables, etc. had "vanished." Even Motoman's two wheels had not escaped the magnetization. The bike had bounded up the porch and smashed through front door in order to dive into the depths of the Octagon.

Something was pulling the building in on itself and devouring everything in the process.

And this something had chosen to hide out in the foundation.

"Damn, it took my bike!"

After a brief moment of hesitation they decided to go down. Qube transformed his suit into one less metallic. Then the group took the back stairs that went down to the laundry room. They had to watch out for the debris that was tumbling down the steps. Attracted by the magnetic field like moths to a flame, pieces of the building were quivering like they were alive. The most dangerous were the shards of iron flying through the air to get to the boiler room. All the Kidz suffered minor injuries during the descent. They were in the midst of a vortex, a scrap iron cyclone.

When they reached the hallway on the bottom floor, they were ready to collapse. The Octagon, too, was soon going to collapse. An incredible amount of rubble was flying all over the place. In the middle of the storm the Kidz realized that the floor of the boiler room was sinking.

Qube transformed his helmet to use a telescopic sight. Like that he could tell them what was happening farther away so they could stay a safe distance from the phenomenon. He had to yell to be heard.

"There's another room under this one. Looks like a cell from the asylum. It's hard to see what's in there, it's too dark. But there's a bunch of weird writing on the walls. And metal tubes on some of the walls. It's chrome. I see a magnetic cloud! A ball of energy that's vibrating... It's getting bigger... It's... argh!"

The magnetic flux got suddenly stronger and Qube was thrown to the ground, his face dragged across the floor. He barely had time to change helmets when the Urnus talisman became a lethal trap. It, too, was attracted by the devouring magnet. Marino grabbed Qube by his arms. He tried to yank him back into the hallway but the talisman, pulled by the energy, was being turned into a chainsaw. It was digging into the poor kid's neck, ready to cut off his head to get to its new master. But Qube could not let go of the legacy of Urnus. He held onto the pendant with all his strength. His neck was bleeding. Marino slipped on the concrete.

A second shock wave. The fate of the Kidz teetered on the edge.

The railing on the stairs tore off and smashed Motoman's right knee. As he jumped out of the way, already feeling the pain, his helmet crashed against a wall and he passed out.

"It's... it's taking shape," Fl@mbo warned. "We have to get out of here! Hurry!"

The entity had gathered enough material. All the debris was packing together to form a shell around its heart of energy. Blocks of concrete piled up like a spinal column, electrical wires became its veins, kitchen appliances its organs and the computers with their chips formed a brain. What was not just a simple bloop had turned into a fearsome anaconda of debris! A snake!

Marino's veins were strained to popping. His feet sunk into the cement as he tried to remain standing. With all his strength he dragged Qube who was on the verge of passing out as well. He stopped when he got to Tommy, lying motionless, and tried to grab him with his other hand.

"Let me go, buddy," Qube said.

"No way!"

"You'll never get both of us out of here. I might be able to escape if I use the talisman but Tommy's screwed if you leave him. Do as I say for once in your life!"

"No, no!" Marino shouted. "I'm not leaving anyone behind!"

"Too late," Fl@mbo said.

The girl's body was transforming against her will. She was turning into how she looked when she entered cyberspace. When she changed into a conscious electron she could get into computers, to hack data, to travel through fiber optics and satellite links. Her skin was a flux of blue energy scrambled with incomprehensible data in black. Fl@mbo was just an electric silhouette, a sophisticated program that was starting to be drained of its substance.

"It's going to absorb me," she said.

Her body was turning into sand whose grains were flying off towards the magnetic reptile.

"Let me go, Marino, I can help her!" Qube's chest was heaving in his bloody shirt.

The aquatic teen had grabbed Motoman. He was too exhausted to go any farther.

She cried out, "This monster needs a body. It's going to transform the whole building. You're all going to be trapped inside." Fl@mbo was worn out. Her voice was cutting off. Most of her body had already joined the creature getting stronger from the inflow of vitality.

Tommy opened his eyes. His entire body was in pain, making his heart race. His knee was a wreck. He was being dragged across the floor by the ocean giant.

"It's more electronic than organic. I'll buy you some time," the teen girl panted. "Get out! Run!"

She vanished, ingested. Motoman screamed.

"You're really pig-headed, Jacques Cousteau," Qube sneered before twisting Marino's fingers. He had no choice but to let him go and Tom Tanner rose up in the air with the Urnus Talisman on his chest. He barely had time to wink to his friends before he disappeared into the heart of darkness.

The two surviving Kidz were still as statues in the basement hallway. In the midst of this disaster neither had the courage to reach the emergency exit. Tears clouded their minds. The bitter taste of metal had filled their mouths. The Octagon was collapsing. The concrete swallowed them up like a carnivorous plant.

Outside the building the people who had not yet left the island witnessed a crazy sight. The huge building was run through with spasms. A giant wave shook the structure. All the windows shattered. Then it tore itself from the ground and reared up like an insect before twirling around. The Octagon was now a tall, concrete cylinder twisted like a dishtowel. Small debris rained down on the ground as the New York fire fighters backed away.

The building was alive. It was a colossal snake, a monumental monster crawling over Roosevelt Island. You could make out eyes in what looked like its head: a mass of cars from the parking lot. The light coming out of the narrow slits was eerie.

The magnetic creature headed for the Coler-Goldwater Hospital just next to its birthplace. It was still hungry. The police helicopters were brought down by giant's energy. They folded in on themselves without exploding before being flung onto the new skin like magnets on a fridge. Then it was the turn of the hospital buildings to uproot and join the titan, one by one like Lego pieces. The patients' screams were carried away on the wind. The more the python destroyed, the bigger it grew.

The first Air Force jet to reach the site suffered the same fate. But its missiles remained intact and became part of the dragon's arsenal.

After a little more destruction, the ophidian monster lost interest in the place. Its head swung around toward the East River to gaze upon the Manhattan skyscrapers. Its phenomenal mass rippled and squirmed as it dove into the water. It was big enough to touch the bottom and its head rose up 200 yards over the surface. Its enormous weight carved a highway through the silt.

But while it moved towards Carl Schurz Park on the other shore, its energy drained.

It groaned.

What remained of Fl@mbo had decided to put an end to the fiasco. Parts of its concrete armor dropped off its skeleton and splashed into the water. The monster was disintegrating, one piece at a time. When its jaw snapped off it could no longer cry out its rage. A blue energy flux, charged with computer code, was running through the creature. The giant snake came apart as quickly as it had been put together. Unable to get away it was reduced to the size of a poodle before it reached the other side of the river. Then its belly exploded.

Motoman remembered snapping awake in the ice-cold water of the East River. His injured leg made swimming impossible and he dropped like an anchor. He felt Fl@mbo's last burst of energy before disappearing for good. The magnetic reptile was nothing more than a puny iron worm. It made ripples on the surface of the river, then escaped into the depths. The water poured into Tommy's lungs as he sank dying.

He woke up five minutes later, lying on the docks. He could hear sirens. It was the Apocalypse. Marino was next to him, trying to resuscitate Qube who had managed to escape the creature. He had manifested a golden diving suit to keep from drowning but water had got into his mask.

As he had done with Motoman, the merman was struggling desperately to bring Qube back to life.

Breaths, chest-pumps, breaths, chest-pumps.

Tom Tanner spit out river water along with a groan of pain and sorrow. He was weeping.

"I couldn't save her... I couldn't..."

The Urnus medallion was still there but no longer glowing.

Without saying a word, Marino stood up and looked out over the East River. Tommy tried but could not get to his feet. His head was stuffed with cotton. Nothing mattered anymore.

"That thing is still alive, Tommy. Somewhere out there in the ocean," the teenager said. His face had changed. His voice too. "I promise you I'll catch it and destroy it. Even if it takes the rest of my life! Take care of yourself, Qube old friend."

Marino dove into the water, swam at superhuman speed through the waves, then disappeared. Motoman never saw him again.

Until today, thirty years after the death of Fl@mbo.

Still sitting on the parapet of the new Octagon, rebuilt exactly the same, the weary biker finished his smoke. He flicked the butt into the gutter then looked at his bike. The corpses of Qube and Marino lay in front of it, watered by a light drizzle. Motoman looked disappointed. He pulled himself up and started towards the building.

Qube was the first to wake up.

When he opened his eyes, he saw the strange color of the asphalt, then the walls of the buildings. Everything looked so hazy, transparent. The sky was like tracing paper laid on top of the complex mesh of a huge machine. The entire environment was just scenery hiding some monumental machinery.

"What'd you do to me, asshole?" he swore.

Marino jumped up next. He saw the same thing. He touched his forehead to feel the bullet hole but there was nothing there. No blood, no wound. He pounced on Motoman. Tommy did not react when his strong hands clutched his neck. The old sea dog still had plenty of strength despite the 30 years spent chasing a monster that did not exist. Big, yellow fingers suddenly pulled Marino back.

96

"That's enough!" Qube said, wearing his combat armor with giant fists.

"But he tried to kill us!" Marino shouted furiously.

"She's here, Marino. Can't you see her?" Qube pointed to the Octagon. The slim figure of Fl@mbo was waiting for them on the front steps.

The amphibian hero squinted, still upset. Motoman coughed. Then he took a deep breath.

"I know you're pissed off but it was the only way. I had to know if you were my real friends or just another illusion. Anyway, I'll tell you this first: it's no use trying to kill me. You'll never do it. Not here at least."

"Why?" Marino asked.

"I'm already dead. For ten years now. On my bike. One night, I was so drunk I ran head on into a truck. I was completely smashed, dragged a hundred yards. But I woke up before the ambulance arrived. Uninjured. That's when I understood. And don't lie to me, Captain Ahab. I can't believe for a second that a hunter like you, diving deep in unexplored waters, never once died. You're not like Qube here who's always protected by bodyguards."

Marino calmed down and nodded feebly.

"Where are we, Tommy?" Qube asked.

"We never left the monster, is that it?" Marino said dejectedly.

"No. We've just been swallowed by the Octagon. Everything we remember, everything we lived through these past thirty years is a lie. We're not in 2041. It's barely been ten minutes since Fl@mbo was absorbed. It's electroshock."

After a brief pause, Motoman went on, "I don't know what this 'thing' is. It's like some vengeful creature invoked by an old patient from a cell in the 1830s. An evil spirit that took all these years to manifest itself in our reality like the light coming from distant stars."

"Is it too late?"

"I think it was the boiler room explosion that stopped the invocation. It wasn't the monster that destroyed the basement but a simple gas leak. But the explosion woke it up. Professor Beckett explained to us that every explosion could cause a re-action, create something somewhere else. And he was right."

"That doesn't explain why we're stuck here?" Qube said.

"Because this monster is just a ball of energy and it needs a body. Remember how it used every piece of the build-ing to build an organism? It did the same with us. We became its memory, which it's using to learn about the world and about humans. To anticipate their attacks. It's racking our brains, our memories to learn, to get smarter. We're in a per-manent dream that's controlling us to test our reactions, our emotions, our fears and failures. It's done to us everything we hate the most. You, Marino, a lone hunter gone back to the wild. You, Qube, a hated CEO of a multinational corporation. And me, an old wreck who can't even ride anymore. As long as it needs us, it won't kill us."

"And Fl@mbo?" Marino wondered.

"She, too, became part of the beast. She copied herself as many times as possible to become its mental network. She's the one who make the link between it and us, transmitting in-formation like a neuron."

"I understand why I saw her. She's trying to wake us up, isn't she? And like a stupid jerk I wanted to forget," Qube said.

"Yeah, she doesn't have much to work with. She's drained and it's destroying all her seditious backups that try to communicate with us. She can't hold out for long. Her minutes are numbered. But she still managed to get enough info to me for us to attempt an escape."

"How?" the Kidz asked.

"I didn't kill you with a bullet. It was a scrambler, a mini-system that broke the creature's hold over you. I don't have your genius, Little Cube, so it took me ten years to de-sign it. Ten years during which I had the necessary means to keep track of you two."

"Don't call me... whatever, go on," Qube smiled.

"Anyway, here it is." Motoman took a piece of paper out of his jacket and put it on a spot of dry land. It was a drawing of a bomb. "It's a magnetic grenade. It's the only way to reverse the polarity of the creature in order to destroy it. Qube, you're the only one who can make such a complex device. I need you to memorize this blueprint in every detail. When we're back in its belly, you'll have to use your medallion to create it."

"OK." Tom Tanner started studying the sketch.

"How do we get out of here?" Marino asked.

"We just have to get back to the Octagon's basement. Fl@mbo will take care of the rest by activating our scramblers."

"And how can you be sure that the basement still exists? Look, the building was totally rebuilt. Nothing was left of its original foundations."

"Except that we've got a billionaire friend who owns the apartments. Isn't that right, old boy?" Motoman turned to Qube.

Not looking up from the bomb blueprint the superhero in the golden exoskeleton nodded. "It's still there, yes. In the same place. I bought the whole shebang in 2018 and I've got the only key. It's my personal sanctuary. I come here sometimes when I'm feeling down. When I start thinking about Fl@mbo. I wanted to know what happened. Why I failed. See, the cell didn't move. Everything was put back in the same place as before. And I never do things halfway."

"Thanks, Qube," Motoman said.

"Oh, it's nothing. Thanks to you for killing me. I knew there was something wrong with my life: in 30 years I never had a girlfriend."

"Me neither."

"Me neither."

"Well, what are we waiting for? Let's get out of this Hell!"

An instant later, the three teens opened their eyes in the bowels of the beast. The shock was hard. The mental scramblers gave them the worst migraines of their lives. They were in a dark hole, sliced through by metal shafts. Electrical wires were stuck into their heads and old pipes poured plumbing fluid into their dungeon.

Qube looked disgusted. "This sucks!"

Motoman quickly found the only spot of light in the room. It was the old hallway of the Octagon which had become a huge digestive tract, the tube that went right up through the throat of their giant captor.

"There's our exit," he said.

Marino flexed his muscles and broke his straps. Once on his feet he twisted off his teammates' constraints to free them. The heroes were floating in a repugnant pool. It took them a minute to realize that they had not grown a day older.

"I can finally run again," Tommy rejoiced. "Your turn, Qube!"

The little genius materialized a magnetic grenade with the help of his pendant. He activated it right away. An invisible explosion, like a shock wave, shook the hyper-structure. The Kidz immediately felt the creature in pain.

"Turn on your cell phone and connect to Archie's secure server!" Motoman ordered. "We need an anchor point for Fl@mbo. She's going to have to copy herself before everything falls apart."

Qube did so. He had barely connected to their protector's network when his smartphone registered a massive input of data. Fl@mbo was downloading herself onto the hard drive located in the Englishman's luxurious mansion.

Part of the ceiling collapsed.

"It's too steep, we'll never get through," Marino snarled. "There's no way we can climb up the throat."

The monster was coming apart. Its energy had been blown out by the bomb. Its huge, makeshift body was nothing but a house of cards ready to collapse.

"Over there! My bike!" Tommy shouted.

The Flying Red Devil had dropped from the ceiling of their prison where it had been tangled up with blocks of cement and twisted iron bars. One of its wheels was bent and its turbines were shot, but it still worked.

Everything was about to come crashing down.

Motoman turned to Qube who was checking the data transfer. The bluish, three-dimensional face of pretty Fl@mbo appeared on the screen. She was safe and sound.

"Without me you boys are really pathetic," she said as a thank you.

"Tom!"

"What?" Qube was distracted by his joy at seeing Fl@mbo.

"Now's the time to put your money where your mouth is! Get out of here as fast as you can!"

"I'll bet ten bucks I can break the sound barrier!"

"Dare you!"

"You're on!"

The Urnus talisman was glowing again. Qube now had big, golden turbines on his back. His rocketman suit started spitting out sparks.

Marino ran over to bike and with one hand bent the wheel back in shape before hopping on behind Motoman who was already gripping the handlebars. He had lost his helmet in the battle and had to rely on his reflexes to maneuver through the hallway. He revved the engine and the back tire started skidding.

The three of them shot through the monster's throat as it decomposed. Huge blocks tumbled down around them.

The Octagon had only started walking less than ten minutes ago. It had not even touched the hospital yet or claimed any victims. The police helicopters had barely taken off.

When the Flying Red Devil reached the serpent head it broke the sound barrier. The colossal skull of the beast exploded. The motorcycle's wings deployed and the three friends flew off over the East River.

The Octagon was reduced to piles of harmless debris spread over the ground all the way up to the hospital parking lot.

"You owe me ten bucks, Motoman!"

The Kidz went soaring through the clouds with smiles on their faces.

Fl@mbo by Alfredo Macall

The Other by Luciano Bernasconi

The Other *was the second envoy of the Great Mind, sent to Earth after Wampus to accomplish the same mission. Originally, however, he was Golden Boy, a superhero on another Earth, before he became corrupted by the Great Mind. This story is about how he crossed over to the dark side.*

Raphaël Lafarge: *Rules*

The Great Mind was spreading slowly but steadily through millions of universes, its mental claws planted in billions upon billions of heads of all shapes and sizes, a mane of raw energy spreading over its servants who needed its omnipotence.

The Great Mind was thinking. It never stopped thinking. It was, after all, thought rather than body, pure mind, the raw power of the intellect. A single will: to spread farther and farther, to infiltrate all thinking and within this vast network, it was unleashing a perpetual storm of ideas. A sense of humor sometimes, that cruel humor that remains the privilege of the alpha predators. A lot of planning, manipulations through the web of time, endless crisscrossing; some things taking shape when its single will was fulfilled; other things bound to vanish when they proved failures.

The Great Mind detested failures. The worlds it had not yet conquered were a thorn in its side, a constant reminder that it was not perfect, that it could still fail. Spread over the multiverse, it pained it to feel the presence of dimensions that resisted it, like hard lumps beneath the skin, worlds where its opposing cosmic force, the Universality, had triumphed.

The Great Mind hated the Universality. And right now, in this fraction of eternity, it hated it more than ever. How dare it stand up against the inevitable, against logic itself, the triumph of pure thought! "The Universality," just think about it! Even the name was an insult to its grandeur. The Great Mind was the only universal unification that could be imagined. The final result of evolution. Living beings became intelligent, then they became conscious, and finally they submitted body and soul to the Great Mind, adding their intelligence to its own, their knowledge to its own, contributing to the boundless fresco of its supremacy.

The Great Mind groaned and its discontent reverberated in the myriad minds of the myriad worlds that it had enslaved. The situation was too balanced. Each of its successes was off-set by a new victory of the Universality. It needed to outsmart the entity opposing it, to find a new configuration of ploys that would assure a constant victory so that the infinite universes would be nothing more than defenseless prey without unwanted surprises, without future failures. It needed a solution.

The Great Mind thought of making a new champion.

But there would be rules.

There always were rules.

"You don't deserve any pity. You blew up Big Ben! Big Ben!"

"That was the order!"

The iron grip squeezed the criminal's throat. It was crushing him.

"Whose order?" Golden Boy asked.

"The usual crime bosses," the man splurted. "The Weasel... Big Ted... Kickstarter..."

Another squeeze.

"I already know them. They're into racketeering, drugs and heists. Why would any of them want to blow up a historical monument?"

"I don't know."

A golden apple appeared in one of the costumed hero's bloody hands. "This is a low explosive grenade. A little explosion... but enough to kill a mangy dog." The golden man shoved the apple between his victim's broken teeth. "You have ten seconds to give me the next target. After that, you swallow it. And I'll wait for you to choke and set it off."

"Hou han't ho hat," the wounded man moaned out of his stuffed mouth. "Hou are Gohen Boy. Hou hon't hill…"

"You know what they say: accidents happen."

He pushed the apple in deeper, scraping the inside of the man's mouth.

"Well?"

"I hon't ho hothing…"

"It's going to be tough cleaning all your guts off the sidewalk."

The man wanted to say something, but his mouth hurt too much for him to talk. The hero pushed the apple in farther.

"Golden Boy!"

The golden man stopped. The Cossack was there, proud and surly, as big as a bear, in baggy clothes, with a long, bushy moustache under this furry hat.

"You've wrecked the guy," the Cossack groaned.

"All part of the job."

"Look, he's already wet himself and you're still torturing him? And now you're threatening to kill him?"

"We're at war against these lowlifes, Ivan Karine," Golden Boy said. "How are we going to know where they plan to strike next?"

The Cossack crossed his arms.

"There are people who only care about getting results, but we don't really call them heroes, do we?"

"Maybe sometimes we have to get our hands dirty," Golden Boy replied.

The thug trembled.

"Maybe a real hero doesn't care whether he's called called a hero or a villain," Golden Boy continued. "Maybe he only cares about saving innocent lives. If Tower Bridge or London Bridge blows up tomorrow, what will you say? What will you tell the families of the dead victims? Lofty ideals lead to the worst massacres, comrade."

The Cossack put his big, heavy hand on Golden Boy's shoulder.

"I'd still choose a man who plants bombs for money over one who tortures out of conviction. You don't want to become that man, Golden Boy."

The golden man suddenly looked less tense.

"You're right, Cossack. I don't know what came over me…"

"We'll talk about it later, Golden Boy. I hear the police sirens getting closer."

Jean Vlad went back home with a migraine, a bruised body, and tired all over. When you walk through the door in this condition, the last thing you want to see is a little girl wrapping herself around your legs.

"Unca Jean!"

"Hey, easy on the tackles. Hard day at work…"

He forced himself to smile before squatting down to look into the small, radiant face.

"You're still up?" he asked.

"It's not as late."

"You mean, it's not *that* late. And I guess you did all your homework."

Corvine walked away without answering but giggling.

Jean searched through the pile of comics on the living room table while waiting for his sister, Mircea, to get back. Jean, Mircea and Corvine Vlad shared an apartment in a quiet Parisian neighborhood. The big bay windows let him enjoy the last rays of the summer day. In this light, the face of *Francix the Gaul* on the cover of *Leader* looked sickly yellow.

"Exactly what Golden Boy needs to forget the job," Jean grumbled, starting to read the latest issue.

Lucky Raspberry was a little more lighthearted. Humor from the far right, for sure, with a hero who repented of his tolerant past and now fought for white supremacy, but easy humor, full of simple jokes for the tired worker.

He heard keys jangling in the lock.

"Corvine! Your mother's home!" Jean shouted and the little girl came running.

The front door opened and Mircea Vlad got her daughter tangled in her legs. Jean laughed with his head still buried in the comics.

"And I bet dinner's not ready," Mircea said with feigned severity. "Corvine, did you do your homework?"

Corvine went away with a giggle that Jean could swear was a recording. It was identical to the one he had just heard without the slightest variation in tone.

"I'll take care of it," he said, getting out of the chair.

"How did the reporting in London go?"

Reporting was their code word for "catching criminals." Jean did not want Corvine to grow up knowing about his double life.

"I got a lot of interviews," he said while putting on his apron. "The last one was a real killer."

His sister forced a laugh.

"Anyway, I've got an hour flight behind me," he continued while cutting potatoes. "I tried to sleep..."

"A plane trip is never relaxing. I read a study about it."

"Babe, in my line of work, you sleep whenever you can."

As Jean sautéed the meat in the sauce, he looked at his sister. Not much younger, with the same black hair and just as good-looking, Mircea was his spitting image. They could have been twins. And Corvine, at five years-old, was Mircea in miniature.

"How was your day?" he asked.

"Not much better than yours. The Ministry is being infiltrated by the Coalition. I feel like it's the same throughout the government. Luckily, the President is on our side."

While the dish was cooking, Jean prepared an endive salad.

"You must see a lot nasty business."

"Indeed. It's the advantage of a job like mine. All the mail going by gives me a view of the whole thing. The extremes are taking control. We're going to end up like the US."

"C'mon, you're exaggerating!"

"Oh, you think so?" she replied. "Today, I was forced to get a Coalition card! Me! The perfectly neutral person, the mediator of the government..."

"Dinner's ready."

When he called Corvine to the table, he saw that the girl was reading *Lucky Raspberry* and she was laughing. Jean winced. Maybe it was time to cancel their subscription to *Leader*. Some strips were not that good... for adults as well as for kids.

In the smoky bar, Ivan Karine was wearing his "civvies." His shabby coat looked as good on him as a pink tutu on an elephant. Beneath his thick neck, his moustache drooped on the table, soaking in the alcohol. How the hell did he ever stay incognito?

"You went too far," the Cossack growled. He downed another glass of vodka. "I come from the Russian steppes. I know history. The Great Purge. The Gulag. I saw what noble ideals can produce."

"I think... you're right, Ivan," said Jean Vlad. "This time I was really on edge. There's a lot of tension at the paper. My boss wants to change the name of *The Universe* to *Great Minds*."

"You shouldn't let your cover job influence your real work," said the Russian.

"You didn't bring me here to tell me I'm turning into a thug."

"No, Jean, but let's talk about what's happening in London right now. It makes no sense. Even CRIMEN would never do that. No one's getting anything out of these attacks."

"You mean, why blow up Big Ben?" Jean said.

"Exactly. Our investigation turned up nothing worthwhile, even with the Flambo's help. But she should've found something. She always finds something."

Ivan Karine swallowed another full glass of vodka.

"So, instead of looking into the present, I tried looking at the past. You know, the old habit, hit the archives. That did us good against the Bloody Puppet and Tenebras..."

Karine knocked over the bottles to clear the table so he could spread out some newspapers that were more yellow than the walls.

"These senseless attacks started about four years ago. The atomic lab at Guen. The dam at Vourd. The bridge over the Gard. The Arc de Triomphe in Paris."

"I remember the Arc de Triomphe."

"Then the attacks stopped. The culprit was that young man, Sten, an up and coming agent of Department X, gone completely bonkers. First, they locked him up in a psych ward. Then they hanged him."

"Finally, a happy ending."

"No, Jean, because the attacks have continued for four years. They stopped in France, but they kept going elsewhere. In Germany at first, then in America. Everywhere. Senseless attacks, never justified. No one claiming responsibility. The the same thing, the same goal, the same chaos..."

Jean Vlad went home with a heavy heart, growing heavier by the minute. His blood was saturated with alcohol. He had to stop three times to take a piss. It made him feel worse. He thought of himself as a good citizen and hated to dirty the streets of the city.

In front of his building, he saw three vans with turrets parked at the curb. They were new vehicles that the police had gotten last year. They were armored and came with a plasma cannon on their roof. The secretary of the Coalition had sworn to high heaven that it was only for "deterrent purposes."

He pissed one last time on one of the vans.

The big windows were opened onto the night. Jean closed the door softly. Feeling around in the dark, not wanting to wake anyone, he went to the bathroom where he managed to throw up a little. Drinking with the Cossack was never a

111

good idea. He decided to turn on the lights before wiping off his chin. He opened the cabinet looking for a towel.

He saw the body of his niece stuffed onto the bottom shelf.

The world blanked out. Jean disconnected from reality, then reconnected with painful awareness. The little girl was naked and pale, rolled up like a fetus. Her skin was bruised in places and her neck black and blue from strangulation. She was as dead as could be. She had been the most beautiful little girl, and she was now the most beautiful corpse. And the ugliest as well. She was cold and her eyes were closed; there were circles under her eyes, from lack of oxygen; her limbs were thin and fragile, and a fingernail was torn out. She had fought, yes, fought against her attacker, but she had lost. A little girl could not win. She was five years-old and she was cold, and broken in several places. He could not look at her.

He turned away from the cabinet and vomited out everything inside him. Vomit mixed with tears. He staggered, covered in vomit, the world was spinning. He had stepped in liquid, was it vomit or blood? He moved forward, moaning, unable to control what came out of him—noise, yes, noise, he wanted to make noise, but he was choked, he swallowed hard, stumbled into the living room and finally he could wail.

He wailed. Nobody came. He paid no attention to the soiled carpet. He had not sobered up. He wanted to sober up. he should have called Ivan Karine, his best friend, not the police but Ivan, who would know what to do about the cabinet and where to hide the suitcase with his costume during the investigation… no, wait, it was Golden Boy who had to investigate, the police were useless, only good for driving armored trucks with war cannons and playing with their igneopters.

Hands on his cheeks. Lips that kissed him gently. Arms that hugged him. It was his sister finally. She wiped off his face and his shirt.

"Now, now, calm down."

"Sorry…"

"You had some bad booze. That's the last time you're going to drink so much. Our parents didn't raise us to be like this." Her reproach was couched in her words, but her voice expressed nothing but sympathy.

"Corvine…"

"Hopefully she didn't wake up."

Mircea led Jean to the kitchen sink.

"You need to hydrate. Drink."

She refused to talk to him until he gulped down some water. He coughed and held back his tears.

"Mircea, your daughter…"

"Corvine. Her name's Corvine."

"I know… I…" His gut wrenched but he did not throw up again this time.

"Unca Jean?"

Jean wept again, uncontrollably.

Corvine was in the doorway, unharmed, in her pajamas.

I hope you're feeling better. A doctor came by. We feared it might be alcohol poisoning. I was afraid for you but that doesn't mean I'm not angry with you. This is an appalling example to set for our little Corvine.

Mircea

Teetering, on his feet, but his whole body feeling intoxicated, Jean pocketed Mircea's note.

Spots of vomit from last night had soaked into the carpet, leading straight to the bathroom. In the gray light of the new day, Jean followed the trail and opened the cabinet.

His niece's corpse was not there. Where Corvine had been huddled up, under the shelves with the towels, the space was almost empty, only two bottles of bleach, a rag and a small bottle of dissolvent. He could not remember seeing these things last night, but he remembered the pale skin and the bruises.

He felt nauseous again. He bent down to inspect the space. It was tiny. Was there enough room for a five year-old girl? The sides showed no signs, but the wood was varnished, easy to clean. Was the corpse just an alcoholic hallucination?

Mircea had left for work at the ministry and Corvine was at school. If it was Corvine... and not a zombie, a vampire or the ghost of Corvine...

Taking advantage of the empty apartment, Jean looked for signs of some crime. He found nothing bloodier than leftovers from the chicken in the garbage.

After a quick shower he looked at the morning paper. *Le Matin*, March 24, 1973.

France: President Duclos confirmed "The Coalition is a necessary phase." Work, family and nation are still the main concerns of the party.

Cuba: Batista wants his territory to become the 54th state of the United States. The US government will study the issue after elections.

Korea: Opening of the new space center to support the Soviet bloc in the lunar conflict.

Italy: The mysterious death of Cardinal Faria. The Partito Luminoso refuses to comment.

Syria: Vietnam adds its missile batteries to the Americans'.

Slowly, methodically, Jean Vlad folded up the newspaper and placed it in the fireplace. He put three logs on top of it with enough space for air to circulate and went to find some matches.

On March 27, Jean Vlad went to Spain under the guise of having a new story to cover. He met the Cossack there in a big Catalan restaurant. Sitting at the same table were the two heroines Flambo and Night Princess. All of them were in costume.

Jean liked Flambo a lot... even if he had never seen her without her black and electric blue costume. Her helmet covered her face completely. He only knew her voice. But he had often imagined her smile.

She showed some interest in the possible name change of the paper from the *Universe* to *Great Minds*. "Words are important. I entered the data from the latest publications, books, magazines and newspapers, from various countries in my calculator recently. I do it once a year to keep an eye on the changes in the lexical field on every level, regional, national and global."

"I see," Night Princess laughed. "You want to become a French teacher."

Flambo ignored the woman dressed in black and red with dark glasses. She went on, "There's a serious change in ideology going on. You can see it in politics: Europe and Africa are toughening up to form a 3rd and 4th bloc to confront the USSR and the USA. The marginal states, like in Oceania, are turning into pawns. The *zeitgeist* of the day is a desire for unity, a frightening unity."

"So a German teacher?"

"On a cultural level, you can see all kinds of simplistic works with purely evil enemies fighting against allies of light, paragons of righteousness. It's propaganda, not artistic expression."

Jean thought of *Lucky Raspeberry* and *Francix the Gaul*.

"Everything about empathy and sharing is gone, being replaced all over the place by 'spirit,' 'soul' and 'mind.' Ideas about perfection and completion are everywhere. Most countries have been infiltrated by one party that calls itself revolutionary. In France, it's the Coalition; in England, the New Wing; in Italy, it's Il Partito Luminoso; here in Spain it's simply El Partido, the Party... It's taking control of the media and the economy and it's backed up by a militia that fosters a climate of terror."

"Like the Nazis in Germany," the Cossack grumbled. "Or the Communists in the USSR. Doesn't matter the ideology. The process is the same and we know the results."

After the waitress came and took their orders, the Russian continued.

"Flambo found the date and location of the next attack. It's the day after tomorrow, and it's not in England. It's in

Germany. In the city of Sarrebrücken, at the Flüssigkeitfabrik."

"It's an important building," Flambo explained. "An architectural and technological wonder, a factory that resulted from a complicated political compromise, one of the sensitive spots for the European alliance. The USSR has tried several times to bring it down. The recent attacks of our mysterious enemies in England, and before that in Sweden, have upset different factions and weakened..."

"In a nutshell, please," Night Princess cut in.

"The date, like the place, was not chosen at random. The destruction of the German Fabrik would result in an all-out war between the Soviet and Pan European blocs. Then all it would take is one final push, a lunar attack and..."

"Short and simple. I know I'm no genius but..."

"Total nuclear war."

Jean Vlad got back from Spain on March 28 during the day, feeling even worse than when he had left. The seeds of global totalitarianism divided into a few "blocs" that were always just two peas in a pod had been planted even before he was born. So, when had the nightmare started?

When he entered the front door, he found his niece standing in the middle of the living room waiting for him. A fire was going in the fireplace.

"Hello, Uncle Jean."

"Hello. You're being so polite this afternoon!"

"Have to," the girl smiled, "you're my favorite uncle."

Jean went into the kitchen to make some coffee. He felt Corvine's eyes follow him. She never called him "Uncle" Jean, always "Unca."

When he got back to the living room, Corvine was lying on the carpet reading a book, a real book, about the rise of the Coalition.

"That's not age-appropriate. Don't you have school today?"

"Sorry, Uncle Jean, I forgot."

"You missed the bus?"

"Yes."

Jean looked at the low table. He snatched up the copy of *Leader* and threw it in the fire. That mockery of a magazine had sullied the room for long enough. Corvine stared at him again.

"You can stay home today, but tomorrow you're going back to school. It's important. You can't *forget*."

"Yes, Uncle Jean. Sorry."

Corvine's voice sounded emotionally sincere, but with an emotion that was not like her. Jean stared as she turned her attention back to her book. The hair was Corvine's, the face was Corvine's, the right clothes, the right size... Everything was Corvine, including the measles scar on her cheek. It was Corvine in every detail. But her behavior was not right. The life was gone, the energy was gone. Corvine did not come running, and then run away instead of saying sorry. It was like another kid had been put into her body. Or the image that an outside observer would have created of the niece of Jean Vlad. A well-behaved child.

He stood up. "Would you like some water?" he asked.

"Yes, Uncle Jean. Thank you very much."

Jean shuddered again. If this was an impostor, if Corvine had died that night, he had no idea what to do. He knew nothing about this creature, not even how to expose it.

Or had he become totally crazy?

Jean called the ministry and left a coded message for Mircea. He went into the kitchen, filled a pitcher with water and took two glasses. The faintest sound echoed in the apartment. He heard pages turning in the living room. He went back and poured Corvine a glass of water.

When she drank, he thought he saw something reflected in her eyes, for a split second.

Arrows pointing down.

The train arrived late at the German station. Igneopters, squat and chromed with fire cannons on top and a jet engine in the rear, swept the skies with their searchlights. The buildings in Sarrebrücken flashed white before sinking back into darkness.

Golden Boy ran as fast as he could through the ectoplasmic city that swam in and out of the bright beams. The presence of the police igneopters meant something was wrong.

When he got to Ludwigsplatz, the golden man saw the Flüssigkeitfabrik in all its glory, giant glass tanks standing proudly in the façade sweeping along their blazing plasma, outlining the contours of the rough concrete. All the strength of man and the new ideologies gathered together into a huge conglomeration of geometric shapes.

The Fabrik exploded. Jean was cast into an apocalyptic nightmare: white and gray buildings were shattered by the wreckage before being hit by pure plasma, the fiery, explosive liquid that fed all of modern Europe's industry. A volcano had erupted in the middle of the city.

My friends are in there!

Jean started running again into the ruins of the Fabrik. He dodged a block of cement that crashed into the pavement and kept running heedless of the other meteors. The igneopters were not so lucky. One of them was about to crash into Fröschengasse; another had destroyed the Friedenskirche church.

Around the disaster, the city was in flames. Defying the hail of falling debris, Jean had reached the front walls when the plasma poured into the Sarre river. He heard a hissing sound and knew what it meant—and he ran the other way.

Burning steam flooded the mangled square. Screams of people spewed out of the building. Jean had to stay on the far edge of the square, listening to the people run away behind him and watching the burning steam in front of him.

He had to wait. If he ran forward, he would die and no one would help.

Jean was sweating. The foul stench of the scorched Sarrebrücken inhabitants in the torrents of lava were mixed now with a more appalling odor, that of steamed meat. His stomach turned.

He should have been organizing the evacuation. But his friends were in there.

The steam cleared a little. His eyes stung. He forced himself to walk into the steam, a sea of fog where pieces of concrete were floating like islands. The façade came into view, shining with wide plasmic veins.

Streams of industrialized lava wound through the ruins. Jean made his way past the assembly lines calling out to his friends. Every shout made his throat drier and his voice hoarser but he could not stop calling out to them.

He got to the oldest part of the factory where it was joined to the foundations of an ancient church. Raw concrete pillars stood atop the sculpted stone effigy of a God who had long ago abandoned the dreams of humanity. Between the long worktables, the altars to the glory of Industry, they lay. Barely recognizable, marked by the stigmata of a battle they could not win. His friends.

He found the Cossack first, sitting against a wall. His legs were there but his upper body and head were no longer visible, covered by a mass of melted metal.

Then he saw Flambo, skewered by a girder. Acting on impulse, he took off her impenetrable helmet and at last saw her first, saved from disfiguration. She had been beautiful. She had a small mouth with white teeth and he could only imagine the smile he would never see. He wanted to cry but his face was seared and his eyes felt completely dried out.

"I was waiting for you, Jean Vlad!"

Jean's reflexes went into action. He rolled away from a twirling blue beam that struck one of the columns. The concrete crumbled and the metal cable attached to it melted, just like the steel that had covered and killed the Cossack.

The thing that came out of the columns of steam and streams of lava had been the Night Princess in a distant past. You could still recognize the feminine curves in the black and red costume, but the latter was torn in places and revealed disgusting limbs, waxy, purplish, with twisted, swollen muscles and tendons. The ligaments bulged and shrank, dancing like tentacles. Jean could see right through the tendons of her arms and legs.

"What *are* you?" he asked.

"The hero you know."

Her voice had not changed and her face was still human, as well as one of her breasts, which only made this parody of humanity even more obscene.

"Don't get upset with me, Jean Vlad. You, too, feel the beauty of what I have accomplished."

"What *are* you?"

Night Princess shot a blue ray out of her gloved hands. Jean dodged it and tossed a grenade. The *thing* jumped in the air and its rubbery legs wrapped around a thin girder. The golden apple exploded near a steel cabinet, scattering tools in every direction.

Night Princess hissed like a snake.

Jean barked, "Come down here!"

A second apple blew up the girder, dropping the creature at the feet of Golden Boy. It was on its hands and knees, but not like an animal; its chest and face were facing up instead of back, while its flexible limbs scurried it away frantically.

"Now you're a contortionist? Come back here!"

Jean tried to toss another grenade, but another blue ray hit him and the apple exploded in mid-air, throwing him against the wall where the Cossack's body was slumped.

A damp heat spread through his body. Had he been irradiated? What kind of ray was this abomination casting?

"Now you're joined to the cause of the Great Mind," the monstrosity cackled. "You're going to fulfill its will. You're going to…"

Jean pitched one last grenade into one of the plasma streams. The blazing splatter sprayed his enemy who fell, writhing on the ground, screaming and spitting…

Jean went over to the wrecked cabinet and grabbed a big hammer. He came back to the creature who was trying to drag itself to safety. The hammer landed right in its belly.

"Answer me and you'll suffer less. What is the Great Mind?"

"How can a creature of this feeble world understand It?"

Jean brought the hammer down on one of its deformed limbs. "Answer me."

"Our god. The Great Mind rules over an infinite number of worlds..."

"Alien worlds? Where?"

"You're thinking too small, Jean Vlad. The power of the Mind rules over parallel worlds."

Jean stroked the monster's face with the sharp end of the hammer, then he lifted off the dark glasses.

"Where I come from, Jean Vlad, I am really the Night Princess, the Night Princess of another reality. I came into your world one year ago and after destroying the Night Princess you knew, I took her place quite easily. After all, I knew her... she was me..."

"What do you want?" Jean growled as a chill ran through his entire body.

"For the cycle to continue. Don't worry, there's nothing you can do. We've already won. On this world, the envoy of the Great Mind faced himself and defeated the champion of the Universality. It was a decisive victory."

"What are you talking about?"

"It's finished, Jean Vlad. You were hit by my ray on the orders of Great Mind."

"Your ray didn't do anything to me. It shatters rock and melts metal, but it left me untouched.

The monstrosity had a cruel laugh. "No, Jean Vlad, the ray did affect you. You've been contaminated, corrupted by the power of the Great Mind and there's nothing you can do. Soon you will kill. Your path will become drenched in blood. You will destroy all those dear to you, and in the end you will bow down to His Omnipotence. I have accomplished my final mission for the glory of the Great Mind."

Jean gulped, remembering the heat he had felt. But his grip on his weapon tightened. He was bound to become a murderer? So be it, he would become one of these abominations.

"I can now return to my world," the Night Princess murmured. "Content with having spread the word of the Great Mind, the path of total unification."

"You will never return to your world."

Jean raised the hammer high.

When it was over, when he had stopped swinging, after his hand opened up and the weapon fell to the ground, he wept. Over the corpse of the monster he poured all the tears he could not offer to the remains of his friends.

Because the Night Princess's dark glasses had hid something that he had already seen... sickly yellow pupils with irises in the shape of inverted arrows.

The little girl walked fearlessly, full of curiosity, through the hallways of the military base. In front of her was Colonel Steber, a high-ranking officer in the Selenite division, radiant with his austere uniform and his short, silver hair. She looked at the propaganda posters, the images warning against the various dangers of life on the Moon, the reminders of the international issues at stake in space. She was so curious that the officer had to keep pulling her by the hand.

It took all morning to get through the procedures. Procedures that the girl did not understand. They had promised her a guided tour of the base, organized by the Young French Action Committee, but this field trip was not like the others. Her schoolmates were not there and the colonel had taken her on her way to school. She did not understand why so many people looked startled or amused by the "unusual situation." She did not understand much of what Colonel Steber was saying or why sometimes he took those people into another room to talk only to come back out alone.

She was starting to get a little scared.

They finally arrived at the boarding room, a huge hangar full of machines that the girl knew nothing about. She was only five and did not think it strange that there were no employees or security guards.

The colonel smiled while gazing at the Nova rocket. "Just look at that ship, the apex of human knowledge and know-how. It's going to take us to the stars."

"Not if I can help it."

A golden apple sent the girl and the colonel flying. The latter did not get up. But Corvine did. With a bruised knee, she looked at Golden Boy, a positive figure whom she had seen so many times in magazines. But this could not be him. Superheroes did not attack little girls.

"That's better," Golden Boy said with a cold smile. "Your eyes look human and your voice is… a perfect imitation. I guess you're satisfied, bitch? Do you know how many soldiers I had to kill to reach you here?"

He jumped on her.

"Why Corvine? Why?"

He was pinning her to the ground, strangling her.

"Why the Great Mind? How many of you are there?"

She did not understand the questions. Her neck was hurting and she could not answer. Her little hands beat the ground and tried to hit him.

"I can't," Golden Boy went on. "Accursed creature, you look so much like her. I can't… do this…"

At last, she recognized him. The mask fit tightly over a face that she knew. And the voice… now her uncle was repeating, "Why? Why?" She wanted to ask him why too, why choke her, was she a bad girl?

He was crying now, crying while killing her. She could not fight against him. She had no more energy. The pain in her neck had stopped and purple flowers were spinning in her eyes. She could not really see or hear anything. She gave up. Unca Jean was crying and she could not say anything to comfort him. She wanted to tell him it was OK, she was proud of him because she loved Golden Boy, he was the best of all the superheroes.

She wondered one last time, "Why?"

Her uncle asked her one last time, "Why?"

And that was her last thought.

Corvine's heart had stopped beating. Jean felt sick. He disgusted himself. It had been a perfect imitation of his niece, down to the smallest detail, and she had almost managed to fly to the Moon. Up there, she would have carried out the last attack needed to start a nuclear war. He did not like the world, but he had to fight for it, no matter how ugly it might be.

He wanted to die. No, he couldn't die. Someone had to keep on fighting.

He got off the corpse of his fake niece. He had loosened his grip on her neck several times as his resolve had almost... but he had remembered the body folded into the cabinet and the way her eyes had briefly flashed inverted arrows when she drank water. And he had killed her. He wondered if Mircea was also a monster, a monster in the shape of his beloved sister. He wondered how many people around him were monsters.

He, too, was a monster. He had killed in order to get through the Paris spaceport. He should have shut down the alarm system, then snuck in, but he had killed humans. Before today Jean Vlad had never killed. He always figured out how to knock them out, tie them up, gag them, use chloroform, whatever. But his speed and his success at reaching Corvine and his killing her were the keys to survival for humanity. If he had to dirty his hands to save others...

He heard a laugh.

Colonel Steber had crawled away while Jean Vlad was killing his niece and now he was getting up. Every one of his movements looked artificial, jerky, either too fast or too slow. His body was swaying and his limbs bending in ways not possible for human bones as he struggled to his feet.

"Little girl... So fragile... So full of sickening beauty..."

Jean had run out of grenades. He stepped back, sizing up his adversary. In Steber's eyes, he could see the sparkling, inverted arrow-shaped irises. The creature answered Jean's unspoken question by bowing melodramatically like an actor at the end of a play.

"Glad to meet you more formally, Jean Vlad, Jean Vlad the idiot, Jean Vlad the murderer, Jean Vlad the powerless..."

"Who are you, monster?"

Steber took out his pistol. Jean jumped to the side to avoid the bullet but Steber... shot his own hand. The hole in his hand grew larger while the uninjured hand made a hole in itself. His clothes melted like wax as all his limbs stretched out, mutilated into multiple articulations.

This was the final form of the organism Jean had confronted in the Fabrik. A more evolved specimen of the same, ageless evil, a foul, mangled, slimy creature covered with rustling, twitching tendrils.

"*I am Wampus!* I created the human species with my hands. Without me, you would be nothing but filthy slime. While traveling through time, I altered your history. I led it in the direction desired by the Great Mind."

The pale creature laughed again, which was not easy to do since the fleshy coils across its mouth were like prison bars. The jagged hole in its face covered by bluish ligaments was, along with the inverted arrow-shaped irises, what was most human-looking about him.

"A path of technological development, a metaphysical ascent," the monster went on, "because it's only by progressing that you can reach the stage where you will make the choice, the free and voluntary choice to turn away from the complexity of existence and submit to a single greatness. To go backward, one must first go forward..."

"I don't understand what you're talking about."

"Totalitarianism is a cry for help. The last crimes of cowards, the negations of existence and of thought..." Wampus' voice turned falsetto. "I feel so bad! I can't stand getting out of bed in the morning having to think about others.

I don't want to admit they may be right, that I may be wrong, and to think that the approaching death is unbearable. Give me simple reasons, even if they're false, responsible parties, better still, guilty parties who will soon become targets, enemies. Give me a purified, mechanical society founded on obedience to superiors, where art would submit to precise standards and serve only ideology. I desire only to obey, to serve, to destroy. Make me a robot, to liberate me, make me a machine free of pain, make me a gun to kill everyone who might subvert these ideas, everyone who might show me another way is possible, a way that I am even more scared to follow..."

"That's a pretty speech... coming from a monster who wants to manipulate us into our self-destruction."

"Ha ha! What did you not understand? You are all responsible for me being here. When humans evolved to the point of explicitly making this existential non-choice, when totalitarian ideologies appeared, the Great Mind finally had the right to come into your world for its own good, and I was sent here to fulfill my destiny, according to the Rules. *You called me!*"

Wampus took a step toward Jean and the corpse of Corvine. There was a big, inhuman smile on its fungal face. Jean looked desperately for a weapon within reach as he spoke.

"You say we had no choice?"

"You always have a choice. And it's always interesting to know what you do with it. There's nothing more enjoyable than seeing a human being sink into chaos and destruction on his own... Tell me, why did you kill your niece?"

"She was an imitation. Like you."

"Oh, right," Wampus chuckled. "The body in the cabinet—*that* was me."

"I know it was you," Jean replied coldly. "You killed her, the night I came home drunk. You took her place in our life..."

"No, my friend. I was only the corpse. You just killed your real niece."

Time stopped. Started again. Jean's heart was racing in his chest as the revelation sank in, and worse, the awful certainty that he could have guessed, if he had taken time to think, to ask, if he had not killed...

"I was the corpse," Wampus walked toward him. "I left your niece sleeping peacefully in her bed and I squeezed into the cabinet looking like her. After you saw me, I just had to escape through the pipes."

Jean backed away,

"That's impossible. Corvine had change when I got back from Spain. And for an instant, her pupils turned into inverted arrows, like yours."

"Yes, that was me again, 'Uncle Jean,'" the abomination said mimicking the little girl's voice. "It was a school day, you remember? You even scolded me. That day, your niece was really at school and I was told by the Great Mind to get into your home and sow the last seeds of your paranoia."

Jean moaned, a sound that he himself barely heard though it went on and on. Why was nobody coming? Why was there no soldier in the boarding area?

"Don't you remember?" Wampus said as if reading his mind. "You've killed them all. It was for the good of humanity!"

"I did what I could," Jean said. "The Night Princess' ray contaminated me. I told myself that, if I was forced to become a murderer, I could at least put the murders to good use. I turned the Great Mind's curse against it!"

"You think so... Tell me, how many people did you kill on this base?"

"Nine... teen."

"Nineteen! Hell of a score, friend. Congratulations, we are witnessing the start of a promising career. All for the greater good."

"You made me do it. You poisoned my mind..."

"No, we just pretended to."

Jean's vision started to blur. "No..."

"No trick from the Great Mind could make anyone do such a terrible thing. It goes against Its most basic principle. Anyway, why trick you into becoming a murderer when you did it so well all by yourself?"

"But you…"

"We did nothing! Our ray only affects stone and metal. It's useless against living beings. You killed because you believed we infected you mind. That's all it took. A simple suspicion of mental corruption. In fact, it was only a pretext, a convenient excuse to convince you to take the easy way out, the way of violence. You've killed these men because you wanted to achieve your goal."

Jean was becoming dizzier. He could not look the creature in the face.

"And what a goal! The murder of Corvine! Oh, Jean Vlad, it wasn't a wasted day. You've proved yourself very gifted indeed. The Great Mind was right to choose you."

The obvious question got stuck in Jean's throat.

"Why you?" Wampus asked for him. "But, my dear Golden Boy, because you're magnificent! When the Universality loses a world, when a champion like me has defeated the other side's champion, things change, evolve... Maybe you haven't noticed it, but over the last four years, mindsets have started changing. It goes beyond your meager terrestrial ideologies; it's the result of the pull of the Great Mind. Your entire world becomes but a pawn, cannon fodder..."

The monster, still stretching out, stopped at Corvine's corpse.

"But you, Jean Vlad, you're different. This world's greatest hero. The Great Mind wants to use you as its champion."

"Never," Jean managed to speak, flat against one of the hangar walls. "I'd rather die."

"You're already dead, deep down in your heart. You're beyond redemption, Jean Vlad. But I can give you thousands of reason to serve us."

Wampus raised his crude, pale face toward the sky.

"The Moon is a full of mines. Since the super powers got there last decade, they've been fighting over territory. If I or one of my agents who works there, you know what will happen. The Sarrebruck attack was the last stage in the fulfillment of my plan."

"The destruction of humanity."

"You can stop it, Jean Vlad. The Great Mind doesn't want to destroy the planet. One planet more or less doesn't matter to It. But champions, good champions, are rare. Give It your allegiance, Jean Vlad, and your planet will survive."

"A planet of sheep, of Nazis…"

"That you have already decided to save at the cost of twenty dead today. Were these innocent people killed in vain, hero? Was your niece killed in vain?"

"You're taking the world hostage."

"Oh, not just the world," Wampus jeered. "Your sister, too. Your only family. What do you imagine she'll think of you after the massacre today?"

The monster knelt on Corvine's body.

"I tell you, Jean Vlad, you do have a choice. You've always had a choice. Humanity also has always had a choice. You can deny me. But what's the point since I've already got agents on the Moon, men like in London, quasi-men like the Night Princess, who will act alone. And before the world is consumed by nuclear fire, you'll have time to taste the tears of your weeping sister. To feel her boundless hatred."

A human-like thumb, with a fingernail, but soft like a mussel, slipped into Corvine's mouth.

"But everything can happen differently. The world can survive and grow in the shadow of the Great Mind, and Mircea can see her daughter again."

Wampus tasted the saliva from the child's corpse and shrank down, shriveled up, until he was the same size. His slimy skin turned into the clothes of the little girl.

"What do you choose, Jean Vlad?"

The Great Mind was spreading slowly but steadily through millions of universes, its mental claws planted in billions upon billions of heads of all shapes and sizes, a mane of raw energy spreading over its servants who needed its omnipotence.

The Great Mind was sated. It exuded miasmas of suffering like gas from decomposing bodies. The remains of Its last hunt, Jean Vlad's world. Soon the human hive would be in perfect harmony, all its thoughts in tune, its madness. Because after a period of necessary chaos, the cycle would create unity, peace. This was the goal of evolution, the path that all intelligent beings ought to take.

It stretched out a lazy tendril toward the next universe. Ah, there was an interesting Earth...

Its new champion would have to prove his loyalty. The rules said that Its envoy would have to kill his twin in the parallel world, his unsullied double, a sacrificial lamb, an ignorant servant of the Universality.

Jean Vlad versus Jean Vlad. The Great Mind never missed this kind spectacle.

Jean Vlad would have to kill himself in a fair fight, of course. Not only in accordance with the Rules, but also with Its own principles.

After all, the important thing is to have Rules.

*The historical **Dragut** was born around 1485; he was a freebooter in the service of Khayr ad-Din, aka Barbarossa, Sultan of Algiers. Later, he became admiral of the Ottoman fleet and was killed by a cannonball at the siege of Malta in 1565. The fictional Dragut of the Hexagon Universe has met Wampus, the evil wizard Maleficus, the seductive **Scarlet Lips**, Stormshadow, Captain Hook, and many other legendary figures....*

Jean-Marc & Randy Lofficier: *Dragut and the Sea Serpent*

"I seek the human known as Captain Dragut," said the Sea Serpent.

The creature had suddenly burst out of the water and towered over the ship, terrifying the sailors who were already signing themselves and confessing a vast litany of sins.

"Dragut, you say? No, can't say I recognize the name," said Dragut, without losing his cool. He turned towards his first mate and not-so-secret lover, the beautiful *lamia* Scarlet Lips. "Does that name ring a bell, darling?" he asked her

"I can't say that it does," replied the scarlet-tressed woman.

"Sorry, can't help you there, mate," said Dragut to the Serpent, flashing what he hoped would look like a convincingly sincere, warm smile.

"What a bother," said the Serpent. "If you could help me find that pesky mortal, I might be prepared to be generous..."

The Monster tried, but utterly failed, to look sympathetic.

"Generous, how so? asked Dragut, raising an eyebrow.

"I will promise you a quick and painless death instead of chewing on the marrow of your outer appendages," suggested the Serpent.

"A tempting offer, indeed, but I still find myself oddly unmotivated," said Dragut. "Perhaps if I were to know more about your quest... Why exactly do you seek that Drago...? Cragut...?"

"Dragut. It has come to my attention that that wretched little man has had the temerity to slay some of this world's greatest denizens."

"Ah!—you mean Monsters."

"Watch your tongue, manling. I mean creatures such as me, who are ancient, learned and beautiful..."

"Sorry to interrupt," interjected Scarlet Lips, "but we've just met the Zombie Master of Saint-Domingue and, Lord, he was *uuuugly*!"

"Well, perhaps not zombies then," said the Serpent.

"And what about that mangy Kroatoan wolf-creature, flea-ridden and slobbering like a dog in heat," said Dragut, snapping his fingers. "Have you ever seen anything more pathetic?"

"...Or the Sirenids..."

"And what about the mud-men of..."

"Enough!" shouted the Sea Serpent, causing the ship to almost capsize. "I'll grant you that not all of our races are truly beautiful..."

"Or learned," said Dragut. "You should have tried talking to the Last Ghoul of Twilight. She could barely spell her name in Sanskrit."

"...Or learned," grudgingly admitted the Serpent, gritting his teeth, producing a noise not unlike the screech of chalk on a blackboard. "But we *are* ancient!" he finished in a triumphant tone.

"Yes, you are that. Can't argue about that, can we, darling?" said Dragut to Scarlet Lips.

"Nope. Some of these monsters are really really old," she replied. "In fact, I've heard—but no, it would hardly be impolite to mention this before our towering scaly guest here."

"What have you heard, female?" roared the Serpent. "And be careful. I have a mind to end this most annoying of conversations right now and consign you all to Davy Jones' locker."

"But then, you wouldn't find out what she knows," pointed Dragut.

"If you insist..." said Scarlet Lips.

"I do, I do," said the Serpent.

"Well, it's been said that some of you elder creatures are so old that... that... well, you know..."

"No, I don't," said the Serpent.

Scarlet Lips tapped her forehead slightly in an unmistakable gesture.

"...That you've all gone a little ga-ga," she finished.

"Ga-ga?" roared the Sea Serpent, causing a tear in the mizzen sail.

"Senile. Doddering. Feeble-minded."

"I know what 'ga-ga' means, female! I mastered your inane language three hundred years ago!"

"Sorry," said Scarlet Lips, looking properly apologetic.

"She's right, you know," interjected Dragut. "I've even heard some no doubt misguided souls claim that you can't even remember your own name."

"Of all the stupid things! That's absurd! I am Jörmungandr, also known by the secret name of Uroborus and..."

Suddenly, there was a long silence. The Sea Serpent had realized that it had said too much, for his name was his secret, his secret was his name, and there was much power in both.

Dragut smiled. It was a mean, triumphant smile, nothing like the smile with which he had first greeted the Serpent.

From his pocket, he produced the bottle that Stormshadow had given him; it was made of a substance that might have been glass, except that it was totally dark and did not reflect light.

It was a matter of mere seconds to incorporate the true name of the Sea Serpent into the eight conjurations that the great shaman of the Twilight People had taught him, recite them aloud, and thus force the creature inside the bottle.

"So much for the Sea Serpent," said Dragut to Scarlet Lips. "He was much easier than I thought. They may be ancient and learned, but they sure are stupid. What's next on the list?"

"Something about a giant white whale, I think..."

Dragut & Scarlet Lips by Alfredo Macall

Aster and Pinky by Juan Roncagliolo Berger

*An alien from the negative universe of Zhud, **Aster** came to Earth in order to find a cure for the sterility of his people. Here, he met the beautiful and charming **Pinky**, became a superhero, and was even for a time a founding member of the Hexagon Group. This adventure takes place soon after their return to Zhud.*

Ghislain Morel: *Programmed Decay*

Dedicated with affection to Chloé Relaño.

The alarms went off all over the ship. While the screens flashed red and gold lights, casting a sinister tint over the cabin, Pinky jumped into the copilot seat and pulled up the response system of the onboard computer. An impersonal, feminine voice sounded in the cockpit:

Alert! Receiving a distress signal sent to the Zhud Monitors. Attempted boarding of monitor ship XV-108 by unidentified pirate ship at 57 astro units from the orbit of Aavera on the directional vector of the Sextan System.

Aster came into the cockpit just in time to hear the cause of the alarm.

"We should go. We're the closest ship and the only one in this sector. The proximity of Aavera keeps space travel to a minimum around here to avoid the risk of detection."

"I'll enter the coordinates," Pinky said, working on her nav-console.

The saucer fired its reactors full speed ahead toward the location of the call for help.

Ten minutes later, the young Earth woman got her first visual. The situation was indeed alarming: the Monitor ship, a patroller, a spherical saucer just like theirs, looked like it was drifting, seriously damaged. A flexible bridge had been hooked up to its airlock from the pirate ship—a long cylinder tapered at the front with three stabilizing fins in the rear and a proton cannon on top. Several turrets stuck out like warts on its surface. At the approach of their ship, they immediately started turning and within seconds, energy beams were shooting through empty space at them.

Pinky had never faced this kind of situation and her navigation skills were relatively new, but she adapted quickly and her reflexes compensated for her lack of experience.

"You're doing fine," Aster said. "I'll get on the weapons."

He crossed the cabin and jumped into the seat in front of the targeting system. His fingers flew over the keys and the tactile screens of the different weapon systems. A flood of energy from the enemy ship struck their shields when three cannons opened fire on the same point.

"I'm going to concentrate my attacks on their rear. Sometimes, there's a weak point in the shields because of the reactor flux. I'll try to destroy their generators to strand them there and shut down their weapons system."

Pinky's face was covered with cold sweat. She was fully aware that the slightest mistake could spell death for their ship. Nevertheless, she piloted expertly out of the enemy fire helped by the fact that their attackers' movements were hampered by their hookup to their prey.

"I thought I saw some shapes moving through the bridge to the pirate ship," she said.

"We'll lose our tactical advantage if they can take off!"

Aster decided to risk it all. He sent two missiles to the same coordinates as all his other shots. The first missile finally brought down the energy shield protecting the pirates. The second exploded between two fins, opening a breach in the hull.

Then the menacing cylinder lit up its reactors and pulled in the bridge from the patrol ship before shooting off toward the Sextan system. With cold shivers running down their spines, Aster and Pinky could see a thin mist leak out of the monitor ship's airlock only to crystallize immediately, probably the atmosphere from the cockpit.

"We have to help them."

"No, Pinky, it's too late. They must have died instantly from the decompression. Let's catch those pirates and try to find out why they attacked a Monitor ship of Zhud."

The young American woman immediately set a course to chase the enemy ship, which was trying to pick up speed but was obviously slowed down by the damage from the missile. She reacted instinctively to all the counter-attacks and zig-zagged between the energy bursts, urged on by the desire to make the murderers pay for the lost lives.

Aster focused and targeted the turrets one by one, following the rays back to their point of origin. Each cannon could only shoot once, so Aster destroyed them methodically after each firing. The enemy ship looked like it was going up in flames, blazing at every point of impact and losing its weapons with every explosion. Then it abruptly changed direction and headed out into empty space with all the power of its reactors. Under its belly, out of sight of its attackers, a trap door opened and dropped a small vessel, a replica of the pirate ship but ten times smaller.

Aster thought for a second of using the time ray. It was the most powerful weapon on the Zhud ship, a flux of chronotons that aged its target at hyper-speed rendering the material obsolete and killing all living things with old age. But the possibility of interrogating the prisoner made him change his mind.

"I'm going to destroy their reactor. That should immobilize them long enough for reinforcements to get here."

Aster selected one of his last missiles and sent it just above the main reactor at the base of one of the fins. The weapon hit on target and destroyed the rear of the ship. The fin was torn off by the explosion and went twirling off into the void. A series of explosions ran all along the side of the ship until the whole thing blew up, creating a giant ball of fire that lit up the darkness separating the planetary systems. Taking advantage of the burst of energy, the small ship hiding behind the momentary sun fired its reactors and plunged into hyper-space before the explosion dissipated in the cosmic vacuum.

Pinky circled the last position of the pirate ship while Aster maxed out the scanners to analyze the remains of the enemy vessel.

"There's nothing left. The explosion evaporated every-thing. No survivors, no sign of life at all."

As he was examining the screens, Pinky suddenly thought of the Monitor ship and sped back towards it. She slowed down at the last minute and drifted up to the gaping airlock.

"I'm going to manually dock since the locking beams from the airlock aren't working."

She stuck out her tongue while concentrating hard, which would have looked hilarious in any other situation. Aster came behind her to watch the maneuver.

"You're full of surprises today. Yesterday, you could barely steer, and today, it's like you've been doing this your whole life."

"The battle gave me confidence. Besides, there's no time to lose. Maybe there are survivors in some sealed compart-ment."

Aster quickly buckled into a seat before responding.

"You're right. Pump some air into the ship. When the airlock is pressurized, I'll go look for survivors."

A metallic noise and a green light turning on in the air-lock signaled that the ships were docked. Aster activated the forcefield of his suit and opened the first door. He stepped into the wreck and hurried down the corridor leading to the cock-pit. The airlock and the door had been destroyed with thermal weapons and the melted metal had hardened in the passage-way. When he entered the big, glassed dome, he saw right away the five corpses of the crewmembers, hideously mutilat-ed by the decompression that had happened when the pirate ship had violently broken off.

Some of them also showed signs of being hit by thermal fire and must already have lost their life before he arrived, but

Aster could not help feeling somewhat responsible for their deaths.

The cockpit had been looted. Obviously the pirates were interested in the equipment and had ripped out control panels and screens, leaving a mess of cables and electronics strewn around.

Aster turned on the sensors on his Thorion belt to analyze the inside of the ship. Normally a Monitoring crew was made up of five people, but for some reason, two more passengers were on board.

A voice came out of his belt, warning, *"Presence of antimatter detected behind a fluctuating, compression field."*

Aster understood right away and ran back to his spaceship, "Pinky! Disengage from the airlock! That ship is booby-trapped with an antimatter bomb!"

The navigator cut the moorings without a second thought and fired up the reactors as Aster ran down the corridor. As the two ships slowly separated, the atmosphere between them started leaking off into space. Aster used his belt to go into flying mode and slipped through his ship's airlock in the nick of time before it sealed shut.

In the meantime, Pinky pumped the reactors to full power and almost instantly put several miles between them and the wreck. The explosion was colossal, using the patrol ship itself as an explosive it blew out huge amounts of energy thanks to the antimatter from the magnetic fields that kept it from reacting with the matter in our universe.

The explosion was strong enough to catch up to the saucer and shake it as it zipped away close to the speed of light, headed for Aster's home planet—Zhud.

"Our Monitors have analyzed the site of the attack. There's nothing left, the antimatter totally consumed our saucer."

Councilor Karzul was pacing his huge office while talking to Pinky and Aster who were seated in comfortable, antigravity armchairs.

After a short pause, he went on, stroking his beard, "Also, there's nothing left of the pirate ship but the images your vessel got. We're trying to identify it with the help of our allies. Initial information seems to point to the infamous space pirate Captain Glautekas, a Xan who's been plundering worlds for decades. But this was far from his usual territory."

Aster did not try to hide his feelings, "I don't get it either. This pirate was heavily armed and what would he want with a Monitor ship from our fleet?"

"That's not the only mystery we're up against. They told me this morning that on Durkania, the museum planet, someone tried to steal some artifacts from our planet's collection of antiquities."

"Durkania? I've never heard of it," Pinky looked inquisitive.

Aster told her right away. "It's a museum planet set up on a dead world. All the peaceful cultures of the galaxy have a collection there to present their histories to the rest of the cosmos. There are also the archeological remains of vanished races discovered throughout the universe. It's a world of wonders. And of course, it's well guarded, both the museums and the individual collections use the latest security equipment."

"It's the kind of world that I'd love to visit," the young Earth woman mused.

"Well, I don't know if we'll have time to do a lot of sightseeing, but we will have to go there to investigate this attempted theft. Councilor, I'm going to run some checks on our ship and then, we'll be out of here within the hour."

"The Council has complete confidence in you, Aster. May the gods of Zhud protect you!"

Thanks to the automatic pilot, Pinky and Aster had a chance to rest and get a few hours of hard-earned sleep. The computer woke them up when they entered the solar system that was their destination. After washing up and getting dressed, Pinky took her seat at the controls.

142

"I've never seen so many ships in the same place. Space is swarming with all kinds of vessels. It's like an armada here," she observed.

"I told you, Durkania is one of the most visited planets in the galaxy. There's a multi-planetary protection fleet, there are cargo ships carrying provisions for the workers, scientists and tourists, there are star cruisers bringing in visitors, archeological expeditions and scientific researchers coming and going and a whole bunch of people profiting off the traffic."

"It's impressive, especially for someone who never even suspected, just a few months ago, that there was life beyond her own planet."

She looked out of the transparent cockpit at the seemingly anarchic movements of the thousands of tons of metal floating around in space.

"You should pay attention to the controls. Despite the apparent chaos, the trajectories are assigned to avoid collisions. Contact the navigation authority and program the autopilot for the Zhud Embassy on Durkania."

After a brief conversation, the young pilot entered the route in the computer and left the control of the ship to the autopilot, which allowed her to gaze in wonder at the ceaseless traffic of the system.

After docking, a security officer from the space museum took them to meet the Ambassador appointed by the Supreme Council of Zhud who went with them directly to the security office.

Standing in a cold room, they stared at weird corpse lying on the autopsy table. Pinky was not used to this kind of situation and her uneasiness showed. Obviously, the weird body on the table was not helping.

In the room, an alien doctor who looked like a praying mantis (despite the fact that its eight legs ended in six long fingers, each with five phalanges) was maneuvering jointed manipulators and remote-controlled nano-probes to examine the body.

The security chief, Captain Sominn, spoke first.

"It was hard to identify the thief. At first, the DNA looked similar to ours, but in fact, it's unlike anything we've seen before. It's most likely an artificial creature, some kind of clone specialized for this mission."

In a squeaky voice, broken by clicking mandibles, the alien doctor started speaking.

"This body is not meant to survive. Its lifespan is very short. It can't eat or digest. It doesn't even have a mouth. Its DNA proves it's a female, but all its genitals are atrophied despite extremely elevated levels of hormones."

While talking, the insectoid brought up a hologram zooming in on the organs and cells to illustrate his explanation.

Captain Sominn went over to a glass cabinet and pointed to the clothes inside.

"The most interesting thing is what it was wearing. The suit is hermetically sealed to let nothing in or out. It's equipped with an osmotic breathing system that filters the air and even changes dangerous particles into a breathable oxygen-nitrogen mix. There are multiple sensors in the 'ears' that keep it at such a constant room temperature that it was undetectable by thermal sensors. The outer structure, with a strange defensive field, suppresses 97% of air movement, and also serves as armor against most conventional and energy weapons, absorbing or dispersing most of the damage. Plus, it's covered in a mimetic camouflage that makes it virtually invisible, and it has a cybernetic, prehensile tail controlled by thought, not to mention retractable diamond claws in the gloves, making it agile and lethal in a fight. This suit alone is worth more than most of the objects exhibited here."

Aster was fascinated by the suit.

"What did, er, *she* try to steal?"

Captain Sominn went over to the controls and typed something in, bringing up another holographic image: a stone cube with one side missing; inside it was a huge book made of metal paper.

"When the first ships able to travel faster than light took off from Zhud, many centuries ago, the explorers used ultra light, metal sheets on which they wrote with thermal pens so that, in case of a wreck, their logbooks would survive the ravages of time and space. These indestructible books mostly ended up here, even though some of them have remained on abandoned colonies, lost ships, or deserted planets. The discovery of these ancient logbooks is a gold mine of information regarding the history and daily life of the ancient Zhudians.

"The thief broke a votive stone and tried to take the book hidden inside. I don't know how she knew what was in there. No one ever suspected there was a metal logbook inside that stone, even after all the detection equipment it'd been passed through. Even the ultra-X-rays never revealed the presence of that book."

"Lucky for us," the Ambassador said, "she set off an alarm when she broke the side of the box. The automatic defense systems were activated and she was forced to flee, but a guard managed to bring her down with his Thorion rifle."

"Where's the book now?" Aster asked.

"A team of historians is reading it right now to figure out what's so interesting about it. It turns out the text is about your home planet, Miss Bolan—Earth. It would've been written by a member of one of our scientific expeditions sent to your universe to test the compatibility of its inhabitants with our race."

"That's amazing!" said Pinky.

"Yes, and that's not all. According to the log, the scientists left a genetic bank inside a stasis field hidden in a 'temple of life' dedicated to a goddess worshipped by the local Earthmen at the time on what you call the Indian sub-continent."

"Aster, before leaving Earth, I heard an interview on the radio with some archeologists who'd found the ruins of a legendary temple of Shakti in the jungle of Maharashtra. That could be it, couldn't it?"

"Either way it deserves to be checked out," replied Aster. "Plus, these archeologists might be in danger if others are after this genetic bank. Besides, this discovery could save the people of Zhud. These genes could produce enough new life for us to thrive again."

"And that would keep you from having to import pretty Earth people for your personal needs, right?"

The sarcastic young woman headed toward the Embassy without turning around. The Ambassador stared at the ground for a moment before following her. Aster sighed and went with them.

The next day, a Zhud saucer entered Earth's atmosphere, flying towards India. Pinky was getting the hang of piloting and made a perfect descent. She soared over the jungle at supersonic speed, close enough to the ground to see the ruins and the archeologists excavating them. Aster took care of the sensors this time. After thirty minutes of searching, he jumped up in his seat.

"Something flying right at us at Mach 7!" he shouted.

"A missile?" Pinky asked, worriedly.

"It's strange. Despite its size, it seems to be piloted."

"Evasive maneuvers?"

"No, it just veered off to take a course parallel to us."

Through the transparent cockpit, they saw a strange being in a golden armor being propelled by two sparkling blue flames. The fists of his metal suit looked like ram's heads with the horns curved to form two small shields on either side of the wrists. His helmet was in the shape of a lion's head. At the same time, a screen signaled an incoming radio call. Without hesitating, Aster pushed the receive button.

"I'm Agni, protector of India," a voice said in English with a strong Indian accent. "Who are you and why are you flying over our territory?"

"I am Aster, protector of Zhud and member of the Hexagon Group. I'm here on a mission to find an artifact from our people that was left here a long time ago, and also to protect your archeological expedition that is about to find it from hostiles who wish to steal it. Can you assist us?"

For a few seconds, nothing but static could be heard, then Agni's voice came through again.

"Follow me!"

The superhero in golden armor turned south, followed almost at the same time by the flying saucer; which stayed in his wake.

After a few minutes of flying in total silence, Aster said:

"I'm detecting a lot of activity in front of us. A big aircraft is approaching us from the northwest. I'm also picking up some alien signatures coming from south of the ruins. From what I can see, the archeologists are on site. Pinky, open the airlock, I'm going to fight the ground troops. You take care of the enemy ship. Agni, a little help would be welcome."

"Got it! See you down there!"

Aster ran to the airlock and jumped out. His Thorion belt went to work and let him fly to the ruins that he could now see clearly through the thick foliage of the trees. Pinky swung the saucer around to face the enemy ship, which looked like a long drop of water lying horizontally, but with a front that had been partly cut off and replaced by two black glass domes that made it look like a giant flying serpent.

No doubt about it, this was one of Melanos' ship, the diabolical enemy responsible for many attacks on Zhud and Earth, including one not long ago when he had allied himself with the Xans, a reptilian alien race. Aster had saved the world by leading the Zhud fleet into battle. That's when he had found Pinky in the ruins of the city and brought her back to his world.

Pinky did not even blink an eye; she opened fire on the enemy immediately. The ship made evasive maneuvers, but kept heading for the trees across from where the ground troops were fighting. A big, metal door opened and dropped out two strange, steel objects shaped like diamonds, ten yards high and wide. Before landing, long, metal legs and turrets sprang out of trapdoors and the weird machines started marching slowly toward the temple, searching for targets.

147

In the meantime, Agni saw the terrifying creatures that were running toward the temple, sometimes on four legs, sometimes on two. Despite clothes that were probably not from Earth, he could see that their bodies were both feline and humanoid, covered with black and yellow, tiger-striped fur.

He circled the ruins and used his flamethrower to make a barrier around it to slow down the enemy. Then he hovered at the edge of the site, ready to face off with the strange hybrids.

Aster went straight into battle. He charged the first man-tiger and used his momentum to give it a wicked uppercut, hurling it against a tree trunk. Two others took its place and pounced on him, but the Thorion belt's forcefield blocked them in mid-air and they fell to the ground. Aster grabbed a fourth hybrid and threw it at two others who were trying to get through the wall of fire, sending all three into the flames before they went running into the jungle with their fur on fire.

Meanwhile, the Indian superhero was shooting flames at the man-tigers who were too zealous. He almost missed seeing the fresh troops arrive, equipped with ray guns this time. He dodged their first volleys before rushing at these new, much more dangerous adversaries. He flew between the trees shooting flames that hit their target every time, burning the clothes and fur of the soldier cats.

Pinky shot up vertically and went back to the first warship while firing all the guns. The cannons of the other ship turned on her and fired. Only a few shots hit their target and the shields held up, but the young Earth woman was a little shaken by the impact. On the other hand, her attack was more effective and the ship in her sights started to smoke and stand still. The second craft, however, was still shooting at the ruins.

The two superheroes had their hands full with the ground troops which kept growing in number. The enemy fire forced Agni to land and he knocked out a few hybrids with his ram-fists before burning a few others when they came out from under the cover of the trees to shoot at him.

Aster was having trouble in his fight. His forcefield had been shot down and he barely got rid of the three hybrids who had pinned him and were attacking him with their razor-sharp claws. Now he was running toward the man in the golden armor.

"Agni! Turn your flamethrowers up to full power! Fire at me, a few feet over my head!"

For a second, the armored superhero questioned the order, but decided to do it anyway, trusting in the Hexagoneer whose exploits were well known on Earth.

Aster used his Thorion belt to create a small forcefield around his head. The jet of flame struck him and exploded into thousands of burning sparks that rained down around the two superheroes creating an umbrella of fire, burning the forest and their enemies for around ten seconds, just enough time to make sure the troops had definitely dispersed.

At the same time, Pinky was turning her attention to the second ship of Melanos. She saw that it had reached the dig and its guns were now aimed at an excavation that had uncovered a polished metal surface.

Melanos' voice boomed out from the speakers of his strange craft.

"Aster, you have lost! Give up or I will destroy the precious genetic bank that could save our race."

Aster rose out of the jungle with Agni right behind him. He looked grim and showed the fatigue from combat. Suddenly, a smile lit up his face. A strong ray of energy shot out of his Thorion belt and struck the genetic bank, melting it and destroying it completely.

In the saucer, Pinky froze in amazement. Agni struggled to understand what was happening before his eyes.

"Aster, fool! You... you've just condemned our race," Melanos stammered, apparently more disturbed than the Protector of Zhud by this act of sheer destruction.

"Ha, Melanos! Your trap was almost perfect, and I have to admit that I fell for it at first. This genetic bank never existed. You're the one who created it. And I'm sure that it contained some horrible genetic retrovirus meant to enslave the people of Zhud. But later, I understood why these space pirates took one of our Monitor ships. You needed a time weapon to artificially age your evidence, the metallic book with the coordinates of the temple, and the gene bank itself, so that our scientists wouldn't suspect that you put them there only days beforehand. The theft on Durkania never happened—quite the opposite, in fact! You brought the fake book to the space museum to make us believe it had caught your interest, but in reality, you wanted us to find it. Then you set up just enough opposition to make us believe this site was valuable, but there's nothing here for us to overcome. You're not even here physically. You're just talking through a giant robot because you knew the defeat of your troops was inevitable."

With these last words, another energy ray shot out of Aster's belt. Agni focused his flamethrowers on the legs of the marching war machine while Pinky aimed at the body with the saucer's weapons. The robot had barely time to point its own cannons at its attackers before it was turned into a big ball of fused plasma, putting an end to Melanos' latest scheme.

In the cockpit the three allies had a drink of sweet alcohol that came from Aster's home planet.

Agni, a.k.a. Professor Radesh Shrankar, took off his helmet to reveal his hair plastered to his skull by sweat. He sipped the delicious beverage while Pinky also wet her lips with the glass.

Then she turned to Aster, sounding worried.

"Doesn't it bother you that Melanos got hold of a time weapon?" she asked.

"Not really. Those weapons emit chronotons that our Monitor ships can easily trace. A message from the fleet has already informed me that our weapon was found and destroyed before Melanos had time to move it. And he was too busy to try to discover its secrets. We still have this technological advantage over our enemies."

He turned to the superhero in golden armor.

"Thank you, Professor, your help was much appreciated."

150

"It's my duty to fight that kind of tyranny. We won this time, but there are still a lot of dangers for your planet, and ours."

Pinky raised her glass.

"To our success, then! To peace and life!"

"To peace and life!" the two superheroes chimed in perfect unison.

Roxy and Jessica Puma by Anne-So Doligny

Roxy and Jessica Puma are members of the legendary Twilight People, capable of changing into lycanthropoid hybrids. Roxy is the assistant of their great Shaman Stormshadow and works in the Twilight library. She is also Dick Demon's girlfriend. Jessica is Harry's (Dick's brother) girlfriend, and works for them at The House in Santa Monica, CA. Like the two Damon brothers, they're both descended from famous heroes of the Old West.

Blanche Saint-Roch: *Monsters, Twilight & Co.*

Lying in my bed, my mind still a little foggy, I watched the shadow puppets projected by the sun through the curtains dancing on the ceiling of my studio apartment in Venice, CA.

My alarm clock read 2:47 pm. The familiar sound of traffic and honking horns did not disturb my peacefulness. The beach communities of Los Angeles slept little, day or night, but I was used to it. The smell of grilled chicken wafting up from downstairs tickled my nostrils. I closed my eyes, sniffed and savored it with delight. Marvelous! I was going to get up, put on a sweater, and go downstairs to buy a box. No, two. Or maybe just spend the day in my cozy bed. After all, it was the weekend and I had nothing to do, no one to see today. Tough choices to look forward to...

I turned over and took a deep breath of serenity. The previous evening talking to Dick had ended up rather passionately. No troubles or particular problems bothered our people—the Twilight People—at the moment, and when Dick had peace of mind...

The sound of footsteps in the hallway shook me out of my pleasant thoughts. I furrowed my brow. *Her? Here?*

Three sharp knocks rapped at my door. I sat up immediately. *She* was really coming to see me! Crazy!

I scrambled out of bed, dragging my comforter and the cord of the alarm, barely catching the latter before it crashed to the floor. I held back a curse knowing that *she* could hear me and ran my hand through my messy red hair, trying to give it a semblance of order as I ran to open the door.

She was standing there, as straight as usual, gorgeous in her cream-colored business suit that highlighted her nut-brown skin. Even with her hair up in a tight bun, she still had the look of a wild cat. Her black glasses looked like jewelry on her face. *She* may have been only seven years older than me, but I always felt like there was an entire world between us.

She stared at me serenely, unblinking.

"Hello, Roxy," she spoke softly.

"Uh… Hey, Jess," I stammered. "How are y…"

"I woke you up, from the looks of that old t-shirt and your panties."

"No, no, not at all, I…"

I broke off. Jessica Puma showing up at my place was such a surprise that I had opened the door in my underwear! Damn! Well, today wasn't the day for me to impress her. I pulled myself together and stood up straight.

"What can I do for you?" I asked, trying to retain a little dignity despite my old t-shirt and panties.

"Can I come in?"

I stepped aside and she walked into my apartment. Her disapproving eyes gazed at the mess, the clothes strewn all over the place, and the dishes from last night (or before) piled up in the sink. I kept a wary eye on her, ready with thirty different answers to justify the state of my apartment. After all, it looked exactly like a human's studio apartment should look for a nineteen-year. The least you could say was that I had taken pains to fit in! Well, OK, maybe not taken pains, but still.

However, Jessica made no comment and sat delicately in an armchair near the television. Her calm exterior did not fool me. A vein was pulsing in her neck and the air around her was quivering with pent-up anger. She was boiling over with rage. A connection with the dirty plates in the sink? I hoped not!

"I need your help," she said flatly after crossing her long legs.

I stood there speechless with my mouth open. Jessica needed my help? Jessica Puma, the were-woman, one of the strongest women I knew among the Twilight People, the girlfriend of Dick's terrifying twin brother, Harry, needed *me*? Maybe I had misunderstood…

"Really?" I blurted out. "How's that?"

"A new drug has just shown up in the city," she explained in a monotone that meant *I am beside myself (with anger)*. "There are a lot of victims. The addict himself, of course, who dies from severe, internal dislocations, but also, and more importantly, from the people around them who are found disemboweled or beheaded, as if they were ripped apart by giant claws. A few buildings have suffered damage as well, found with windows broken and walls slashed."

I nodded, hanging on every word. Her past as secretary of Dick's late father who dealt with the such troubling cases and the crimes of or against our people had gotten her used to being precise in her explanations.

"The addicts did that?"

"According to the few surviving witnesses, yes. Whoever ingests the drug transforms into a kind of huge, orange demon with fangs."

Her hand gripped the arm of the chair. Oh, now I understood why that new drug bothered her so much! Harry looked a lot like this, minus the fangs. How to ask the next question tactfully…?

"Do you think our people are involved?"

"No," she was firm on that. "And I mean to clear this up before the brothers hear about it."

I nodded. Dick and Harry would not, in fact, appreciate it. Therefore, Jessica couldn't ask them for help as usual…

I felt my chest swell with pride. "You're asking *me* to help you solve this case, is that it?" I tried my best to restrain my enthusiasm.

"You might say that. I need you to find the drug dealers who are selling this crap. You should know where to find this kind of person, right?"

My shoulders slumped. Jessica came to me because she thought *I* was taking drugs?

"No idea," I scowled. "I don't hang out with that kind of person."

She raised an eyebrow. "Really? Oh... In that case, sorry to bother you. Especially on such a fine morning."

She got up to leave. I grunted, annoyed.

"All right, I don't take drugs, but if it's just a matter of finding a few dealers..."

I jumped up to follow her but stopped when I remembered one important detail: I was still in my underwear. Damn! Where did I throw my minishorts before collapsing on my bed last night?

Half an hour later, we got off the Santa Monica freeway to venture into the seedier parts of South Central L.A. Here there were two kinds of cars: gorgeous, brand new sports cars (stolen) and old junkers built before the Peloponnesian War (431 BC). The buildings seemed to close in on us the farther in we got. Jessica had refused to change her clothes and her tailored suit clashed dramatically with the new scenery.

"I don't like to show off my body," she declared with her eyes raised at my minishorts and blouse when I suggested she should wear something more appropriate.

The men we passed watched us with hungry eyes and twisted grins. A few whistles pealed out. I shrugged every time. I wasn't too worried. They were just humans, after all, and even if Jessica hadn't been here, I wouldn't have been much afraid. My little were-fox fangs and claws planted in the right place were always enough to remind overeager guys to act like gentlemen.

My nose soon picked up a familiar scent.

"He's over there," I pointed to a young man in sweats standing on the street corner.

156

"Great," Jessica congratulated. "For someone who doesn't know how to find a dealer, you did pretty well."

"Hey!" I was riled up. "Don't get any weird ideas! I had to do a favor for a friend... once..."

"Sure, whatever you say."

I scowled. I could tell from her smile that she didn't believe me.

"Anyway," I grumbled, "we'd better get him before he sees us, because the last time we met, I smashed his face on the sidewalk. He might not want to see me again..."

A sparkle of interest glistened in Jessica's eyes, but we had no time to discuss it further. The dealer spotted us and his jaw almost dropped to the ground.

I quickly raised my hand to give him a friendly wave.

"Hi there!"

A waste of time. He turned tail and ran like a rabbit.

"Aw, shit," I mumbled.

I took off after him without even looking at Jessica. With her heels, she had no chance of catching him. I turned the corner just in time to see him disappear at the next intersection. I raced after him, my sneakers barely touching the ground. When I turned the next corner, I stopped short. The dealer was there. Jessica, too. She had her hand around his throat. My eyes almost popped out. When did she pass me? Where? How did I not see her? Did she fly over the rooftops? In her high heels and tailored suit?

"Hello, young man," she said politely to the dealer while crushing his throat between her fingers. "I'm sorry for bothering you on this very fine day but I'm looking for a drug that turns people into big orange monsters. Do you know what I'm talking about?"

The dealer was beet red and choking in her iron grip.

"No? Come on, try a little harder."

"You have to let up a little, Jess," I intervened. "He can't talk like this."

"If you say so."

157

A feline smile crossed her face. Yeah, she was doing it on purpose. So, she had a thing about dealers... But she loosened her grip and the guy gulped down some air.

"You'd better not piss her off," I whispered to him in confidence. "She gets ugly when she needs a fix."

Jessica shot me a look, but the dealer wriggled nervously.

"Be cool!" he whined. "I don't know what you're talking about! But if you want, I've got some good shit..."

"We don't care about the rest," I shrugged. "Too bad. Have fun with my friend."

Jessica's grip got tighter.

"No!" the guy screeched. "OK, OK... it's... it's some new shit... Everyone says it'll get you high like a kite, but I swear it's a bunch of crap! It kills you and that ain't good for business..."

"Name and supplier?" Jessica asked."

"I don't know the supplier. No one knows. You're looking for him to get a cut, right? He's dealing on our territory, so he's got to pay, but no one's ever found him. The drug's called Isadora."

"Isadora?" I was surprised. "Sounds like an old ship."

"Or a little girl who likes to visit museums," Jessica said.

"Yeah?" the dealer muttered. "I thought it was the name of an angel."

Jessica squeezed him hard. "Nobody asked your opinion."

"Where are we most likely to run into users of this Isadora?" I snapped.

"I don't know," the guy sputtered. "Look, they say you don't find her. It's her who finds you. But I have the feeling that there are more users in Inglewood."

Jessica brought her face close to the dealer's. "You're not saying that just to get rid of us, are you?"

"No, of course not!"

I frowned, skeptically. Given the two slaps that rattled his teeth, he could have confessed to being Princess

Mononoke and believed it. He wasn't going to be back here selling dope anytime soon, I thought.

We were not much more successful in Inglewood. The few drug dealers we managed to get our hands on, thanks to our highly developed sense of smell, were small fry and knew no more about Isadora than our first catch.

The sun was setting behind the skyscrapers when Jessica finally let out a sigh.

"I'm afraid we'll have to go talk to *them* after all."

She meant Dick and Harry. I nodded. What else could we do? Their net of informants was vast, even amongst humans.

"If you want," I offered timidly, "we could…"

I was interrupted by a scream. We both turned in its direction. It came from the next street.

"We could what?" Jessica raised an eyebrow.

"We could go and see if that scream came from a drugged up little-girl-angel-visiting-a-museum-ship?"

Jessica smiled in the growing darkness.

"See, you can come up with some good ideas once in a while."

We ran to the next street and my heart froze in terror. In front of us was a ten-foot tall orange monster, as wide as two cars, glaring at people petrified with fear. It had huge hairy feet, red eyes sparkling with glee, and goo dripping from its long fangs. He also stank of sulfur and charred flesh. I gagged.

Where did it come from? It loomed over the pedestrians, its eyes burning with a morbid appetite. Paralyzed, I watched its claw reach out for them. It was going to snatch them up!

The sound of rustling clothes next to me snapped me out of my daze. Jessica had just transformed. She rushed at the creature and let loose her own claws, jabbing it away just as was about to reach the two humans.

The monster grunted in surprise. Jessica lost no time. She grabbed the pair of terrified bystanders and shoved them toward me. I caught them before they fell down.

"Save yourselves," I said. "Run as fast as you can and don't look back!"

One of them, a kid who couldn't have been older than thirteen, nodded his trembling head. He appeared to understand. The other, even younger, was wide-eyed and panicking. The first kid grabbed his arm and dragged him away. I shook my head, but I felt relieved. What the hell were these two kids doing here?

Jessica was back at my side in her were-puma form. Her yellow eyes glistened in the shadows. I glanced down at her naked legs and scanty suit, low-cut down to the belly button, which left nothing of her voluptuous shape to the imagination.

"Who's showing off their body now?" I mumbled.

"Very funny. Do you want to help me or would you rather just stare at my gorgeous body in action?"

"But Jessica... I'm not as strong as you..."

"Come on, help me!"

Six feet over our heads, the monster was searching for its prey, looking puzzled. Then, it saw us. Its face convulsed in fury. I felt myself shrink away while Jessica yowled and got ready to leap at its throat.

I took a deep breath to clear my head and let my red ears rise out of my head while my fangs and claws grew out. Every part of my body changed completely to make me stronger, more agile, more supple. The were-fox in me was awake.

Jessica jumped on the creature's arm just as it swiped at her. She shimmied up to its shoulder in a split second. The monster tried to shake her off, but Jessica buried her claws in its flesh and hung on. It roared in fury and turned its head to snap its jaws at her while she sought its jugular vein.

The creature was paying no attention to me. I ran up and bit it behind its knee as hard as I could. It howled in pain, but I did not let go. I dug in deeper, then yanked out its tendons.

Not able to stand on one leg, the monster collapsed in agony. Its head hit the ground hard. Jessica had leaped off at the last second and landed right on top of its face. The creature groaned, but stopped fighting.

I remained alert. Jessica did not move. The monster's breathing grew faint. It reached out for the wall, but only scratched it, making an awful screeching sound. Then, its throaty panting stopped. Jessica jumped down from her improvised perch.

"It's dead," she stated.

As if to prove her wrong, the mountain of orange flesh shuddered. We tensed our muscles for another attack, but its body went limp. A wisp of black smoke rose up as its claws and its fangs disappeared. The beast was turning back into a human.

A minute later, we were staring at the corpse of a young man who looked like the older brother of the two kids we had just sent running away.

"Surprising," Jessica said calmly. "What do you think, Roxy?"

"Er... not much," I muttered. "Anyway, at least now we know our people have nothing to do with it. There's no one who looks like that among us. Do you think we killed this guy?"

"No, I don't think so. Look, the only wounds we inflicted are there, and behind his knee—which was well done, by the way!—and on his arm. Back to human form, they shrunk in proportion and they don't look that serious. Not enough to kill him, anyway. His internal injuries, on the other hand..."

She pointed at the bruises on his abdomen and then at his joints twisted out of shape.

"That killed him."

I thought for a minute.

"So, Isadora makes our addicts look like monsters, but when their bodies can no longer put up with it, they die?"

"It would seem so," Jessica agreed.

"There's a substance that can do that?"

She shrugged, "You still think it's a drug?"

I didn't know what to say. Jessica wasn't thinking of a drug anymore. Then what?

"Magic?" I said timidly.

"Possibly. Without completely dismissing the drug trail, I..."

A wail interrupted our discussion: "THOMAS!"

The two kids we had saved a few minutes ago were running back. They fell on top of the corpse, crying.

"Thomas!" the older one said between sobs. "Wake up! Thomas!"

The younger just wept at his feet. Jessica and I frowned at each other. I retracted my ears and became human again before going to squat next to them.

"You know him?" I asked as gently as I could.

"He's our big brother," the older one muttered with pleading eyes. "He's not really dead, is he?"

I didn't answer. After a few seconds, I tried not to sound too cold-hearted, "Did he have any problems? Did he take drugs, for example?"

The kid suddenly straightened up, dried his tears and looked hard at me.

"He quit! He quit so he could take care of us! He went to see Pastor James for help... He saw him... Just yesterday and... and... and..."

He broke down in tears. I didn't take him in my arms. His grief was painful for me to see, but what could I do for him?

Standing behind us, Jessica, also back in human form, had found her suit, heels and sunglasses by some miracle that escapes me even now. I wrinkled my nose. She has to teach me how to do that. My shirt was ripped up. I would probably have to take it off to keep from ruining it altogether. I saw my partner write something in a notebook. Obviously, she already had an idea of where things were going.

She tore out the page and came up to us.

"Take this, kid," she handed him the piece of paper. "Tomorrow morning, you and your brother go to this address. Tell them Jess sent you and they'll take care of you. Got it?"

He nodded without saying a word, with tears still streaming down his face. Despite her cool composure, I could feel

Jessica's emotion when she pushed a loose strand of hair behind her ear.

"Now, tell me, kid, where can we find this Pastor James?"

Sitting alone outside, back against the cold wall of the local church, I contemplated the stars and listened closely. On the way over, Jessica had explained to me that if Thomas had decided to stop taking drugs in order to take care of his brothers—and therefore, to protect them—the kids would not have been able to tell us whether he had used Isadora, or dabbled with magic. On the other hand, the man who had helped him get off drugs should know something. And that was Pastor James. Who better than a man of the cloth to help in those matters!

Jessica had insisted that I wait outside. Grungy girls like me didn't belong in the House of the Lord. I stood there, a little baffled, as she entered alone. Me, "grungy"? But I found a comfortable spot on the grass, against the wall, and listened to what I could hear coming from inside.

"So young Thomas is dead," Pastor James grieved after Jessica finished her story. "What a tragedy... and yet, his will to live was so strong! He drew his motivation from his brothers' smiles. I thought his true nature would help him overcome his ordeal, with the aid of the Almighty, of course."

The wind kicked up some leaflets in the park. I watched their chaotic dance without thinking of anything.

"Did you know him well?" Jessica asked.

"He came to see me a few times because I have a program to help young people get off drugs. What a shame... Could you tell me exactly how he died, please?"

Jessica did so and I winced. Why was this man interested in the details of such a terrible death? Did he want to suffer along with the boy he couldn't save?

One of the leaflets fluttered down by my leg. I snagged it under my foot and grabbed it. It read: *Express your true nature!* The photo showed a man about 40 years-old, smiling, crew-cut, right out of a toothpaste commercial. It was Pastor James. Around his face there were a few carefully placed slogans describing how he could help junkies escape the hellish world of drugs. I started to feel a little sympathy for the man. If there were more people like him, maybe the world wouldn't be so messed up.

"He really decided to quit?" Jessica asked again. "Was there anything that could have pulled him back? Looking for newer, better highs?"

"I don't know, my child. The ways of the Lord are mysterious, even to me. I could only encourage him with all my heart to express his true nature…" Obviously the good pastor was a little obsessed about true nature. "Lately, he seemed determined to start a new life, but he relapsed, just like the others."

My sixth sense kicked in. I turned away from the leaflet and looked up. *Like the others*? Jessica had felt it too.

"You've had this happen before?" she pressed him.

"Sadly yes. Lost little lambs who are not strong enough to express their true nature…"

Jessica wrinkled her nose. What did he mean by all this talk about "true nature"? Was "true nature" some kind of orange demon? If so, they sure could do better!

"Have you ever heard of Isadora?" Jessica went on.

The pastor didn't answer. Now, I was liking him less and less. This guy might not be the boy-scout I had imagined at first. I examined the leaflet more closely. I had a good idea how to check the suspicions now taking form in my mind—but what would Jessica say?

"The ways of the Lord are mysterious," he repeated softly. "You should go home, child. This sad news has left me very depressed."

I had about twenty seconds before he sent Jessica away for good. I had no choice if I wanted her to stay close by and watch my back. I ran to the front door of the church and stumbled inside. It looked exactly like what I had imagined: a bare room with rows of benches, an altar, and a simple wooden cross on the wall. The harsh light reflected off the varnished wood and, in the middle of it all, Jessica and Pastor James stood, looking at me in bewilderment. I had just enough time to notice that the pastor looked a lot not very much like the toothpaste salesman from his photo before I limped towards them, leaning heavily on the benches, holding the leaflet out in my hand.

"Are you Pastor James?" I groaned, dropping onto a bench ten feet away from them.

"I am, my child," he answered in a gentle voice. "What can I do for you?"

"Help me! Please, help me! They want to take my baby!"

Jessica's eyes almost popped out of her head as the pastor came over to me.

"Calm down, my child," he cooed. "Tell me everything from the beginning."

"It's all Carrie's fault," I shouted, rolling my eyes and waving my arms. "She called Social Services! They're gonna take my baby if I'm not clean by tomorrow. Tomorrow! I can't do it!"

Behind the pastor, Jessica raised her eyes to the ceiling. I could almost hear her thinking that, for a girl who never took drugs, I was doing a really good job playing a junkie. Oh well. Now that I was here, I was going all the way.

"Help me," I begged, wringing my hands.

"I understand," Pastor James soothed me. "You have nothing to fear, child. You knocked on the right door. We're going to pray together for the safety of your soul and…"

"Pray? No! It's tomorrow! I can't… They told me you could work a miracle for me. Please, I'll do anything you want, but it's absolutely necessary … I want to be clean! With all my heart!"

He looked at me for a minute. I was panting, staring at him eagerly and trembling. If I'd been any more strung out, I'd have overdosed! I didn't dare look at Jessica.

"You seem very, er, motivated," he mumbled.

165

"Oh, yes! I'll do anything to give my baby a good life. I'll be the best mother. I promise. I'll take good care of him. I'll... I..."

"You want to get through this... and live..." he muttered.

"Oh, yes! Whatever it takes!"

He straightened up a little. He had the smile of a cat who has just cornered a mouse. Was he hooked?

"My dear child, I think it's time for you to express your true nature."

Bingo!

"Yeah, sure," I squawked.

"Come with me."

He dragged me to the empty space in front of the benches. Jessica raised an eyebrow.

"What are you planning to do to her?" she asked like any normal witness would have.

"You wanted to know if I knew about Isadora," the pastor replied with a barely visible, but wicked, grin on his face. "You're going to have your answer. The angel Isadora is going to accomplish a miracle for us tonight."

The angel Isadora? One point for my favorite dealer. Next time, I'd tell him that before smashing his face.

I let the pastor put me on the tiled floor and my sharp eyes glimpsed the pentacle hidden in the grooves. Malevolent vibrations made the hair on the nape of my neck stand up. Churches were pretty bleak to start with, but this was starting to stink of black magic.

"The angel Isadora?" Jessica sounded skeptical. "Isadora is a drug. You can't cure one drug with another."

The pastor glared at her coldly.

"A drug?" I whispered. "No, you're not gonna give me more drugs, are you? Aren't you gonna save me?"

"Of course, I'm going to save you, girl," his voice was comforting again. "Isadora is most definitely not a drug. Don't listen to that woman. She works for Social Services and is only interested in how she can take your baby away."

I threw Jessica a look full of horror and hatred, as best I could, while she kept talking.

"I could turn you in for this," she threatened.

"Oh, my child," the pastor smiled sweetly. "You will be turning nobody in."

I stiffened up. In one way or another, he planned to get rid of my partner. Sure, he didn't have an army with him to do it, but I really didn't like guys who wanted to kill my friends.

He took a small box out of his pocket, opened it and picked out a blue pill.

"Don't do it!" Jessica warned.

I took the pill cautiously. So this was it—Isadora. The evil aura it gave off would have made me run if Jessica hadn't been here. What was it? A demon? Was the pastor trapping demons in pills and giving them to his flock so they would hatch inside their bodies? No wonder humans couldn't cope!

"Gulp it down!" he ordered, paying no attention to Jessica. "Then think hard about your baby and your desire to live."

I nodded. Maybe the will to survive could make an organism hold out longer. Pastor James selected guinea pigs based on their will to live. But his experiments had killed them all. I was going to rip his head off...

I let the pill roll in my palm and only pretended to swallow it.

"No!" Jessica yelled.

I gulped as convincingly as possible and waited while I kept the true Isadora pill hidden in my hand. Pastor James had a big smile, but it looked nothing like the friendly smile on the poster. He turned to Jessica and gloated.

"My child, you're going to be the first real witness of the power of my servants from Hell. Unfortunately for you, you won't have time to appreciate it."

"Your servants from Hell?" Jessica repeated. "You trap demons inside those things?"

So we'd come to the same conclusion. Damn! I was hoping to impress her!

"Brilliant deduction, child," he congratulated her. "My servants just need a body to come into this world."

"But human bodies die quickly. You're going to have a hard time conquering the world."

He shook his head solemnly. "That's correct. And it really pains me to see all these young people die. It pains me even more that my servants die with them. I'm searching for the ideal host. Who knows, maybe I'll find it tonight?"

He turned back to me, his eyes ablaze with evil joy. I was trembling, but it was just pretend. The demonic vibes around us made my blood run cold.

"Any second now…" the pastor mumbled.

Jessica shot me a look that wasn't hard to understand. If I didn't turn into a demon right away, he would know I was a fraud. My heart was racing. I let my body change shapes and my ears popped out.

"There it is!" the pastor rejoiced. "It's coming! Listen to me, child of Baal! Obey me! I am your master! Come to me!"

My eyes sparkled. I let my teeth turn into fangs. The pastor—or rather, sorcerer—was getting more and more excited.

"Yes, that's it! Come on! Rise up, demon from the outer spheres! Come and feed on fresh blood to get strong!"

He pointed at Jessica who was calmly smoothing out her tailored suit.

"Protect me and kill her! I command you to do it!" he ranted on.

I hesitated. Should I pretend to attack Jessica just to keep my cover?

"Go on, Roxy," she urged me when she felt my indecision. "Our friendly preacher would be very disappointed not to see a complete transformation this evening. I'll let you do it. You have to teach him."

The sorcerer looked at her with a bewildered grin on his face.

"What are you talking about, woman?"

Hmm, no more 'child,' no more niceties? OK, Jessica was right. I didn't want to let the bastard down.

168

I went full on were-fox and gave the guy a second to look at me. He lost his arrogant attitude. Did he understand? Even if I didn't look completely human, I certainly didn't look like the demon he'd been expecting. Well, I was a lot sexier for one.

"Surprise!" I smiled at him.

And I pounced.

He had just enough time to mumble some kind of ineffective spell before I sliced his throat and his blood came spurting out. His body collapsed under the weight of my own. I rolled off and jumped up right away, all my senses on alert. There was no need. His eyes were glassy and his body became motionless after one last convulsion.

I sniffed scornfully and growled, "He was a terrible sorcerer, wasn't he?"

"Yes, he was," Jessica said. "Otherwise, I wouldn't have let you do it alone. Dick would skin me alive if anything happened to you."

I looked a little horrified at her. With someone like Jessica at my side, there was no risk of me getting a swelled head.

It was late at night when we got back to my place. Jessica had kept silent the whole way and I didn't try to break the mood. One quick phone call to Mr. Baratini had be enough to make sure that the pastor's body would be disposed of and all traces leading back to us would vanish.

We stopped at the door to my building.

"Well, then," Jessica finally spoke up, "that's that. Good job for both to us."

"It'd probably be better if we were to keep this to ourselves," I remarked.

She nodded, her eyes still staring. Was she expecting something else?

"You want to come up for a drink?" I offered.

To my great relief, she shook her head and gave me a little smile.

"Let's leave it here for tonight. Good night, Roxy."

She turned and walked into the darkness without waiting for my response. In the blink of an eye, she was gone. I let my breath out.

In the end, I hadn't done so badly. I promised myself that, from now on, I would clean my apartment before her next unexpected visit. Starting tomorrow. Or maybe the day after. Maybe. Ah, come on! I was half-fox, after all!

ROXY -

Roxy by J.-M. Arden

Wampus by Luciano Bernasconi

*A terrifying shapeshifting monster, **Wampus** is the agent of an evil cosmic entity known as the Great Mind, who sent him to Earth to sow chaos and spread his master's dominion. However, he is bound to fight his own "twin," in Earth's case, former French secret agent Jean Sten. The issue of their battle shall decide the fate of our world. This adventure takes place long before their final confrontation...*

Artikel Unbekannt: *Strategic Showdown*

For David and Sandra

Italy, 1975

The heart of Lingotto was nothing but a pile of smoking ruins. This proud symbol of the Italian auto industry had survived Fascism and World War II, but now the birthplace of Fiat looked like a shapeless, smoldering quagmire. As if bombed over and over, the two huge buildings housing the production lines had toppled onto the office building and the three of them were now reduced to rubble. If the site had been located near Naples, it would have looked as if it had suffered from a devastating eruption of Vesuvius, but this was Turin, and the famous volcano was five hundred miles away.

The alarm had sounded early; apparently, several fires had broken out at the same time, creating one, long fire trench melting up steel and concrete. Despite their courage, it took the firefighters hours of desperate struggle to control the inferno. It was a bittersweet victory, because several of them had perished in the attempt...

With his clenched fists stuffed in the pockets of his old raincoat, Chief Inspector Merenda looked on silently at the terrible sight. He didn't flinch when the hot gusts of air whipped his suntanned face; he just stared at the destruction with his hard, dark eyes, thinking of the workers who had died, trapped inside the buildings.

After a minute of silence that felt like an eternity, the policeman turned to his right-hand man, Inspector Testi, and asked for a cigarette. Merenda had quit smoking after the massacre at the Fontana Piazza in 1969, but he inevitably relapsed with every new attack—meaning that he never quit for long.

His second-in-command was used to the ritual and took out a pack of Lucky Strikes and handed one over discreetly to his boss.

"So, you think this wasn't...?"

"No, Testi, this was no accident, I'm sure of it. You know, I only consider this when all other avenues have been exhausted. Well, we live in a wonderful time when 'accidents' like this have become the norm. And we just can't accept it. I'm going back to the station to do some research—it could be political activism, or terrorism. I'll try to cross-reference it with other recent attacks. You stay here and draw up a detailed report. Be specific, deductive and quick. I'll be expecting your report..."

"...An hour ago, I know," Testi cut him off with a smile.

Surprised, Merenda paused, then a glimmer of amusement briefly softened his hard eyes. After seven years of working together, the two men had ended up so much alike that they could have passed for brothers. Tall, brown-haired and with the same thin, athletic build, they were a dynamic duo, even though the chief inspector was always in charge due to his rank and experience. He reminded his subordinate of this with: "If you know this, then why am I still waiting?" before walking off to his car.

Testi knew that Merenda's coldness was a poor cover-up for wounds that would never heal. His wife and five year-old daughter had died in a terrorist attack in 1972. He never talked about it, but since that tragic event, he had thrown himself headlong into the battle that Italy waged as best it could against terrorism. Like a hungry snake devouring its own tail,

174

this desperate energy fed on his inner rage, but the chief inspector found some kind of perverse balance in it. His second-in-command often wondered what would happen to his boss if the threat was entirely eliminated someday. But there were more pressing questions that day, and Testi now stepped into the devastated factory without suspecting that there was a stranger who had heard every word of their conversation.

The man looked like one of those young *ragazzi* dragging their arrogant boredom around the city. No one could say exactly how these kids supported themselves, and no one really cared, that is until they got conned by one of them. The kid watching the two cops was but one man wearing shabby clothes, lost in a crowd of onlookers. No one paid any attention to the strange glimmer in his eyes. There was something of the predator in the intensity with which he looked at the inspector who was walking into the ruins. Then, as if he had just realized that his hungry stare might be noticed after all, he hurried away from the police cordon.

A few hours later, when Testi was back at the station, Merenda immediately noticed his colleague's unusual attitude. They knew each other too well, had worked together for too long, for him not to spot the slightest mood changes. For instance, the deputy inspector was always a sucker for the charms of Dellera, the red-headed clerk at the front desk, but this time, he walked right past her desk without saying a word, without even a flirtatious wink. Testi was ordinarily a lively character, not at all cocky, and when he found himself in a tough spot, he was able—unlike his superior—to defuse the situation with good humor that never failed to lighten the mood. This virtue seemed to have mysteriously vanished in the ruins of the factory. Merenda would have been even more worried if he had seen the odd glare, hard and cold, gleaming like molten metal in his partner's eyes.

"So, any interesting finds?" he asked, trying not to sound concerned.

"Not much," Testi replied. "The crime scene guys are working on it, but we shouldn't expect any miracles. Everything burned and the place is total havoc. You'll have the details in my report, but I can already tell you that just the identification of the bodies is going to take some time."

"Really?"

"Yes, The whole building literally melted. All the steel and plastics formed a kind of lava that covered up everything and most of the corpses are stuck in it," Testi reported, as he shut the door of his office.

The two inspectors were supposed to meet again in the afternoon prior to a television interview. All of Italy was panicking because of this new attack and was waiting anxiously for the police report. The wave of blind violence that kept hitting the country was also a cause of concern abroad. Merenda was well aware of the stakes as he reluctantly prepared to attend the press conference. During an ongoing investigation his cautious blend of obfuscations and doublespeak usually pleased his hierarchy. Not being very sociable, he did not relish this kind of exercise, as opposed to Testi, who never minded facing a media storm.

Today, however, his partner appeared to go along with obvious distaste. Merenda realized again that Testi was not acting like his usual self, but could not figure out why. Hundreds of miles away, however, there was a man who knew why…

In Paris, that same evening, Jean Sten, a former agent of the French counter-intelligence service, was following the news reports of the Italian attack with great interest. After reading the first newspaper accounts of the Lingotto fire, he had wandered all afternoon along the Seine, searching for distraction among the bookstalls. Finally, as night fell, he decided to return to his cheap hotel room and, like millions of others, he turned on his TV. He had not been expecting any extraordinary revelations, and had yet no idea how wrong he was.

Although the report in itself was of little interest, and the investigator in charge gave nothing to the journalists but the usual banalities, the attitude of his partner, on the other hand, was rather odd, to say the least. Introduced as Inspector Testi, the man stubbornly refused to talk, and stood as far away from the cameras as he could. He tried to keep his face covered and would obviously have stayed in the shadows if his superior had not turned to ask him for a cigarette. Merenda was about to light it when one of the journalists bumped him and he dropped his lighter. Jumping as if he was scared of being burned, Testi stepped into the light for an instant, revealing his face to the cold stare of the *paparazzi*.

"Those eyes! It's *him*! Wampus has infiltrated the Italian police!"

Jean Sten turned off the television. He had no need to hear more because now he knew. He knew what was hiding behind Testi's face. He knew the cause of the senseless, murderous attacks. Only one creature was capable and guilty of such dreadful deeds... Wampus!

The ex-agent had already faced off several times against the diabolical entity from Outer Space who had come to wreak havoc on Earth. Wampus was a shapeshifter focused entirely on destruction. Using water—or blood—he could make himself into an almost perfect copy of any living thing, except for that awful glimmer in his eyes, the windows to the human soul that even he could not duplicate.

Jean Sten would never have realized this if he had not personally seen Wampus in action. Dealing with fire, however, was another story. Simple contact with a flame forced the monster to relinquish his borrowed form. Sten would never forget his first, terrifying encounter with the strange, protoplasmic creature that had come to spread doom on Earth.

In fact, Wampus was only vaguely humanoid. The creature had long, thin limbs, as if stretched out, and the structure of its body was a mystery: the flesh without muscles looked stuck in the air with no support; one could see right through some spots and it apparently had no skeleton. The extraterrestrial was also incredibly strong and that, coupled with its cunning and fanaticism, made him one of the most dangerous enemies of humankind that had ever walked the Earth.

Jean Sten was the only one still alive that had ever seen the true face of his enemy, and he paid dearly for this dubious privilege. His superiors had refused to believe him, and even thought that he'd been losing his mind. As a result, he had been suspended, but this had not prevented him from tracking down Wampus whenever and wherever he popped up. He felt this was his sacred duty, although he didn't quite understand why, even if he did it against all odds.

The day after the press conference, the Turin police raided the usual haunts of the Red Brigade and the local neofascist gangs. Despite the vague conclusions of his report, Testi had managed to convince Merenda to give him free rein to obtain more information. There was a lot of political pressure coming down hard from above. The mayor was pressuring the police chief, who in turn was harassing his subordinates to get results, especially if it was an act of terrorism.

In the morning, dozens of anarchist and fascist militants were brought in. Testi had insisted on being alone to interrogate the leaders while the rank and file were being questioned in their cells. Merenda wanted to consolidate all the information himself, so he personally supervised all the activity, while slowly growing increasingly nervous.

The day went on, in a plodding, tense and yet futile manner. Worse still, the investigation revealed that the Lingotto attack had claimed more victims among the militants than the workers! It turned out that they had infiltrated sleeper cells in the local trade unions, and the autopsies revealed that many anarchist militants had perished in the explosion. This made it unlikely that their organization had ordered the attack. Even if the "red moles" had been found out by the fascists, there were better ways of disappearing them.

Even though the interrogations had led nowhere, Testi kept his suspects in custody. On their way back to the cells, they passed by Merenda's desk, one by one, as they used the wall phone near his office. The chief inspector was surprised and a little sickened to see cuts and bruises on their faces. Of course, the Italian police were not known for their kindness, but Merenda had never seen Testi display such brutality before. Therefore, without a moment's hesitation, he called his subordinate over to explain himself.

"What's with this crap? Why were you so rough with those suspects?"

"You gave me carte blanche," Testi replied, unflustered. "And this 'crap,' as you call it, is exactly the kind of thing these people deserve."

"Oh, yeah? Let me remind you that we have no proof that any of them are behind this. And vague suspicions are not reason enough to start acting like Maurizio Merli in an Umberto Lenzi movie, especially since this makes you look like a thug! Let me make myself very clear: I don't want to see this happen again, or your carte blanche will turn into a red card!"

"Don't you worry, I'll lighten up now that they got the message. You wanted results? We'll have them very soon, and I bet they'll surprise you," Testi concluded by staring at his boss with an intensity that had nothing human in it.

The next morning, downtown Turin was in total chaos. During the night, no less than ten fires had erupted in various buildings, including city hall, three banks, the welfare and city planning offices. The fires had started, one every hour, which had created such panic that the firefighters had a hard time controlling them. In fact, there hadn't been enough of them to cover them all so the mayor had declared a state of emergency.

Jean Sten arrived in Turin at dawn. Not even bothering to pack, he had jumped into his car and driven all night without stopping. Alarmed by the sight of the devastated city, he went straight to the police station. Thanks to the news on TV, he knew the name of the man in charge of the investigation, and asked to see Chief Inspector Merenda. Unfortunately, Officer

Dellera was not at the front desk and the officer on duty just glared at him. The Frenchman was persistent and finally convinced him to notify his superior that he had important information. Many long minutes later, Jean Sten was introduced into the office of the chief inspector who spoke without looking up from his stacks of files.

"As you can imagine, I'm pressed for time," said Merenda. "Who are you and what do you want?"

"My name is Jean Sten. Until very recently, I used to work for the French counter-intelligence service. Thank you for seeing me. I know you're busy so I'll get straight to the point. I think the wave of attacks hitting you has nothing to do with anarchists and other extremists. The raids you've ordered won't produce anything but more disturbances."

Merenda became suddenly attentive and looked up to examine the man sitting across from his desk. He was solidly built, over six feet-tall, with a square jaw and determination written all over his face. He looked a little like that French actor, Jean-Paul Belmondo. Intrigued, the chief inspector waved his hand for the visitor to continue.

"I suppose you're considering prosecutions, but I don't think this will get you anywhere. All the radical leaders are now in your cells. Such quick and brutal response as those fires from last night couldn't have been organized without time to prepare and complicated logistics. And those extremists don't act without instructions from their *capos*."

"I see. So what are you thinking?"

"That you've got to look elsewhere for the guilty parties. I've dealt the same kind of terrorist attacks in the past, but before I tell you what I know, I'd like to ask you a simple question: do you trust your partner?"

"What do you mean?" Merenda asked, thinking of Testi and his recent unusual behavior.

"I'd just like to know if you've noticed anything strange, unpleasant even, amongst the members of your team since the tragic events began."

The policeman tensed up but did not answer. He had gone to see the prisoners that morning and he thought of the confusion and strange fear they all displayed. These men were all as hard as nails, but somehow the shock treatment they had received from Testi had produced bizarre results. Some of them went as far as pleading with him not to make them suffer at the hands of that "monster" again. Even if their fear seemed irrational, Merenda had to admit that, deep down inside, he thought his partner had changed.

"Your silence is an answer," Jean Sten went on. "Still, you have some reservations and I understand. That's why I suggest that you organize, let's call it, a little test that won't cost you anything or harm anyone. Call in Inspector Testi and watch how he reacts when he sees me."

Merenda thought about it. Hesitating, he played nervously with his lighter while staring at the man sitting across from him. He was suspicious of this Frenchman appearing out of the blue and knowing more than he did. As strange as his request sounded, he ended up agreeing to it. After all, if meeting with Testi turned up nothing, he would have lost only a little time and could get rid of this lunatic. So he rang the intercom.

Five minutes later, Testi entered the office of his superior, As Sten had surmised, there was no need for an explanation... As soon as their eyes met, the two enemies recognized each other. Pure hate burned in the eyes of the creature that was not Testi, and his reaction was as sudden as it was violent. Wampus pulled out his Beretta M 1951, the pride of the Italian police, and pointed it at the two men. Sten was not armed and Merenda was so startled that his hand had moved too slowly toward his holster.

"Don't move if you value your life, chief inspector!" Wampus ordered. "So I see that you've figured it out. I guess you saw me on TV last night, Sten, but it no longer matters. I should kill you now, but that would attract attention and I can't change my appearance here. Handcuff yourselves to the radiator. My 'partner' have some on him and here's another," he tossed a pair of handcuffs on the desk. "Unless, of course, you'd rather see me kill the entire police force here..."

"You've gone mad," Merenda growled, before turning to Sten, "You, what is your game?"

Anticipating the Frenchman's answer, Wampus broke out in a diabolical laugh.

"Jean Sten knows that you are powerless against me! You still harbor doubts, but soon, you will see more examples of my power. What you've seen so far was but a small sample! Your world is doomed, little human," concluded the creature hiding under Testi's skin, stopping only to smile when he heard the clicking of the handcuffs. "And I promise that, before I'm done, it will pay a heavy price in blood and tears!"

"I don't know if I should be laughing or crying," Merenda said after the fake Testi had left, quietly locking the office door behind him. "He must've seen a picture of you somewhere, even if that doesn't explain his behavior. All these deaths... He's lost his mind. If I were a shrink, I'd say the helplessness of the police before terrorism has given him some kind of guilt complex, but I'm a cop, so what I worry about is keeping him from hurting anybody else..."

Sten chose his words carefully before answering. He understood the officer's rational response and did not want to aggravate him by breaking down the unpredictable suspension of disbelief.

"Prepare yourself for another nasty surprise because your 'partner' will be impossible to catch, even if his description is sent out everywhere right away. Anyway, I'm sure we won't have long to wait before we hear from him again. Right now, let's hope your colleagues won't take too long to come and free us... In the meantime, please listen to what I have to tell you..."

The course of events did not take long to confirm Jean Sten's pessimistic prediction. Three days later, all of Italy was in shock again. Two very violent attacks had taken place on the same night in Rome, the targets being none other than the

Vatican and the Cinecittà studios! Even though these two sites were among the most guarded in the capital, it took hours to get the fires under control. Some firefighters gave unexpected reasons for it. None of them talked about a "capricious" or "unusual" fire, but when questioned, they all blamed the strange behavior of their chief, the esteemed Captain Milian.

When Jean Sten heard that, he understood knew that Wampus had again changed identities. Poor Testi was too compromised so he had "dropped" him in order to carry out his great work of spreading chaos.

Before the office door was unlocked by Officer Dellera, who had come in to give the chief inspector some files, Jean Sten had had time tell Merenda the story of his fight against Wampus. Even though the policeman had reacted with legitimate skepticism, at least he had not looked at the Frenchman as a complete lunatic. So, Sten had had no need to explain why he knew the theater of operations had moved on. After three days of spinning their wheels, waiting for new clues, they had decided to get to Rome. Although he did not fully accept Sten's account, the Italian policeman had decided to go along with it for the time being. Besides, he had no other leads at the moment, and he wanted to stay close to Sten until Testi was found, hoping against reason to get some logical explanation from his former partner.

Thanks to the chief inspector's Lancia Beta, the 450 miles of highway separating Turin from Rome were swallowed in record time. After an hour of silence, Merenda relaxed and started up a friendly but guarded conversation about their respective jobs.

Just before midnight, the two men entered the police headquarters. After introducing themselves, they were notified of the latest developments. Captain Milian, their only suspect, had almost been caught that night, but had managed to escape. The neighborhood in which he was hiding was being searched thoroughly, and the *carabinieri* were on high alert.

Sten and Merenda insisted on being taken there and spent a long night of hunting, their nerves on edge, though only one of them understood the true nature of their prey.

In the early morning, a figure came out of the shadows of an abandoned building. He had brown hair, Latin looks and a strange and cruel flame burned in his eyes. When the police saw him, they recognized Captain Milian and ordered him to halt. Surprised but unruffled, the suspect ran off and disappeared down a nearby alley. Twenty men went in pursuit, soon joined by all the others scattered around the area, and they chased him tirelessly through the streets of Rome.

As if spurred on by superhuman energy, Milian managed to reach the small square where the majestic Trevi fountain sat. Despite his unusual stamina, the fugitive was not far ahead of the cops, who did not worry when he slipped out of their sight behind an egg-shaped stone to the right of the sculpture. Their surprise came when they reached the spot, but in truth no normal person could have witnessed such a spectacle without being thrown off balance.

Milian had disappeared, but a gorgeous blonde dressed in a slinky, almost indecent black dress had come out from behind the fountain! A crowd gathered quickly around the newcomer. Tourists, passers-by and the police, everyone stood transfixed by this sudden manifestation of near supernatural beauty. Jean Sten and Merenda were also stunned by the spectacle unfolding before their eyes.

Time appeared to stop. None of the spectators questioned this miraculous event, watching in reverential silence as the object of their collective desire took the opportunity to walk away.

After the woman had gone, slowly, the charm wore off and the police resumed the chase, but it seemed, with much less enthusiasm.

"Wampus!" shouted Sten, just as the woman was about to turn the corner.

As dozens of baffled eyes turned toward the Frenchman, connecting his primal scream to the visual shock they had all just experienced, another set of eyes turned his blood cold... The stunning woman had turned around by reflex and showed him the look of pure hatred he had expected to see!

"It's him," he told Merenda. "Follow me."

Sten did not have time to explain the situation to the Italian police so he decided to forego their help. After a moment's hesitation, Merenda joined him and they went running after the woman. They lost sight of her several times on the paved roads, bordered by pizzerias and bright tourist shops, but thanks to the people on the street who had all noticed the beautiful blonde, they found her trail again every time. There were a few rare couples who pretended not to have seen anything, and one or two matrons who thought they were crazy, but most of the passersby answered answered them with stars in their eyes when they asked if they had seen a woman who looked like Anita Ekberg in *La Dolce Vita* go by.

Finally, after a long game of hide-and-seek in the back alleys winding through downtown Rome, Wampus revealed his destination by heading for the docks.

"The Tiber! He wants to get to a source of water so he can change shapes again," Sten said, panting. "We can't let him, or we'll lose him for good."

Being focused on his running Merenda did not respond. His side was aching, but he was hoping he would catch a second wind and cursed the tobacco industry. He was looking forward to closing this case so he could question the Frenchman about what was really going on. His story of a shapeshifting alien seemed completely absurd, but he had to admit that there were some very unnatural things happening. Besides, Italy had been under attack for too long for him to simply ignore any possible lead.

And Testi had disappeared, damn it! Vanished in thin air!

The chief inspector thought about what he would write in his report when his superiors would ask for one. What would he tell his chief when asked if his partner had been found...

In the meantime, Wampus was taking one of the bridges over the river to Tiber Island. Seeing that the two men were not gaining on him, he leaned over the railing with the obvious intention of jumping.

"Shoot him!" Sten shouted, being unarmed himself. "Shoot him, or he'll get away!"

The chief inspector drew his gun and aimed carefully, but hit the railing. The fugitive then ran off onto the island, a few seconds ahead of his pursuers, but with just enough time for him (her?) to disappear behind the only building standing there.

"It's a dead-end," Merenda said. "Let's split up and we'll have her cornered."

The chief inspector rushed off to the left, followed by Sten who snuck along a parallel wall to the right, being more cautious than his Italian partner. When he reached the back of the building, he saw right away that Merenda was alone... and that an evil glimmer now sparkled in his eyes!

"Monster!" shouted Sten. "Once again, you've accomplished your goal! But don't think you're going to get away so easily. You might be able to change shapes at will but I've still got one trick up my sleeve..."

Sten pulled out his lighter.

"Your threats are empty, Sten" hissed the monster. "You've lost to me before, and you will lose again until I decide to put an end to you. My powers are limitless. I don't need to get rid of you today, because whatever you decide to do, you're doomed. If you attack me in this body, the Italian police will accuse you of trying to murder Chief Inspector Merenda. And don't forget, Inspector Testi disappeared under mysterious circumstances—you were the last person to see him alive... It won't take long for them to connect the two. You have no witnesses and you'll look like a madman if you tell them about me. Let me go and maybe I won't order my 'colleagues' to arrest you."

"Why do you do that? Why not just kill me?"

"To enjoy your helplessness for a little longer, and to have you be the last human witness of the apocalypse I'm prepared to unleash on your world," Wampus replied.

This was too much for Sten. Without thinking of the consequences, he lit his lighter and threw it at the monster. What followed was the same gruesome transformation he had seen before. Merenda's body quivered and jerked frantically, then stretched out and pulled apart, before finally exploding into the nightmarish, protoplasmic figure with empty limbs.

"Ah! You will regret this, Sten! You will regret this!" Wampus howled before diving into the Tiber, leaving only a foaming, bubble in his wake.

"Regret this? Maybe. But it's better than remorse," Jean Sten said as he watched the spot where the monster had disappeared. "Besides, something tells me that I'll soon have another chance to show the world the true face of Wampus."

Agent Joanni Bourask par Juan Roncagliolo Berger.

Joanni Bourask is descended from the famous Johnny Bourask who settled in Virginia in the early 1600s. She is a field agent of C.L.A.S.H. and has met many superheroes in the course of her assignments, such as the Strangers and Kit Kappa. Here, she happens to be in the African Republic of Karunda, an opportunity for her to work with Jungle Lord Zembla, whom she dated for a while...

Patrice Verry: *A Nice, Quiet Village*

I am...?

The question came out of nowhere when she regained consciousness.

...a woman.

Unquestionable biological signals gradually restored her identity in her mind, along with a painful physical reality—stiff in the neck, groggy in the head, numb in all her limbs, and a throbbing, burning pain in her belly.

Suddenly, she realized that the groaning she heard was coming from her own constricted throat.

Joanni, what did they do to you?

Remembering her name filled in some holes in her memory. She opened her eyes, then closed them right away as they hurt in the bright light that illuminated the place, making the shadow in the room darker still.

Behind her eyelids Joanni Bourask focused her thoughts on her vague memories: C.L.A.S.H.[2], Miss Kiss, the reconnaissance mission, going undercover...

What mess did I get myself in this time?

However, she could not remember what had brought her here. She warily opened her eyes again, then sat up. The pain

---

[2] Consortium for Law Enforcement And the Security of Humanity.

in her belly was fading away. She rolled her head, trying to loosen the knots in her neck, and rubbed her bare arms.

Bare?

Suddenly, her other senses returned. She felt/smelled/heard the damp heat in the air, the exotic smells, the cries of wild animals... Too stunned to stand up, she put her feet down on the dirt floor of the sparsely furnished room. Her heart started racing.

Africa!

She remembered those intense moments spent in Karunda a few months ago. Besides her mission, her collaboration with Zembla was imprinted in her memory because of his charismatic personality. The nature-loving Jungle Lord was ready to do anything to defend his home against the vultures who sought to plunder its resources.

Joanni tried to breathe deeply to clear her mind and drain the last remnants of pain from her body. Her brain was starting to work normally again, and with it, the mental reflexes that had pulled her out of so many scrapes before...

Observation, analysis...

Her memory loss made her suspect a drug. She examined herself but found no signs of physical violence.

Stiffness due to immobility, abdominal pain from the ingestion of a drug, nothing I won't get over...

She was dressed in a simple sarong slipped over her underwear; her feet were bare. It was a far cry from her usual C.L.A.S.H. gear. She clenched her jaws at the thought of having been undressed while she was unconscious. If anyone had got a free show, they'd better hope they'd never see her again, at least not if they wanted to keep their peepers.

Her makeshift bed looked typical of Karundian handicraft. The rest of the room confirmed that impression. She stood up cautiously, but could not hold back another moan. Her thighs and calves felt stiff and sore.

Me, stiff and sore! Now I've seen everything! What the hell did they make me take?

She shivered despite the heat. She really did not feel up to fighting against a horde of badly-trained enemy agents. Who knew if there were even people to fight? Right now, she still had no memory of any mission that Miss Kiss might have sent her on.

Disheartened, Joanni dropped back onto the bed. The drug had weakened her physical abilities. Feeling crippled and miserable, she buried her face in her hands and could not help crying like a little girl.

No! That's not me! It must be a side effect of the drug.

She bolstered her will against the depression that muffled her thoughts and dried her tears.

I'm certainly not going to sit here with my arms crossed waiting for them to come and finish me off.

Joanni got off the bed and took a few uncertain steps toward the door, which had been left ajar. Already feeling better, she stumbled through it and blinked in the daylight. Almost directly overhead, the sun was shining on a village she did not recognize. The natives were going about their business, paying no attention to her. Nearby, trees typical of the African jungle formed a vegetable wall that looked impenetrable. She knew that there was no way she could venture into hostile territory barefoot and wearing only a sarong. At least, not before finding out why she was there…

She felt dizzy, so she leaned against the mud wall to keep her balance. Snatches of memory suddenly began flashing through her mind.

"What would you say to a vacation in Karunda, Joanni?"

Miss Kiss sounded mischievous, as if she were in on a practical joke.

She was a very attractive strawberry blonde in her early thirties with a twinkle in her eyes.

"Karunda?" Joanni answered. "Is Zembla in trouble?"

"No, he's in Paris right now. But one of our monitoring satellites has detected an unusual increase in traffic around the mines. The roads are really busy. Maybe it's nothing, but we've seen this type of thing before leading to some problems later. So we need detailed information before deciding to get involved—or not. Don't take any unnecessary risks. And report a.s.a.p. if you find out something suspicious."

Joanni tried in vain to remember more. Had she taken a regular flight, or had one of C.L.A.S.H.'s planes parachuted her directly? In either case, it was obvious she had been expected. Her capture retroactively justified Miss Kiss' suspicions. She had not been killed, but she presented a potential danger that worried someone. Why kidnap her and put her out of commission if not to keep her from discovering some illegal traffic? The calm that reigned in this village was hiding a truth that she had to reveal.

Joanni Bourask was back in the fighting spirit. Her mind was recovering faster than her body. Still, she was not about to jump into a battle without knowing more. Therefore, her mental capacities would be more useful to her right now than her hand-to-hand combat skills. Since they had left her free to roam, she decided to question the villagers. There should be no problem communicating with them because, like many Western African countries, Karunda had adopted French as a second language.

She spied a pair of dusty old shoes and slipped them on before heading for the nearest native. He had very dark skin and was dressed in simple cotton pants. He tried to avoid her but Joanni did not give him time to escape.

"*Bonjour!*" she said in French, "can you tell me where I am?"

The man spread his hands and shook his head as if he did not understand her. He was uneasy, looking around for support from his fellow villagers who just ignored him.

Despite feeling annoyed, Joanni could not help smiling and thinking how out-of-place her western behavior must appear. Karunda was no longer a French colony! It hadn't been for decades. She left her mute acquaintance with a "*merci!*" and approached other villagers.

Surprisingly not a single one seemed to understand her. This was getting weird. In what remote spot of the Karundian jungle had they dropped her?

Something was screwy here. These people's behavior was not normal. She could see that they were embarrassed and… yes, scared!

She wandered around the village for a few minutes without coming up with a plan of action. Her feet led her to the edge of the forest. A big, blue butterfly fluttered by before disappearing into the foliage. The apparent calm of the place was an invitation to idleness. The young woman shook herself.

I'm not on vacation!

She turned around to head back and find the chief. A dozen inhabitants scattered when they saw her, as if she were carrying some kind of contagious disease. A big, round hut sat in the middle of the village square. On a bench next to its entrance, casually leaning back against the wall and smoking a long pipe, a man with a stern face watched her approach.

"Do you understand me?" Joanni pronounced every syllable.

The man nodded. He did not look like he wanted to talk, but the young woman squatted down anyway.

"Can you tell me what I'm doing here? Who brought me here?"

Reluctantly the man took the pipe out of his mouth, blew out a cloud of smoke, and answered slowly:

"We found you in the forest, unconscious."

Yeah, right.

Joanni was sure he was lying. She said nothing for a minute, possessed by the furious desire to shake the truth out of him, but she did nothing. She tucked away her violent reaction in the back of her mind with the conviction that the parties responsible for her kidnapping were not among the villagers.

She stood up slowly, taking a deep breath to relieve the tension. Keeping her eyes on the chief, she said harshly:

"I can help you if you need my help, but don't get in my way. You'd regret it."

Without gear or weapons, Joanni had no idea how she would make good her threat, but she wanted the villagers to know that she meant business. By clearly showing her intention, she was hoping the natives would chose sides in case of a direct confrontation with whoever had orchestrated all this. The Karundians surely knew that she was Zembla's friend, which might tilt the balance of power in her favor.

A furtive movement at the edge of her vision drew her attention. She swung around but the figure had already disappeared around the corner of a nearby hut. It was very brief but she could tell it had been no villager. And she would have sworn that the person was wearing a domino mask.

Ignoring the remnants of pain still coursing through her muscles, Joanni sprinted away, leaving the bewildered chief to his pipe. She was at the hut in seconds, just enough time to see the figure dive into another hut fifty yards away. It only took a split second for her to assess her chances in hand-to-hand combat. He would not be expecting her to arrive so quickly, which would give her a real advantage. So, she ran. Her shoes made little noise but raised a cloud of dust behind her. She ran straight into the hut, ready to swing away at any enemy, but instead she froze.

The place was empty!

Across from the entrance was another door leading outside swinging gently in the warm air. She rushed over there, swearing enough to make even Miss Kiss blush, and had to face the facts: her prey had vanished!

Furious, Joanni dropped into one of the chairs in the room to catch her breath. Sweat was blurring her vision and making her sarong stick to her skin, but at least the exercise had enabled her to test her physical condition. This thought alone gave her strength. She jumped up and examined every detail of the room. Something jumped out at her immediately: the chest along the wall was not Karundian. It looked more like a European steamer trunk.

Curious, the young woman opened it and could not hold back a cry of surprise: she just found her gear! Her heart was racing as she made an inventory. Except for the stunner, nothing was missing—her insulated suit, her backpack with emergency rations, her long distance communicator and—the icing on the cake—a dose of telepaverine!

"Miss Kiss is concerned on your behalf."

Joanni nodded. Behind Mr. Song's charming smile she could sense some unusual tension. Did C.L.A.S.H.'s top agent also think that this reconnaissance mission carried some unsuspected risks?

"Let's not make a habit of this, but I'll give you a dose of telepaverine. You only get one, so use it wisely."

Joanni knew what it was and appreciated this gesture of trust. Telepaverine was a substance derived from the hallucinogenic mushroom Kiaolu—now extinct—that gave the user a minute of almost unlimited telepathic power. The doses created by one of C.L.A.S.H.'s top chemists were scattered randomly over the Earth. There were a limited number of them and therefore, they could not be used carelessly.

Joanni recalled exactly how Mr. Song had gotten hold of the precious substance. Even under torture, no member of C.L.A.S.H. could reveal the whereabouts of the vials. Only the computer, tuned to the psychic frequencies of a few, selected agents, could deliver the locations of the doses.

This prelude to her mission had seemed like a vacation. Mr. Song had taken the young woman to a surveillance satellite in a microshuttle in less than half an hour. The top agent had consulted the computer, which spit out such diverse data as historical dates, mathematical formulas, chemical constants, fragments of biological nomenclature, names of celebrities...

He had spent a good fifteen minutes trying various combinations and finally had hit upon the desired coordinates.

"OK! Ready now?"

Joanni nodded with a smile that was a little bit forced. Mr. Song had a reputation as a ladies' man and she did not want to have to deal with that. While they were putting on their spacesuits, she felt him admiring her attractive curves.

Then they got into the microshuttle and her misgivings vanished.

"Head for the Gulf of Mexico," Song announced.

When you knew the coordinates, getting the vial was just a formality. The microshuttle entered the atmosphere on a trajectory that minimized heating up the fuselage, then dove into the Gulf of Mexico to reach the underwater location where an old Spanish galleon had been rotting away for centuries.

After entering the ship through a breach in the hull, their vehicle deployed its remote-controlled arms to delicately shake loose a small metallic container from a dark corner.

Joanni had never been in such an environment. Far from the technical preoccupations of the recovery operation, she got an eyeful of the remarkable biodiversity of the aquatic landscape. In awe, she watched the diverse varieties of fish scurry away from the spotlights of their shuttle.

"Head back to base," Song said.

The young woman was sorry to have to cut short her reverie. A second later the shuttle shot out of the sea and flew back to C.L.A.S.H.'s Aspen HQ.

Joanni smiled at her memories. Besides the relief she felt at being mentally sound again, the memory of those adventures and the feelings she got from them supported her firm conviction that she had chosen the type of work that she would not give up for anything else in the world. She threw the sarong into a corner and put on her own suit, filling her lungs with scents so different from the noxious fumes of the big western cities. Deep down, she felt sure that she was in the right place at the right time. Whatever criminals were hiding in this village, their misdeeds would soon be exposed and foiled.

In no time, the insulated suit absorbed the excess heat and she felt better. She grabbed the vial of telepaverine, opened it and gulped it down.

Joanni felt dizzy right away and had to sit down to keep her balance. Her perceptions opened up to the whole world in a cacophony that was hard to bear. Mr. Song had told her how to avoid this inconvenient effect. She focused her mind on the mission at hand, Karunda, the mining region, the village she was in. An image appeared before her.

In a large grotto, a man dressed in a toga, his face hidden under a big hood, sat on a rustic throne addressing a crowd of attentive followers. Like the one she's spotted earlier, they all wore domino masks. Moreover, they each had on identical polo shirts with two wavy lines going down from shoulder to waist on either side of the chest. Last but not at all least, a number was pinned to their chests.

Joanni made the connection to what she knew of the history of Karunda. They were members of The Hundred! Zembla had long fought this gang of criminals. If they were back, that was not good news. The young woman did not think she could fight them alone. She focused her thoughts on the vision, trying to learn more.

"This time we shall succeed!" the hooded man was saying. "Zembla is in Paris and the C.L.A.S.H. agent is out of commission. Soon, we will control the gold mines."

The vision suddenly vanished. The power of the dose had worn off. A little dazed, Joanni could feel the chair under her again. There was no time to lose. She grabbed the communicator. A red light was blinking faintly.

They drained the battery!

She flipped it open and turned it on. Maybe there was just enough charge left for one call to C.L.A.S.H. She had to try it. It was her only hope of getting backup. Just as she was about to press the call button, she paused. Wouldn't it be better to warn Zembla first? After all, it was his country!

She silenced the little voice that was whispering to her that the head should come before the heart and she pressed his number on the speed dial instead. While waiting, she kept a wary eye on the battery bars. Would she have time to explain the situation? She had to choose her words carefully.

"Pierre Marais," a distant voice announced.

Joanni took a breath and rattled off:

"Zembla, it's Joanni. I'm being held prisoner by The Hundred who are after the gold mines..."

The communicator died.

That was it! All she could do was wait, hoping the villains would not decide to move. They thought their captive was out of action and would not be expecting her to fight back. An idea suddenly flashed in her mind. Could it really be so easy? She doubted it. How could her enemies be so stupid as to leave all her gear there? In fact, if she had not followed the man watching her, she would never have imagined that the equipment was being kept in one of the huts. Shivers ran down her spine. Could it be that all this had been planned by The Hundred? But why?

Uneasy now Joanni forced herself to think clearly. Since she had run after the spy, she had done one thing after another without taking time to think. Finding her gear, taking the telepaverine that revealed the plot against the gold mines, and the one call she'd chosen to make to Zembla...

An awful doubt seized her. She had not stopped to think about her lack of choices. The chase? The man's weird outfit to draw her attention. Him leading straight to her equipment. Being able to make only one call... To Zembla... The Hundred's arch-enemy...

The Hundred's lack of discretion was bound to attract C.L.A.S.H.'s attention, and her bosses would send their one agent familiar with Karunda... Yes, it was all part of a complex plan. They had brought her here in order to trap Zembla. Knowing him, he would certainly not waste his time jumping on a plane to come to her rescue...

Joanni growled in rage and frustration. She had been gullible and acted as bait. If Zembla were killed, she would be the one responsible and would blame herself for the rest of her life—which would probably not last long once they no longer needed her.

For the first time since joining C.L.A.S.H., she felt alone. Neither Miss Kiss nor Mr. Song were here to back her up. In less than a day, Zembla would be here. If she did not find a way to warn him, even Wamba, his pet lion, wouldn't be able to save him.

She clenched her jaws to repress her need to scream. There were better ways to spend her energy. She checked the emergency rations, but she knew full well that they would never let her reach Somboville. Besides, without the GPS on the communicator, she could never find her way there. She put the rations back in her pack, left the hut, and snuck into the jungle.

"She spent the night in the forest, but we don't know what she did there" reported No. 78. "Right now, she's talking with the natives."

The Hooded Man on his throne nodded and eyed his agent scornfully. Through the holes in his hood, his eyes burned with anger.

"I don't like this," he grumbled. "You're sure you didn't leave her with any other weapon but that stupid stungun?"

"Er, yeah, just a rope and her food. Her communicator ran out of juice after her call. I don't see what danger she could be."

The Hooded Man clenched his fists.

"Zembla should show up soon. I don't want to take any risks. Get rid of the girl and take your positions in the village. We can't screw this up. We've been preparing for too long."

"Yes, No. 5."

The man ran in yelling, "They're coming! They're coming! From everywhere!"

Joanni smiled, then turned to the chief who was puffing on his pipe.

"If I keep my promise, will you keep yours?"

The man nodded without saying a word. With a wave of his hand, the villagers scattered. The place became deserted in no time.

"Even if they're expecting a little resistance, The Hundred won't send in all their troops at once. The effects of my work ought to make them think twice."

At that very moment, screams were heard to the north of the village, followed by shouts coming from all directions. Then there were four explosions, one after the other, which shook the ground. Clouds of dust rose over the horizon.

Five villains, masked and armed, came running out of the trees. They wore numbered badges and looked rattled.

"Your turn, chief!" Joanni shouted.

The man gave an order. The natives immediately jumped out of their huts and captured the gangsters before they could make a move. Elsewhere, ten other bandits had been taken in the same way, stunned by the villagers' defiance.

"Now we just have to pick up the ones trapped in the jungle," Joanni said.

Followed by the chief and a few men, she went into the forest. The sight of the brigands hanging upside down, ten feet off the ground, made the natives laugh. Further away, other attackers were struggling to their feet, still dazed by the explosions.

"They're not so scary like this, that's for sure," Joanni laughed.

"You showed us that the path of fear is not the best path, friend of Zembla," the chief said solemnly. "We will stand by you."

In this first skirmish, The Hundred lost thirty men. Disarmed and tied up, they were put under guard in an underground cell whose only access was a trapdoor nearly invisible on the ground. Joanni knew that it would not be so easy if there were another seventy or so men left. Most of the traps had been tripped. However, some of the villagers were now armed, which would help them hold out for a little, She still had an ace up her sleeve.

She went up to the chief's favorite bench to get her communicator whose solar batteries had been charging for more than an hour. The Hundred might come up with all kinds of tricks, but they hadn't thought of her having enough time to use solar power to recharge her phone!

"Miss Kiss? It's Agent Bourask. I'm surrounded by The Hundred here, and Zembla will be walking into a trap when he returns. A little backup would be greatly appreciated."

She figured it would be at least two hours before C.L.A.S.H. would arrive. Things were going to heat up fast.

The second attack ended up in a chaotic retreat by the remainder of The Hundred—who, as it turned out, had dispatched only about sixty men in total. Joanni had positioned shooters up in the trees around the village. They shot a few enemies, but mostly sowed panic in their ranks. Not knowing where the shots were coming from, the gangsters fled, shooting back randomly. Some villagers were spotted, but made a quick getaway using jungle vines.

This strategy gave them another half an hour of reprieve. The villagers used the time to finish filling the ditches they had dug with flammable resin.

The third attack was a wild charge. The assailants managed to avoid the snipers. When they hit the first wall of flames, they couldn't stop in time. Their clothes caught fire and kept burning until they stumbled into a nearby swamp. The gangsters' morale dropped with every fatal failure.

It was at that moment that Zembla joined the fray.

The roar of Wamba the lion echoed through the trees as he came rushing through the remaining ranks of The Hundred, delivering well-aimed blows. The men were flung away, knocked out before they even hit the ground. Then, Wamba finished them off, scattering the villains, not hesitating to bite a few read ends that passed too close to him.

"So, you can't be trusted to sit still even for a few minutes," Zembla said with a big smile when he saw Joanni in the middle of the village.

With uncontrollable emotion, she threw her arms around him and kissed him on the cheek.

"You don't know how glad I am to see you!"

"It looks like you did most of the work without me," he said.

Pierre Marais had taken off his city clothes and now wore only his leopard skin loincloth. Impressed by his pet lion, who was now lying down nearby, the villagers kept a respectable distance.

"Welcome, Zembla!" said the chief. "You can be proud of your friend."

"I have no doubt," the giant laughed.

A humming sound filled the humid air and, soon, a combat helicopter appeared over the trees. It landed in a clear space. Joanni let out another sigh of relief.

"I'll be surprised if we hear anything about The Hundred for a while."

"They have an annoying habit of coming back sooner than one would expect," said Zembla. "But at least, we settled the score this time. Thank you for your help. You are very resourceful."

"Ha! Some people don't think that a rope could be a weapon. You taught me well, Zembla. Ropes and branches make for excellent traps. As for the C.L.A.S.H. food rations, there are useful explosives hidden inside."

They stood silent for a moment watching the C.L.A.S.H. commando head into the jungle to hunt down the last of The Hundred. There was little hope of wiping out the whole gang, but after this defeat, it will take some time before they could rebuild their forces.

"Joanni?"

"Yes, Zembla?"

"Do you have anything planned for the next few days?"

"Yes, a lot of R&R. I haven't fully recovered from their drug."

"Perfect. I know just the spot for that."

"And where's that?"

"In Karunda, of course."

Together, they burst out laughing.

Zembla by Manuel Martin Peniche

Klang (The Metal Man), Kel, Sibilla and Ozark (The En-chanters) facing the goddess Aruna by Roberto Castro.

Elena Drago, a.k.a. **Sibilla**, *is an investigative journalist of the supernatural whose articles appear in the Italian magazine* Flash. *She is also a talented magician, the heir of Cagliostro whose mystic ring she wears.*

Ozark *is Earth's supreme shaman, protector of our mystic sphere, whose magic knowledge seems boundless. He is often accompanied on his adventures by Mustang, a flying horse who is the incarnation of the sacred soul of the Lakota people.*

Kel *and* **Klang** *are beings created long ago to mediate the eternal conflict between Love and Hate by the powerful druids of New Camelot. Klang fought with the Partisans during the Second World War while Kel helped found the Organization for the Defense of the Environment (ODE), the precursor to the World Safety Unit (WSU) in the 1960s.*

Together, these four mystic heroes team up to form the **Enchanters** *when the Earth is threatened by supernatural menaces. As for* **Dave Kaplan**, *he is a daring photographer who works for the* New York Examiner *and has worked with Sibilla before.*

Nelly Chadour: *Dream Catcher*

This time, my friend, your name will be added to the long list of reporters who died in the field!

Dave Kaplan gripped his camera with his aching fingers. The land around him looked like Verdun during the Great War. The Ukrainian soldiers he was following for his assignment had managed to find a safe hiding place, leaving behind them the corpses of their comrades, along with the American journalist, in the middle of the turmoil. Squatting behind a bombed out wall, he clearly heard the clamor of Russian tanks between two explosions. He had seen some men trying to escape and being crushed under the heavy tracks. The same fate was awaiting him if the bombs did not get him first.

Too bad, Kaplan thought. *Screwed for good, might as well shoot the dead. What an incredible imprint I'm going to leave behind!*

The journalist put his eye to the camera to immortalize the advance of the tanks toward his feeble refuge. Just as he was about to press the shutter, the death machines suddenly stopped as if paused in a video game.

Everything froze in silence.

Stunned, the journalist lowered his Canon and saw he was surrounded by huge, gray and brown flowers—the blasts from the shells suspended in mid-explosion. He tried to get around the wall to get a better look at the phenomenon but the air was as thick as during the worst heat wave.

A neighing in the sky made him look up.

A horse with a shining hide was galloping several feet off the ground. The horseman was stout with long black hair, probably a Native American judging from his features. He was gesturing to the journalist below him.

Horse and rider alit on the pitted ground. The newcomer jumped out of the saddle and walked toward the reporter.

"David Kaplan?" he asked.

The reporter nodded his bewildered head while pinching himself frantically, trying to wake up. The pain he felt suggested a more disturbing truth: his mind was seriously out of whack.

"I'm Russell Red Horse, but I'm usually known as Ozark," the other said.

Something in the back of Kaplan's mind was nudged. The rider grabbed the hand that was not pinching a fold of skin and shook it firmly. The reporter saw then that the bare chest and face of the man was bruised and scratched.

"I froze time but that spell takes a lot of energy. Come with me. Mustang is going to take us far from this hell."

Dream or reality, no matter! A timely savior, even if came out a John Wayne movie on a flying horse, was better than nothing. Kaplan would wake up soon enough from this weird dream. So, he walked up to the horse that the Native

American had already gracefully mounted. Ozark held out his hand to help him up. The reporter hesitated.

"Hurry up," Ozark urged. "Time is about to start up again."

Kaplan noticed that the flowery blasts were gradually blooming and a distant rumble was slowly reaching his ears— the sound of explosions in slow motion.

"Ah, the heck with it!"

Kaplan grabbed Ozark's hand, which heaved him up with a grunt. Straddling the strong spine of the animal, the reporter thought of his camera, wondering for an instant if he should not immortalize the scene.

"Go, Mustang!"

Kaplan let out a frightened yelp when the horse leaped forward, accelerating to an astonishing speed, straight at the tanks that were flickering back to life. The horse sped up and jumped over the war machines, into the murky sky whose ochre tint changed suddenly into clear blue.

On hearing animal noises instead of the roar of cannons, Kaplan looked down and thought he had gone mad. They had left the frozen field of battle to enter a new chaos. The reporter opened his mouth to scream, but fear blocked the sounds from escaping his throat.

Ozark's horse seemed to be galloping on an invisible bridge over a ghastly sea of canine creatures squeezed together into a mass of sharp claws and drooling fangs, and eyes as red as rubies. The journalist hung onto his camera but was so terrified that he did not even think of shooting the macabre pack of hellhounds.

A nightmare, pretend it's just a nightmare…

This childish wish was repeated more earnestly when Mustang began to lose altitude. The snouts were quivering with impatience, the menacing jaws opened wide, ready to snatch up the flying trio. Claws reached out. The horse's bright coat faded as it made its perilous descent.

"Courage, old friend," Ozark whispered into the horse's ear. "Safety is in sight."

Encouraged by these few words, the horse mustered its strength to dive straight into the thick, living mass of hideous hounds. The Amerindian raised his right hand and a thunderbolt struck a huge black dog with its back deformed by tumors. The monster was burned to a crisp, leaving an open space in the middle of the danger. Kaplan screamed when he felt the claws scratching his army coat. The horse landed on grassy turf and reared up once before standing still.

The journalist's legs were shaking as he slipped off the horse's back and he would have fallen like a sack of potatoes if a pair of strong arms had not caught him. He looked up and decided that he must surely be dreaming when he saw the metal face staring back at him.

Ozark dismounted much more gracefully. Mustang neighed before galloping away into another dimension. Kaplan was now alone with Ozark and two other men. The metal man who had helped him to his feet was patting him sympathetically on the shoulder.

"Kel, Klang," Ozark said, "let me introduce you to Dave Kaplan."

"The one who's supposed to save us?" Kel said, looking puzzled.

He wore a headband and was unbelievably lithe and handsome. Kaplan thought he would fit right into a supermodel catalog.

"Nice to meet you," the journalist answered reluctantly. "Now that we all know each other, maybe someone can tell me what all this... pandemonium is?"

With a sweeping gesture, he pointed to the heaps of nightmarish creatures teeming around them, crawling over one another and pressing their deformed snouts against an invisible barrier.

"This place," Ozark said, "is a mental projection of a tormented mind, and it's up to us to make sure this nightmare doesn't get a foothold in our reality."

Dave Kaplan shook his head in disbelief.

"A nightmare? But who could be haunted by such horrors?"

"A friend we all have in common—Sibilla!"

Dave laughed, of course. If there was one person in the world who rose above hideous corruption, it was his friend Sibilla. Ozark, Kel and Klang, the Metal Man, listened to him rattle off his objections without saying a word. They, too, had difficulty believing that the mind of their dear colleague could harbor this dreadful throng.

When Dave finally stopped talking, out of words and breath, Ozark made a simple comment:

"The sleep of reason produces monsters."

"Excuse me?"

"Sibilla is a victim of a curse that is obscuring her reason," Ozark explained patiently. "The monsters around us are the fruit of an ancient, secret fear that goes back to her childhood."

"The spells of Aruna, Goddess of Hate, our common enemy, have plunged her into this haunted slumber," Kel added. "Our mind contains many horrors, Dave Kaplan. Our conscience alone protects us. And when that conscience is no longer in control, terror takes over."

"So, if I get what you're saying," Kaplan said, "Sibilla is sleeping and having bad dreams. She's become a monster factory. And you don't know how to wake her up?"

"Exactly," Klang said. "But a spell is keeping us away from her. Any bearer of magic will be immediately put into a haunted slumber if they touch her. That's why Ozark's horse lost some of its strength."

Dave pointed accusingly at Ozark.

"I knew you didn't save me because of my pretty eyes. You just needed some schmuck like me to do your dirty work!"

Ozark crossed his arms over his chest. He looked tired and his eyes gleamed with fever, but he spoke with admirable calm as if the growling, slobbering canines were just a bad movie not worth watching.

"Believe me, finding you when you were in great danger was just a lucky coincidence. But I would have saved you no matter what... for the beautiful soul of Sibilla whom you adore. As for this mission, we'd take care of it a second if..." He shrugged despondently. "In cases like this, magic can be a handicap."

Kaplan rubbed his face slowly, then said:

"OK! I'll do it. I take back what I said and I'll wake up Sibilla. But afterward, promise me that this stupid dream will end."

Kel and the Metal Man looked at each other baffled but Ozark nodded with a weary smile.

"Sure, you, too, will wake up. You have my word. Now, here's what you must do..."

Dave Kaplan could not help scrutinizing every snout glistening with snot, every blood vessel in every bulging eye, every red tongue drooling on the invisible wall of the dome. He had not yet decided what was worse: that everything might be real, or that his brain was deranged enough to create such visions. The only way to keep sane was to put an end to the evil spell, whatever it was.

He looked over his camera, checked the flash and turned to the three men standing around him.

"I'm ready."

Klang just nodded, looking tense.

"Good luck, Dave Kaplan," Kel said.

Ozark put his hand on the journalist's shoulder and squeezed gently.

"Thanks for all this."

Kaplan forced a smile. He had no time to look back. He held his breath and rushed into the teeming mass. He went right through the magic barrier, which was meant only to block out the evil entities. Right when he hit the first wave, he closed his eyes and held his camera out front. When he clicked, the flash lit up the chaotic horde. Their bulging, glassy eyes melted in their sockets. The beasts backed away.

Their gruesome howling gave a chilling idea of what the chants of Hell must sound like.

A path was now open. Kaplan opened his eyes and ran with fear in his guts. A hound lunged and he burned it with his flash while protecting his own eyes with his arm. Ozark's spell was effective. The shaman had captured sparks of the sun and trapped them inside the Canon's small bulb.

Dave unleashed the lightning a third time and, when he opened his eyes, he saw a mound of sharp rocks in front of him. His goal!

The journalist sped up. The furious beasts were crawling over each other, but none dared to attack him. The entrance at the bottom of the hill was so low that he had to bend over to squeeze through. After he had disappeared, the pack started shrieking even more loudly. The frantic barking sounded like curses to the ears of the reporter.

It was impossible to stand up straight in the narrow passage. Moreover, the walls were covered with razor-sharp rocks. Kaplan crawled through the dark, one hand holding his camera in front of him. The passage was so tight that it would have been nearly impossible for him to turn around if a daring hound had decided to come after him to get revenge for its mates.

A red light was dancing at the end of the tunnel. The journalist could see nothing of what was waiting for him in that weird glow. It looked like the shimmering reflection of a sea of blood. He crawled toward the light, still clutching his Canon.

Despite Ozark's instructions, nothing had prepared him for what he saw. In the middle of a circular chamber built under a high, vaulted ceiling of craggy stones, his friend Sibilla was sitting on a monstrous throne with a crudely sculpted back of sharp swords and grinning skulls. Her head lay on her crossed arms, which lay in turn on the massive armrest of the seat.

Kaplan could not see her face behind her long red hair that formed a thick curtain falling to the black flagstones—the only smooth surface within the chaotic walls. The red glow came from her head, which was pulsating like a monstrous heart.

The young woman's body suddenly stiffened and a bulge swelled out of the back of her head, stretched out, twisted around and growled. Black paws sprang out of her hair, gripped the carved skulls of the stone chair and a new monstrous creature pulled itself out, sniffing the air.

Dave Kaplan stood gaping at the grotesque scene. The creature was pushing on Sibilla's head to complete its spawning, twisting its spine that bristled with thick hairs.

When it finished pulling itself out of its cocoon with a sickening sucking sound, the dog-like monster perched on the eerie throne looked at Kaplan. Its snout wrinkled up and revealed a row of fangs like shards of glass stuck in blackened gums. The beast leaped at the journalist who clicked his flash and barely had time to protect his eyes. A chilling scream answered his attack. His retinas imprinted the hideous shape before it was reduced to ashes.

The journalist rubbed his eyes and walked slowly up to Sibilla with the shadow of the helldog still flickering in his vision. Very carefully, he put his camera on the ground, put his arm around his friend's shoulders and straightened her up.

Her head fell back as fetid breath escaped from her parted lips. Kaplan felt another wave of fear wash over him: Sibilla's eyes were two opals streaked with purple, rolling in the hollow sockets.

"What have they done to you?" he gasped.

Kaplan had no idea what kind of powers Aruna had, nor what she looked like, but if she'd been standing before him he would have strangled her with his bare hands.

The journalist laid the young woman on the smooth floor. Something was moving, pulsing under her hair. He heard a faint whimper, then a long claw parted the red hair and scratched the cold stone.

Kaplan panicked. A silent scream came out of Sibilla's mouth and her cloudy eyes rolled in their sockets. The birth of her creatures was obviously very painful.

A second claw joined the first.

Enough wasting time!

Kaplan fumbled in the pocket of his army jacket and fished out the object that Ozark had given to him. It was wrapped in a small, leather pouch, but when the reporter took it out, he suddenly experienced serious doubts. What could this little net woven of colorful beads in the shape of a spider's web do against these abominable creatures?

You just have to put it on Sibilla's forehead, the Lakota Shaman had said. *Then pronounce the words I'm going to teach you...*

And now, in the pulsing red light, Kaplan was not so sure. The little web looked ridiculous. But when a black head with pointy ears popped out, he understood that there was no time for procrastinating. He put the spider's web on Sibilla's damp forehead and spoke in a clear voice, as the barking of the newborn monster grew louder:

"O Iktomi, mighty dream spirit, spin your web of dreams and come help me close the Gate of Nightmares!"

Ozark had advised him to put the index and ring fingers of his left hand on the pearls and close his eyes. It was hard to do it with confidence when an aggressive hellhound was gradually pulling itself into reality a few inches away, but he remembered the flash, the damn flash, that could fry these nightmarish creatures.

"Please Iktomi!" he called out eagerly.

Sibilla's head jerked under his fingers. The sickening whine of the demonic runt became shrill, pierced his eardrums. Ozark had told him not to look, whatever happened.

But what if the Shaman had been wrong?

Kaplan squeezed his eyelids expecting to feel the crooked fangs clamp down on his neck and tear off his head at any second.

213

"Iktomi!" he cried out again as he felt the rank breath warm his cheek.

The monster howled and the air stirred around him.

Sibilla's head fell back on the stone floor. A dull thud echoed in the distance, then an explosion, followed by the stench of burning that dissipated quickly aroused his senses.

Petrified with fear, Kaplan realized that Ozark had not said exactly when he could open his eyes.

You'll know when the time comes. Afterward, you just have to let yourself be guided, is all the shaman had said.

Clear, crystal clear... To accept such sketchy information had almost been the last straw for the journalist, but he had had no choice.

He felt a hand on his shoulder. It did not belong to Sibilla whose forehead was still under Kaplan's hand. The journalist screamed. He was answered by a mocking snicker. Now irritated, he opened his eyes and saw a stranger standing next to him, hands on hips, looking down on him with a crooked smile. Another Lakota...

Not as brawny as Ozark, the newcomer nevertheless gave off the magnetic charisma of an actor in the spotlight on a stage. He wore the traditional dress, tanned leather shirt and pants dyed white with red and yellow stripes down the legs and arms. His mischievous eyes were circled with black, and four pairs of long feathers were sewn on either side of his back. He was enjoying Kaplan's look of astonishment and laughed again.

"Invoked by a white man! That's a new one! So, what can I do for you, O worshipper of a paper God?"

The journalist opened and closed his mouth. He did not know what to say. He suddenly realized that everything was different. He was no longer inside the burial mound of cutting stones and Sibilla was not lying next to him. The disquieting sound of the nightmarish creatures had also vanished. Now he was on a large prairie. The grass swayed in the warm breeze and buffalo wandered in the distance with their dark wooly skin like negative images of the clouds floating in the sky that was so blue it was dizzying.

"How did I get here?" he finally asked the Native American, who just sighed.

"I'll ask the questions first if you don't mind. But since yours is so easy to answer, here it is: you're on the Eternal Prairies, the sweet dream of the Lakotas' afterlife."

"So everything was a dream…" Kaplan muttered.

"Hey, you haven't answered my question, you damn *Wasi'chu*! All that's happened must've made you a little slow on the uptake. Now why did you invoke me?"

So it was the dream spirit himself, Iktomi in person! Convinced that the nightmare was finally coming to an end, but wanting to wake up as soon as possible, Kaplan decided to play along.

"The shaman Ozark taught me the invocation. He said my friend Sibilla was imprisoned in an endless nightmare that was spawning monsters. You're the only one who might wake her up."

Iktomi smiled just enough to reveal his incredibly white teeth.

"Why use *might, Wasi'chu*? Of course, I can save your friend."

Iktomi spread his arms and the eight feathers on his back clenched up like downy spider legs. The scenery around him changed and they were now back in the tomb. But instead of a rocky throne, there was a small children's bed with midnight blue covers sitting in the middle of the room. A window with white curtains was set in one of the perilous walls, letting in a halo of light from a silvery crescent moon wash over the slumbering face of a little girl around seven years-old. Her long red hair wound around her white ear. Kaplan walked up to the sleeping girl and right away recognized a child version of Sibilla. The soft quilt rose gently to the rhythm of her breathing.

The journalist jumped when Iktomi whispered over his shoulder:

"Aruna has aroused her childhood fears."

"What... what's that?" Kaplan stammered.

"The most frightening nightmares are those that haunt you as children," Iktomi explained. "The Lakota know this. That's why they called upon me to weave the dream catchers they hung over their cribs. The children who don't have my protection grow up with phantoms crouching in the shadows. That's what happened to your friend. Now we have to chase away those phantoms forever."

"Huh? What do you mean, *We*?"

Iktomi sighed again and spoke with his patience running short.

"As an Amerindian spirit, my powers are limited when it comes to dealing with the psyche of a human raised in a different culture. I will need your help. You know her. You're from the same tribe. I think that's reason enough for you to come with me."

"I'm not so sure about that..."

"Hush! She's waking up!"

The little redheaded girl opened her eyes, fluttering her eyelids delicately like the silky wings of a butterfly. When she found herself in a strange place, she sank down under her comforting blanket. Her bright eyes explored the room and her eyebrows rose when she saw the two men at her bedside.

Kaplan gulped, suddenly touched by the child's green eyes staring at him. He recognized certain expressions of the adult Sibilla. The girl sat up but kept a tight grip on the blanket.

"I'm dreaming, right?"

She spoke in Italian, her native language, but Dave was surprised that he understood every word. Then he remembered his own dreams where he spoke fluently in languages that he could barely stumble through in real life.

Iktomi leaned over her and smiled with all his white teeth.

"Exactly. You're dreaming and we are the hunters of nightmares. I am Iktomi." Then lowering his voice, he added,

"You must've seen more than your share, right? Monsters? You're going to help me kill them, OK?"

Little Sibilla nodded looking very serious.

"I see monsters every night, yes. It's because a mean wizard with big dogs killed my mother. And at night, I dream about them."

Once again, Kaplan felt deep sorrow for her.

"Don't you worry," he told the little girl, "we're going to get rid of all those nightmares."

She looked hard at him with a hesitant smile.

"I know you... you're..."

Not yet, he wanted to say. "You must have seen me in the papers. My name's Dave Kaplan, I'm a journalist." He showed her his camera. "And in dreams, this kills monsters."

"We're warriors," Iktomi added, "but we need your help to track the nightmares."

"I understand."

The little girl pushed off the blanket and got up. She was wearing pale green pajamas with Peter Pan fighting Captain Hook. She looked under her bed and found her slippers with fluffy rabbit ears. Kaplan smiled. Now that was the uniform of a ghost hunter. Little Sibilla fished out an old, one-eyed, stuffed cat that was hiding under the covers and straightened up proudly.

"I'm ready!"

"Bravo, little squaw," Iktomi approved. "Let's get on the trail. Show us the way."

The girl headed straight for the window. Kaplan's mind was jumping back and forth between this vision of the past and Sibilla as an adult. So different but with so many similarities.

"Stay focused, *Wasi'chu*," Iktomi whispered. "You're both mortals in the Land of Dream and my powers are limited because you're not from my tribe."

"Now you tell me that?" Kaplan raised his voice.

"Why else would I take you along?" the spirit made a sign to speak quietly so as not to alarm the girl.

She had already opened the window and looked at them over her shoulder.

"You coming? I don't want to wake up before we beat those bad creatures!"

The Lakota spirit glided up to her over his red and white moccasins, clearly bewitched by the child's determination. He took her in his long, supple arms and together they inspected the night. The waxing moon shined down on their brown and red heads.

"Dave? We're waiting for you," little Sibilla said as she climbed onto the windowsill.

The reporter joined them. The kid jumped down onto the wet ground covered with dead leaves. The two adults followed right after her. Kaplan looked around. They were in a forest seemingly designed by Tim Burton, surrounded by trees whose bark twirled into gray and purple arabesques. In the maze of branches, the owl eyes glared like headlights under the glow of five-pointed stars spread around in perfect anarchy.

When Dave looked behind him to make sure the mound was still there, he saw just a tree with a window in the trunk that looked into a child's bedroom.

"This is the forest where the wizard killed my mama," little Sibilla whispered. "He lived in an old ruined castle and unleashed his monster-dogs on people."

She took the journalist's hand and led him through the trees with her stuffed cat held tightly against her chest. Kaplan suddenly realized then that Iktomi was gone.

"Wait! I…"

He looked around as the child dragged him deep into the forest. He noticed a small black silhouette with as many feet as a pincushion following them by hopping from one branch to another. The spider was spinning a silken web that wound through the forest all the way from the tree house and drops of colorful dew glistened on it, forming a delicate, sparkling garland. Kaplan hoped with all his heart that it was Iktomi who had changed shape.

Growling noises put them on alert. Then ghastly barking scared the owls away. Little Sibilla turned pale,.

"Oh, there they are…"

Without thinking Kaplan snatched the girl up in his right arm and ran. He felt the girl's heart pounding against his shoulder. With her arms around his neck she watched behind them. She looked like a frantic kitten.

"They're coming, Dave, they're going to catch us!"

The spider raced ahead on its spindly legs and hung from a tree in front of them. It twisted its web around the branches forming the word "climb."

Kaplan did not question it. He stopped at the foot of the tree and hoisted Sibilla up onto the highest branch he could reach.

"Get as high up as you can!"

He himself put the camera strap around his neck so he could use both hands and feet to climb. Little Sibilla did the same by putting her stuffed cat between her teeth. The hounds were soon at the foot of the tree. Kaplan heard some of them run off but most seemed to have decided to camp right there, waiting for them to fall down like overripe fruit.

"Don't look down, don't look down," Kaplan chanted for the girl as much as for himself.

Above them, the spider was hopping up and down on a bunch of branches woven with vines.

"We'll just sit there," Kaplan said.

He helped the girl up onto a makeshift nest and heaved himself up after her. Little Sibilla cuddled her cat again and looked straight ahead.

"Dave, look! The castle!"

Kaplan turned around to see what she was pointing at. His stomach was in knots. Gloomy towers rose out of the forest. It looked like the witch's castle in *Sleeping Beauty*, except for the big black dogs prowling along the walls or jumping into the moat where they were devoured by giant snakes. His adult mind laughed at the grotesque sight, but something deep down inside him was calling up old images of his worst nightmares.

In the moonlight the dark building looked made of cardboard, but at the same time it exuded a sinister aura. Kaplan felt tiny, vulnerable, crushed under the imposing giganticness of this fantasyland. He would rather have stayed in the tree, but with the monstrous army of canine creatures coming from all sides of the forest, he knew that their real goal lay within the castle's walls.

"We have to get the wizard who killed mama," the girl spoke firmly. "He's the one controlling the monsters."

"OK, that sounds simple," Kaplan said, "but how are we going to get into the castle? Those bastards are swarming around the walls."

"Bad word!" the little girl wriggled her finger at him. "We just have to use the branches. Follow me, potty mouth."

Since things looked so simple to a child's eyes, Kaplan wondered why the girl had not tried to face her nightmares before. But the answer was clear: she needed the supportive, comforting presence of an adult to find the courage to fight her fears.

"It's better that you're in command here," the journalist said, following little Sibilla. "I feel like I'm in over my head."

The tree shook. Some growls sounded closer so they looked down. The hounds were taking on the tree. Their long claws slashed at the bark and they started climbing, their eyes sparkling with hungry excitement.

"Get on my back!"

Little Sibilla tucked her stuffed cat into her pajamas and grabbed his solid shoulders while her thin legs wrapped around his waist. He felt the child's heart pounding as fast and wildly as his own. Without looking down, he balanced himself holding onto the branches above and started walking. He jumped when he got close to the next tree and grabbed another branch to keep his balance while he found solid footing. The branches were cracking behind them.

"Hurry up, Dave!"

"I'm doing the best I can," he grumbled, holding his arms out now and stepping cautiously over their fragile bridge that was becoming more and more narrow.

"Watch out!"

One of the monsters had leaped and landed heavily on the branch, shaking it violently. The shock threw Kaplan off balance and he went flying through the air. Like the coyote in the cartoons, he flapped his arms trying to grab onto something as he dropped like a stone. Little Sibilla was screaming in his ear.

The journalist closed his eyes, praying with all his strength to wake up.

A net stopped their fall. Kaplan opened his startled eyes and coughed when little Sibilla who had been strangling him during the fall, let go of his neck and clapped her hands.

"Bravo, spider!"

The creature hopped onto one of the branches attached to the silken web with colorful dewdrops that had saved them. There was no more doubt: Iktomi had not abandoned them.

"It's about time that stupid spirit was good for something!"

Dave was being unfair seeing that the divinity had been very busy. It had woven a long, silken bridge running from branch to branch all the way to one of the towers of the weird castle.

But they were not out of the woods yet—literally. The hound that had caused their fall also jumped onto the web and lunged at them. Little Sibilla curl up and screamed. By reflex, Dave raised his camera and was blinded by the flash that instantly fried their attacker. The reporter dropped to his knees and covered his eyes. He saw nothing but a bright white glare sparkling with colored dots. A small hand shook him gently.

"Are you OK?"

"No," he groaned. "I can't see a thing. I didn't cover my eyes... Ow! Shit!"

"Don't worry," the child whispered, "I'm here and I can guide you."

What a kid, Kaplan thought. A heroic seed that would grow into a beautiful plant.

He wrapped his fingers carefully around the girl's little hand and stood up.

"Don't worry about walking, the web has no big holes."

Dave trusted her but was still wary—the threads bent under the weight of his heavy boots. He felt in front of him with his free hand and touched bark and leaves. Angry growls echoed in his ears and he suddenly felt cold.

"We're getting near the castle. It's a foul place."

That was a gratuitous comment. An evil aura emanated from the stones. Kaplan managed to see a little through his blinded vision. A dark shape, shimmering with murky colors, was seeping through the kaleidoscope dancing before him. And below them, the pack of hellhounds was yapping.

The girl's hand was ice-cold. The reporter tried to relieve the tension.

"They sound like a bunch of pampered pooches, don't they? They're mad because they want to get us, but with my camera they're not so tough anymore."

Little Sibilla laughed and sniffled together. Kaplan thought he could hear whining down below.

"We're here," the girl said. "We'll get in through this window."

At the same time, Dave felt tiny feet tickle his neck. He slapped at it but the spider had hopped onto his ear.

"The near-genocide of my people was enough of an abomination, let's avoid deicide, David Kaplan," Iktomi's voice squeaked. "Keep reassuring the child; it's our best chance. You can't see it, but your words helped her see those dogs differently. Some of the hounds have changed into puppies!"

"But can't *you* reassure her? You're the God of Dreams!"

"You are called upon to become her friend when she grows up, so show her that she can have faith in you."

Iktomi's voice faded off and Kaplan no longer felt the little feet on his ear.

"Who are you talking to, Dave?"

"The spider."

He rubbed his eyes. The images on his damaged retinas gradually cleared up. He helped little Sibilla climb over the humid stone of a windowsill, then did the same himself. They stood before a narrow staircase that twisted down into obscurity. The lingering glare kept the reporter from seeing the steps clearly, but his eyesight was now better. The girl hesitated before this path that plunged into darkness. Kaplan would have willingly gone first but his eyes could still betray him. He put a comforting hand on her small shoulder.

"I need you to guide me. Don't be afraid of the dark. I'm sure that if there are monsters, they're hiding because they're scared of us."

Little Sibilla laughed again but a low rumble shook the castle.

"What was that?" asked the child, alarmed.

"Probably the evil sorcerer doesn't like to hear you laugh," Kaplan tried to sound as confident as possible. "You know why? Because he can sense that you're not afraid. The nightmares are nothing but junk from your brain that fade away in the morning. They seem scary but in truth they're not even real."

"Junk from my brain, right!" Little Sibilla gloated.

The disgruntled rumbling echoed again but this time it encouraged her bravery and she laughed as she took his hand.

"Come quick, Dave, I'll teach him, that gutless wizard! Mama would be so proud of me!"

The reporter followed the girl down the stairs. His vision continued to improve but the darkness became thicker the deeper they descended into the castle.

Dreams don't pass gently from darkness into light. They were suddenly in a room lit brightly by a blazing fire in a bottomless pit stuck in the middle of the stone floor.

Sitting on a throne, wrapped in a fur coat drenched with blood, an old man with hollow eyes was sneering at them. The tips of his crown were sharpened swords.

"So this is the daughter of Lucia Drago? This is the little girl who thinks she can defy me."

His teeth were bared in a smile like a steel trap breaking through his wrinkled lips. Little Sibilla, however, walked straight up to him. Dave reached out to grab her but was suddenly gripped by uncontrollable fear. Moriarty, Nicolae Ceausescu, Albert Fish—spine-chilling names crossed his mind at the sight of the King of Nightmares. This was the crystallization of Evil, the incarnation of every fear.

"Don't stop her," the voice of Iktomi whispered in his ear.

The spider god was once again sitting on his shoulder.

"If she kills him, is it the end of the nightmares?" Kaplan asked.

Little Sibilla was standing in front of the sorcerer-king who slowly stood up on his throne, unfolding his long body like some creepy bone-machine. With a few snaps and cracks his head rose so high that the pointy crown scraped against the arched ceiling. Under the ermine robe a number of arms shot out, each wielding a bloodstained butcher's knife.

"If she kills him, she will wake up for good and will put an end to her trauma," Iktomi said. "But see that pit? It's the Gate of Nightmares. It has to be closed for good, or else all the dogs your friend spawned will keep on prowling around the world. And that's where you come in, my friend."

"How's that?"

Just then, the sorcerer rushed at Sibilla. His spidery arms flailed and the blades whistled through the air.

"Ozark gave you some artifacts. It wasn't just for fun," Iktomi told him. "Now get to work, Dave Kaplan! I'll take care of the girl."

Without further ado, the dream spirit jumped off his shoulder and landed near the girl, who was not quite so fearless faced with an attacker standing up on long insect legs, beaming with a gruesome expression of triumph.

"Dave...," the girl started to call out before seeing the small spider hop onto the head of her stuffed cat and bury itself inside the toy.

Kaplan tried to rush forward, but something grabbed his ankle. He tripped, turned around and shook his leg to get free from the clawed tentacle that was now dragging him toward the fiery pit. A misshapen head appeared, followed by another. The reporter pointed his camera at them and closed his eyes. Painful shrieks and the foul stench of burned flesh told him that the creatures had been exterminated.

For her part, Sibilla was handling things. The stuffed cat had suddenly come alive, and grown big enough to make a comfortable little horse that the girl straddled. The black circles around its eyes and the feathers attached to its bare tail bore the mark of Iktomi. He pounced on the old sorcerer and clawed at him, spurred on by its rider. A knife slipped out of the hands of the nightmarish creature that the girl swooped up and started stabbing to help her stuffed cat.

She doesn't need you. Do your job, you big idiot, Kaplan scolded himself as he stared at the mortal combat.

He finally searched his pockets for the objects that Ozark had given him. His fingers touched a piece of fabric. He pulled it out and could not help thinking of the old magic trick in which the performer pulls a never-ending scarf out of his sleeve. His piece of fabric also seemed to have no end. How could such a big thing fit into his little pocket? When he had pulled the whole thing out, he unfolded it and found, wrapped inside it, a dream catcher that was even more impressive. It was the perfect size to cover the pit. Kaplan shook out the net like a bed sheet, but the heat from the blazing fire pushed the dream catcher in the opposite direction.

An ear-splitting shriek drew his attention back to the battle. The sorcerer had cut off the giant cat's tail and a mix of stuffing and feathers was pouring out of the stump. It made the toy lose its balance and the monster knocked off the girl with a strong, swift kick. She crashed on the ground and dropped her knife.

"Sibilla!"

Without thinking, Kaplan, who was battling with the dream catcher, tossed over one of the weighted ends of transparent stone. The child grabbed it.

"Go around the pit and come over here quick!"

The sweet little face lit up when she understood what he meant. Holding the net firmly in her fist, she ran by the king of nightmares, who tried to mow her down with his blades. Dave pulled as hard as he could on his end of the dream-catcher and the demon's spindly legs were caught in the net.

Iktomi gave the coup de grâce. He charged headfirst into the tangled sorcerer and pushed him over. But his momentum carried him into the fire with his enemy.

"No!"

Dave ran up to try to save the dream spirit who had turned back into his original form and was fighting with the sorcerer amidst the flames.

"Pull the net!"

"What about you?" Dave cried out.

"I'm a spirit, you big id…"

Iktomi was cut off by a long hand burying itself in his mouth. The sorcerer was trying to choke him. The dream spirit bit off the fingers and yelled out:

"QUICKLY!"

On either side of the pit Kaplan and Sibilla reluctantly pulled the net tight. It stuck to the edges and blocked out the flames. The infernal heat in the throne room slowly faded.

The duo looked on silently as the dream catcher turned red in the flickering flames. Among the tongues of fire they could barely make out a pointy crown trying to stab through the immovable trap.

Sibilla took Dave's hand. He saw that she was back in adult form. He had a twinge of regret—he would have liked to say goodbye to little Sibilla.

"*Grazie*, Dave;" the beautiful Italian woman said softly.

"Those dogs, that sorcerer... they were just the fruit of your imagination?"

The young woman shook her head.

"Unfortunately they were as real as you and I. But in my past."

Yelps echoed down the hallways of the castle. The pack of hellhounds was rushing toward the throne room to avenge their master. The reporter took his friend's arm.

"We have to get out of here, fast!"

"No. I'm the one who gave birth to them, so I have to be the one facing them. You go!"

"What? After everything I did to help you? You must be joking."

A stream of gruesome creatures suddenly poured through the door. The narrow windows also exploded under pressure from the monstrous mob.

"Close your eyes!"

Dave used his flash. Dozens of hounds got scorched, which only made the others angry enough to forget their fear. They ran at the two humans with their claws stretched out and foaming at the mouth.

Suddenly, Sibilla raised her hand and the ring on her index finger glowed with countless shades of green.

"By the power of the Twelve!"

A bright beam, almost as blinding as Dave's flash, enveloped the front line of attackers who were immediately changed into puppies. Some were quickly devoured by their old comrades. The journalist wanted to strike again, but the camera was kicked out of his hand. Something tore at this coat and he saw gaping, hungry jaws bear down on him.

Sibilla shouted and another beam shot out of her ring, freeing Kaplan from the fangs that were instantly turned into harmless puppy teeth. But she could not stop them coming.

A beast jumped on his back and he fell to the floor. Out of the corner of his eye, he saw that Sibilla was also on the ground. He gave her a weak smile as claws slowly sank into his skin.

"It… it'd be nice for you to wake up now…"

The creature on top of him suddenly let go and let out a moan. The smell of burnt flesh made them wrinkle their noses.

Kaplan jumped up with blood flowing from his superficial wounds. One by one, the dogs were reduced to ashes and Dave knew why when he saw the rays from the rising sun passing through the thick castle walls, which were now turning transparent.

All the nightmares vanished with the first light of the morning!

Then Ozark made his entrance, flanked by Kel and Klang. Their footsteps kicked up the thick layer of canine ashes. All three looked in better shape than at the start of the adventure.

"What do you think of the sunrise?" the shaman said proudly. "Thanks to you for opening the way, Dave Kaplan. Once the pit of nightmares was closed up, Aruna's magic couldn't stop us from lending a helping hand."

"And what an entrance!" Sibilla hugged the three of them in turn. "I'm sorry for putting you all through this ordeal," she added, her voice choking. "It put you all in danger."

"It's not your fault," Kel told her.

"Hold on," Kaplan broke in. "Everyone here came through fine except your friend Iktomi…"

He pointed to the pit covered with the huge spider web.

"Don't worry," Ozark said. "As long as there are dreamers, there will be Iktomi."

Kaplan blinked his eyes, suddenly weary of this senseless world.

"OK, great," he finally muttered. "Now, I'd like to wake up from this endless dream."

The four others smiled. Ozark started chanting in the secret language of his people, but Sibilla raised her hand to stop him.

"Dave, before you wake up…" she stood up on her tiptoes and gave him a light kiss on his lips. "Thank you," she whispered. "Thanks to you, I can face my oldest fear."

Kaplan felt himself blush like a schoolboy.

"I hope I remember your wonderful gesture of gratitude when I wake up," he said as he hugged her closely.

Sibilla smiled and tenderly stroked the American's cheek. Cagliostro's ring glowed and drowned the room in blinding green light.

Dave woke up suffocating. His whole body was one big ball of pain. His muscles were in knots, his skin gashed, dust filled his nose and eyes and a loud ringing drilled into his ears and squeezed his head in an invisible vise. He was about to feel for broken bones when someone shouted:

"Don't move! We're taking you to the military hospital in Kiev."

His vision slowly cleared. Everything around him was a blur and he could recognize the deafening whirr of the blades and engine of a helicopter flying at full speed.

"Where...?" he started, but his tongue was sandpaper and his teeth were grinding dust.

"You're safe. A commando team picked you up on the battlefield. They shot at you, but your camera saved you.

They handed him his Canon. He closed his fingers around it, rubbing it gently until he found the hole in the middle of the lens. Pictures flashed and swirled in his mind. The misshapen dogs, the old man with a pointy crown... all these nightmarish visions gradually faded into a more pleasant dream whose vague memory he felt on his lips.

Still, his fingers felt around the bullet hole. He finally raised the ruined camera up to get a good look. He could clearly see the shape of a spider's web whose center was the black eye of the lens staring back at him.

Dave Kaplan by Carlo Cedroni.

About the Authors

Nelly Chadour has been writing since she learned how to handle a pencil, and became a professional writer in 2011. Her works have been published by Editions Malpertuis, Céléphais, Le Carnoplaste, and Rivière Blanche, including (for the latter) a full-length Hexagon novel starring *Sibilla: Deadly Circles*, currently available in translation from Black Coat Press.

Part-time role-playing (*Patient 13, Notre Tombeau*) and comic book author, full-time mad scientist, occasional freelance writer and graphic designer by profession, **Anthony Combrexelle** is also a fan of fantasy movies, comics and TV series. He lives in a strange workshop located on rue www.misterfrankenstein.com.

Robert Darvel, born in 1958, chose this *nom-de-plume* after reading, at the age of ten, Gustave Le Rouge's *The Vampires of Mars*. After working in bookstores and audiovisual marketing firms, he created his own publishing house, Le Carnoplaste, in 2007. He is the author, among other things, of The New Adventures of Harry Dickson, as well as short stories for the Amicale Jean Ray, Malpertuis, ImaJn'ère, Rivière blanche, Black Coat Press and The Eye of the Sphinx. He does not (yet) live not on Mars, but in the Yonne region.

Willy Favre is a role-playing game author and illustrator. He participated in the Chimeric Brigade Encyclopedia and Humanydyne, two universes about superheroes, one of his many and all-consuming passions.

Amaury Fourtet was born in 1982. He is an assiduous fan of role-playing games and comics. He as one of the translators of *Scion, CthulhuTech, Cold City,* and *Lacuna* into French With

231

the exception of one short short story published in a supplement to the *Bardak* game, this is his first published story, and he's really excited that it is a superhero story. He tried to infuse it with that human side that he admires so much in Kurt Busiek's *Astro City* or Alan Moore's *Supreme*.

Romain d'Huissier also comes from the world of role-playing games, having worked on *La Brigade Chimérique*, and designed and written an RPG based on the Hexagon Comics Universe for French publisher Les XII Singes. He has published a number of short stories and novels for Malpertuis, Le Carnoplaste, Critic, Trash and Rivière Blanche. For the latter, he has written two novels featuring the Hexagon group of super-heroes, *Dark Matter* and *The Immortals' War*, and assembled several anthologies devoted to the Hexagon Universe.

Raphaël Lafarge, born in 1985, quickly developed a passion for the creation of fictional universes of all kinds. Strongly inspired by horror cinema and mythology, he has participated in a number of projects: writing, drawing, short films, games. After studying cinema, he published his first novel, *Teliam Vore*, co-written with Vincent Mondiot, at Flammarion in 2011. He is currently working on *Panta-grame*, an interactive multi-support webcomic project.

Jean-Marc & Randy Lofficier have collaborated on five screenplays, a dozen books and numerous translations, including *Arsène Lupin*, *Doc Ardan*, *Doctor Omega*, *The Phantom of the Opera* and *Rouletabille*. Their latest novels include *Edgar Allan Poe on Mars*, *The Katrina Protocol* and *Return of the Nyctalope*. They have written a number of animation tele-plays, including episodes of *Duck Tales* and *The Real Ghost-busters*, and in comics, such popular heroes as *Superman* and *Doctor Strange*. Randy is a member of the Writers Guild of America, West and Mystery Writers of America.

Ghislain Morel discovered comics at age six in a box that belonged to a cousin of his, filled with French editions of Marvel titles. Born in 1971, he is old enough to have bought and read the original black and white mags which featured the heroes of the Hexagon Universe. He has written games, short stories, articles, played music in the groups Maigh Tuireadh, Skøll and Naheulband, and chaired the musical and literary collective, *The Deep Ones*.

Blanche Saint-Roch was born in 1987 in Paris. Successively in love with Prince Charming, Goldorak, D'Artagnan, Sirius Black and Aragorn (to name but a few), she ended up inventing her own stories and took up the pen to make others dream—while pursuing down-to-earth engineering studies. About fifteen of her stories can be found in various anthologies, fanzines, webzines and magazines. Under the nom-de-plume of Roxane Dambre, her first novel *Animae - The Spirit of Lou* was published in digital form in December 2012 by the Éditions de l'Epée. A sequel was released in 2013.

Artikel Unbekannt: behind this strange pseudonym hides the author of numerous stories published in various anthologies, including several by Rivière Blanche. He also edited a horror imprint for a French publisher and currently serves on Rivière Blanche's editorial board.

Patrice Verry, born in 1953, has been a science fiction since childhood, but it was not until the 1970s that he got carried away and started devouring every genre book within reach. He created the now defunct *Vopaliec SF* fanzine, and organized the 1985 Angers SF convention, Since 2011, he has participated in the organization of the ImaJn'ère conventions which take place every year in Angers. He has published short stories at Le Seuil, Voy '[el], Deleatur, Le Petit Caveau, in the fanzine Piments & Muscade and at Rivière blanche.

The Enchanters by Gabriel Mayorga

OTHER HEXAGON COMICS TITLES:

Bob Lance #1: The Round Table. Carpi & Bernasconi. 64 pages b&w. $12.95.
Bob Lance #2: To Seek the Holy Grail. Carpi & Bernasconi. 54 pages b&w. $12.95.
Bob Lance #3: The Ghost of Rasputin. Carpi & Bernasconi. 54 pages b&w. $12.95.
C.L.A.S.H. Frescura & Trevisan. 248 pages b&w. $20.95.

Dick Demon: Vanishing Point. Lofficier, Arden & Peniche. 108 pages color. $26.95.

Dragut/Scarlet Lips. Lofficier & Macall. 68 pages color. $19.95.

The Enchanters. Lofficier, Mayorga & Castro. 88 pages b&w. $12.95.

The Frontiersmen/Codename: Glory. Lofficier, Peniche & Mayorga. 48 pages b&w. $9.95.

Galaor, Warrior of Mû. Lofficier, Macall, Xavier & Peru. 68 pages color. $19.95.

Guardian of the Republic #1. Mornet & Roncagliolo. 48 pages color. $12.95.

Guardian of the Republic/Barbarella. Lofficier & Ruiz. 48 pages color. $12.95.

Guardian of the Republic/Dragut/Scarlet Lips/Time Brigade. Lofficier & Macall. 48 pages b&w. $9.95.

Guardian of the Republic/Phenix/Super-Patriots. Lofficier & Macall. 48 pages b&w. $9.95.

Guardian of the Republic/Kit Kappa/Night Prince. Lofficier, Castro & Garcia. 48 pages b&w. $9.95.

Gun Gallon. Lofficier, Macall & Picard. 48 pages b&w. $9.95.

HEXAGON COMICS: THE FIRST 70 YEARS. Lofficier et al. 300 pages b&w. $22.95.

Hexagon Group #1: The Dark Hive. Lofficier, Roncagliolo & Ruiz. 76 pages b&w. $12.95.

Hexagon Group #2: Hexagon vs. Heptagon. Lofficier, Roncagliolo & Garcia. 96 pages b&w. $12.95.

Hexagon novel #1: Dark Matter. D'Huissier. 300 pages. $22.95.

Hexagon Spotlight on Alfredo Macall. Macall. 68 pages color. $19.95.

Kabur #1. Legrand, Lofficier & Bernasconi. 252 pages b&w. $20.95.

Kidz. Lofficier & Macall. 52 pages b&w. $10.95.

The Lunatic Legion. Lofficier, Bouquet & Lafuente. 52 pages b&w. $10.95.

Morgane. Lofficier & Lirussi. 48 pages b&w. $9.95.

The Partisans #1. Thomas, Lofficier & Guevara. 48 pages b&w. $9.95.

The Partisans #2. Lofficier & Guevara. 64 pages b&w. $12.95.

Phenix #1. Lofficier, Bernasconi & Roncagliolo. 248 pages b&w. $20.95.

Scarlet Lips: Crimson Dawn. Wolfman, Lofficier & Guevara. 48 pages b&w. $9.95.

Strangers Origins: Homicron. Buffolente, Lofficier & Dzialowski. 364 pages b&w. $24.95.

Strangers Origins: Jaydee. Grossi. 260 pages b&w. $20.95.

Strangers Origins: Starlock. Legrand & Bernasconi. 256 pages b&w. $20.95.

Strangers #0: Omens & Origins. Lofficier & Various. 128 pages color. $29.95.

Strangers #1: Strangers in a Strange Land. Lofficier & Various. 160 pages color. $34.95.

Strangers #2: Of Blood and Fire. Lofficier & Various. 160 pages color. $39.95.

Strangers #3: Of Gods and Men. Lofficier & Various. 160 pages color. $39.95.

Strangers #4: The Coming of Starcyb. Lofficier & Various. 118 pages b&w. $12.95.

Strangers #5: The Kingdom of Shivar. Lofficier & Peniche. 94 pages b&w. $12.95.

Tales of the Hexagonverse #1; Mutations (prose anthology). D'Huissier ed. 244 pages. $20.95.

Tales of the Twilight People: Dr. Despair. Lofficier & Agapit. 148 pages b&w. $12.95.

Tiger and The Eye. Lofficier & Ruiz. 136 pages b&w. $12.95.

Time Brigade: The Grail Wars. Lofficier & Green. 48 pages color. $12.95.

Wampus #1. Frescura & Bernasconi. 232 pages b&w. $20.95.

Zembla #1. Oneta & Oneta. 280 pages b&w. $22.95.

TO ORDER: Add $4 first bok, $2 for subsequent books, for p&h. Pay by credit card/paypal direct from our website: *www.hexagon.comics.com/shop.html* or pay by check to the order of BLACK COAT PRESS sent to: BLACK COAT PRESS c/o Mr. Greg M. Seigel, 18321 Ventura Blvd., Suite 915, Tarzana, CA 91356. E-MAIL INQUIRIES: *info@blackcoatpress.com.*